Also by Edward Mathis
Published by Ballantine Books:

NATURAL PREY
DARK STREAKS AND EMPTY PLACES
FROM A HIGH PLACE

ANOTHER PATH, ANOTHER DRAGON

Edward Mathis

BALLANTINE BOOKS • NEW YORK

Library of Congress Catalog Card Number: 87-35628

ISBN 0-345-35901-1

This edition published by arrangement with Charles Scribner's Sons, an Imprint of MacMillan Publishing Company

Manufactured in the United States of America

First Ballantine Books Edition: May 1990

This one is for Dominick Abel

1

THE LETTER FROM WARD BANNION WAS WAITING WHEN I got back from Wyoming. Not a letter actually, a three-by-five card stuffed into a legal-sized envelope bearing a printed return address in the upper left hand corner: Jerico Falls Police Department, One Century Plaza, Jerico Falls, Texas.

His handwriting was small, precise, surprising somehow, for a man his size. The message was typical, terse, cryptic.

Dear Dan:

I used to say a friend in need is a royal pain in the ass. You always agreed, but that was a lot of years ago and maybe we've both mellowed some. I hope so. Don't call, just come if you can and want to, and I don't consider for a second that I once saved your sorry no-good ass . . .

Ward

I was too tired to do more than read it again and wonder. It had been twelve years since I'd last seen him, a one night stopover on a vacation trip to Colorado. His wife and two kids had been with him, a tall brunette with an impish smile and two all-American kids with sandy hair and blue eyes, the girl six, the freckle-faced boy four.

I had been a cop back then, and proud of it, a wife and a six year old son of my own. I was still an oracle for the law, a real gung ho cop, but somehow it shocked me to find that Ward had recently signed on in J. Edgar Hoover's private Army.

I had always had trouble seeing him as an accountant, the profession he had declared would make him rich, but knowing his intense dislike of autocratic authority, the FBI would have been the last place I'd expect to find him. Maybe the CIA or NSA, the State Department, or even one of the sub-agencies that proliferate just below public awareness, the ones that allow their agents a certain measure of personal initiative.

But he had seemed contented with his new niche in life, happy, proud as punch of his family and looking forward to a new posting in Memphis, Tennessee.

He still looked much the same, but I saw only ill-defined flashes of the old hard-drinking, rebellious, fighting man I had known. I watched his slow easy way with the women and kids and thought of domesticated tigers, neutered lions.

Our contact after that had been limited to a few terse words on the inside page of Christmas cards, flowers and a simple message of condolence when my wife Barbara and my son Tommy died. I never knew how he found out.

Even that tenuous link had petered out a few years back, my last card to Tennessee returned stamped: ADDRESSEE MOVED   NO FORWARDING ADDRESS.

And now, in an unusually convoluted fashion, he was asking for help, putting it in the most innocuous terms possible, giving me an out, a way to back away from an unseemly claim on a wartime friendship, a sixteen year old debt. I understood how much the last sentence had cost him in pride, how hard it must have been for him to write it.

Men like Ward Bannion seldom asked anyone for help, and the fact that he had added an undercurrent of urgency to his message pricked my curiosity like the sound of breaking window glass at midnight. I sensed a note of pleading, maybe for the first time in his life.

I popped a Hungry Man TV dinner into the oven, then went into my miniature office and found my Texas atlas. I sat down at the new desk that Susie had bought me and located Jerico Falls. Approximately one hundred and thirty miles southwest of Fort Worth, forty or so miles south of Interstate 20, it appeared to have a population of less than three thousand.

Just another small Texas town, no distinguishing marks, no historical significance that I could find, no notes about epic battles with the fierce Comanche, the wily Kiowa-Apache, no depredations by the dreaded Kickapoo. One footnote of interest: Early in the year 1901 Butch Cassidy and two members of his Hole-In-The-Wall gang had dropped in for Sunday services at the local Baptist church. Just like common ordinary folk. Presumably, a good time was had by all.

Years before I had deer hunted that general area and, to the best of my recollection, it was a rugged monotonous terrain of stunted cedar, oak, and mesquite, a scattering of chaparral where the High Plains stumbles on the Edwards Plateau. I remembered a lot of up and down, small pockets of scenic beauty that staggered the senses after so much blah. I remembered seeing more sheep and goats than cows, more deer than people, less surface water than the spit I occasionally wasted.

I thought about it while I ate my lazy man's dinner, beef and potatoes and decomposed corn. Washed down with beer, it was filling if not palatable, and gave my grumbling stomach something to do.

By the time I finished I had made my decision. There was really no reason why I couldn't go. My Wyoming case was over, and Susie was off gallivanting around the state again, ostensibly to dredge up human interest fluff on the last ditch, blitzkrieg campaign of the republican gubernatorial challenger. Ordinarily she co-anchored a two hour segment of the Texas News Service's twenty-four hour broadcast day, but her boss and co-anchor, a slick conniving son-of-a-bitch if there ever was one, had decided that she lacked her usual verve, that she looked wan and lackluster and needed a little field time to sharpen up the old vitality, bring back the blossom to her cheeks.

It was all a crock and Susie and I knew it. It was payback time. He wanted her and couldn't handle the rejection. After months of heavy-lidded glances and innuendo, he had suddenly opted for shock value and come on with a flat proposition. She had taken refuge in humor, turning him aside like a lovesick adolescent; gently, I thought, mainly because that's the way she did things, partly because she loved her job and didn't want to have to quit.

She told me immediately because she hated secrets in our marriage. I listened and waited for her to ask for help. When she didn't, I volunteered.

She smiled and shook her head. "Thanks, Danny, but I can handle it. Other women cope. So can I. I don't want Sy to be my enemy. If you intervened that's what would happen."

"It's hard to know sometimes what you want," I said, my voice a little rougher than I had intended.

And so the miserable schmuck had her dashing about in the hinterlands, trying to squeeze a bit of humor and human interest out of a loudmouthed arrogant curmudgeon who had about as much humor as an angry wasp, no more humanity than a shark. I understood Sy Deacon's reasoning only too well. With me out of the picture he clearly believed his chances with Susie would rise exponentially. After all, he was younger than me, handsomer, suave, articulate, divorced, with a high-visibility, dynamite job in a glamorous profession, a deep resonant voice that even Susie admitted sometimes made her shiver. He had been well aware of the strain her eight months as a Special Assignment reporter had put on our marriage, the tiny cracks that had almost formed a crevasse. I had no objection to her working if that was what she wanted to do, but conducting a marriage by long distance was no fit way to live. I wanted to wake up beside her mornings, know I'd see her that night.

And, I thought, as I pushed myself wearily through my ablutions and climbed into bed, if he ever tries to hit on her again there will surely be a day of reckoning, a little extremely unfriendly one-on-one.

2

Jerico Falls, Texas. It wasn't much of a town. The word sleepy came to mind as I drifted in from the Interstate, forty miles to the northwest. After one complete turn around the deserted square, I replaced sleepy with coma.

I saw nothing human. Nothing alive except birds and a gaunt black and silver hound lolling dejectedly on the steps of a small pagoda-shaped bandstand near one corner of the park.

The park, obviously the centerpiece of downtown, was liberally studded with blackjack oak, cottonwood, and a scattering of the largest mesquite trees I had ever seen. A stone statue of Sam Houston, huge shoulders forever stained by pigeon droppings, graced one end of the square, balanced neatly at the other end by an only slightly larger-than-life replica of General Robert E. Lee astride his trusty steed—a Texas small town cliché.

Most of the businesses once surrounding the square had gone belly up, doors padlocked, windows loosely boarded, each affixed with its own little white-on-black sign proclaiming this space for rent, this building for sale.

Small town U.S.A. in the mid-eighties. The great American dream gone awry. I could close my eyes and visualize a

6

hundred just like it, the heart lines of this great state, of this great country slowly withering, drying up and curling in on themselves, waiting for the next blue norther to scatter the residue like dead ashes from a forgotten fire.

I parked next to a clutch of empty spaces marked FOR POLICE VEHICLES ONLY. I shut down the engine and lit a cigarette and inspected my end of the square squat building in the center of the park.

Nothing much to see: a flat-topped building constructed of native fieldstone. A set of Spanish double doors with large hammered metal handles. One narrow window to the left of the doors, and ubiquitous ligustrum hedge lining the two walls that I could see. Not aesthetically pleasing, it had obviously been designed for functionability, a sensible compromise between what the city fathers would have liked and what the townspeople could afford. The only hint of pretentiousness was a large shiny brass plaque above the doors reading:

ONE CENTURY PLAZA
JERICO FALLS, TEXAS
A LITTLE CITY WITH BIG IDEAS

I dumped the cigarette and climbed out of the Ramcharger. It was hot for the end of October, the changing tree leaves making a liar out of the summer-like sun.

Dead still. No trace of a breeze. Still no sign of humanity; no noise except the grating sound of my boots on concrete. Siesta time? Poison gas? Vampires? I thought of the dead-town scene in *Salem's Lot* and felt an involuntary chill along my spine.

I laughed out loud, and the short beefy man in a western suit and string tie coming through the Spanish double doors stopped and looked at me inquiringly, then glanced hastily at his fly, obviously convinced he was the object of my mirth. He looked at me again, cocked eyebrows sending a ladder of deep grooves into his bald pate. One pudgy hand held on to the door, the other stroked his neatly clipped beard, fingered

7

a connecting mustache. He had a round face, big ears, and a slightly turned up nose.

"What?" he said, giving me a cautiously optimistic grin.

"Pardon me," I said. "I know this sounds silly as hell, but I just suddenly felt like laughing."

He nodded seriously. "I know what you mean. I do that myself round this time of year." The smile curved upward at the edges. "You been hearing any buck snorts in your sleep?"

"Hey, that's right. Only a couple of weeks until deer season."

He stepped out of the door, holding it for me. "There you go. Man quits gettin a little buck fever, he might as well pack it in, right?"

"That's right," I said and moved to step around him.

"You going in there to see anybody except Lona Alldyce, you're outta luck, partner. Danged place's shut down tighter'n a rusty nut."

"I was wondering about the populace. You're the first human I've seen since I passed the Shell station out on the Farm-to-market road."

"Junior Rodeo Sunday. Near about everybody's out at the rodeo grounds south of town. I just come from there myself. Just come in to bring my daughter—that's the Lona Alldyce I was talking about—well, I brung her a couple of them corny dogs. My name's Theron Alldyce, by the way." He pushed a small plump hand in my direction.

"Dan Roman. I thought I might find Ward Bannion here—"

"Chief Bannion? You bet. Ordinarily you would, probably, but I reckon he's out at the—no, wait a minute. I saw him leave the rodeo grounds a few minutes ago. He was heading east so I guess he was running out to his place for something." He squinted at me. "You don't know where he lives?"

I shook my head. "I was counting on meeting him here."

"No problem. It's easy to find." He grinned cheerfully

and dug around in his coat pocket. "I got a pen here if you got any paper. I can make you a map."

I rummaged in my wallet and produced a blank check. "This big enough?"

"You bet." He placed the check against one of the doors and made several quick bold strokes. "It's a big old yellow house, two stories, kinda sets back off the road but you can't miss it. About eight miles out there, I reckon. It's got some big old oak trees and a few cedar around it. Just follow this map and you got it made."

"Thanks." I checked the surprisingly neat map. It looked simple enough.

"Don't believe I've seen you around here before. You and old Ward old friends?" His small blue eyes twinkled merrily.

"I knew him years ago."

"Don't think I've ever heard him mention your name. Dan Roman, you say?"

I nodded.

His expression altered, became speculative. "You wouldn't be coming in here to give old Ward a hand with them murders, would you?"

"I don't know. Who's he going to kill?"

He stared blankly, then screwed up his face and bellowed a laugh, color flooding his cheeks above the beard. He clapped his hands. "By God, that's funny!" He slapped his thigh, ducking his head, his portly body bobbing like a cork. "No more'n I deserve, too, poking in your business thataway."

"Thanks for the map." I grinned into his beaming face and turned down the walk to my truck. Behind me, I heard him slap something again, sucking air.

"Who's he gonna kill!" He went off into another chuffing gale of laughter.

I lit a cigarette and climbed into the Ramcharger.

Murders? Plural. More than one. I wondered how many and thought about going back and quizzing Alldyce while I had him helpless under the spell of my wit. But the friendly little man had gone back inside, no doubt to tell his daughter about the new stand-up comic in town. I thought about my unwritten rule and the times I had broken it before to my sorrow. I thought about going home, four hours and a pit stop away. I even gave some thought to the honkytonks I'd passed coming in, tossed around the idea of getting drunk and forgetting the whole thing.

But in the end I drove east out of town, following the map.

One life with sixteen years of accrued interest. How much was it worth? A goodly sum. One might say a staggering sum, more than I could jump over or go around. One could say I owed him.

I flipped the cigarette butt out the window, feeling a silly grin breaking across my face.

Okay. One murder, maybe two. Right. No way would I help him kill more than two.

3

WARD BANNION'S HOUSE WAS OLD AND YELLOW AND square. Two stories high with a gabled roof and broad verandas along two sides, it sat amidst stately white oaks already shrouded in their colorful autumn coats, bare limbs poking through here and there like the desiccated finger bones of arthritic old men.

Set into the trailing slope of a towering, heavily forested hill, it had a quiet dignity, an air of invincibility and gentle decrepitude that brought to mind gaunt, weather-whipped faces and dimming watery eyes, gnarled backs and rough, work-hardened hands. I tried to fit Ward into that picture; forty-two year old Ward Bannion with a gleaming head of golden curls, the smooth handsome face that I remembered, and a hat and gun as big as Gene Autry's. Somehow, it wouldn't jell.

The house sat back from the road a good fifty yards and I parked my Dodge pickup beside a rust-colored Ferrari that seemed as out of place here as a pedicured poodle on a coon hunt.

Middle-aged craziness, I thought, climbing out and crunching up the gravel walk, smiling a little, remembering the first time I had driven Susie's Maserati, the gut-swooping thrill as we passed one hundred and ten miles an hour, the powerful feeling that was almost sexual when I realized there was a lot more under that sleek curving hood, that all it took was more guts than sense.

But I had backed off, the decelerating throb of the engine blending with Susie's jeering laughter, admitting to myself, without shame, that I had just discovered another facet of human endeavor in which Daniel Austin Roman, intrepid private eye, did not excel.

My boot heels announced my arrival loudly on the wooden veranda, and I was still an arm's length away from the door when it swung open.

I was grinning broadly, the way you do when you expect to meet a well-liked, long lost friend, and it took a moment or two to adjust my gaze from a six foot-three inch level to somewhere around five foot-five, another second to assimilate dark eyes and a blinding smile, a slender figure sleekly fitted into skin-tight jeans and a darkly hued satin shirt. Light brown hair broke across the ridge of her shoulders and curled carelessly above the swell of bountiful breasts.

I felt my smile slipping and backed a step away as she came through the door, a small airline bag in her right hand, her left holding a collection of jingling keys and a large brown purse. She closed the door and rattled the knob, her eyes still on mine.

"If you're looking for the Chief," she said, her tone caustic, "the big oaf's up on top of this mountain behind the house. Him and that runty salesman are up there playing with guns. If you go up there, and you do see him, will you tell him for me that Carol Anne said to kiss her ass and that she may or may not call him when she gets back off her run to Little Rock?" She dropped the flight bag, smiling winningly, and held out her hand. "Hi, I'm Carol Anne Siever, who're you?"

"I'm sure glad I'm not the Chief," I said, swallowing the small dry hand in mine, squeezing it once, gingerly, then letting go. "In your present frame of mind, I'm not even sure I should tell you I'm an old friend."

"Dan Roman," she said promptly, her full lips coming together as she made a rueful face, one hand striking her forehead in a gesture of mock dismay. "Oh lord, of all the people in the world for me to smart off to, it had to be you. His only hero." She paused, a nervous giggle in her voice.

When I couldn't think of anything to say and the silence began to grow, she rushed on, her voice subtly shifting to the liquid rhythm of the South, attenuated consonants and elongated vowels. "You can't imagine how many times I've had to listen to the stories of what you did in Vietnam, the witty things you used to say, how neat and cool and courageous you were, still are, to his way of thinking. And it doesn't take much to get him started. Like two weeks ago we flew down to Houston for the weekend. He saw an Army helicopter at the airport and that set him off. He talked about you and Vietnam—mostly you—the rest of the night. Saturday morning he started in again." She paused, smiling. "I finally had to threaten him with bodily harm to make him change the subject."

"Nostalgia," I said. "It does funny things to people's minds sometimes."

She shook her head vigorously, impatiently. "He's never forgiven himself for not keeping in touch after Vietnam." Her eyes had become faintly mocking, her short nose crinkling as she made a dimpled face. "I made up my own mind-picture of you . . . somewhere between Charles Bronson and Clint Eastwood, only taller and better looking."

"I'm pretty tall," I said, straightening to my full six feet, tucking in here and there, responding automatically to her critical feminine appraisal, a universal conditioned response that begins along about the first time you notice that girls are softer and prettier than boys.

"Yes, you are," she said, her eyes gleaming. "And handsome too."

"Don't tell me that," I said, "My head's too big as it is."

She laughed, a deep, delightful sound that made me think of Susie. She tugged back the sleeve of her blouse and uncovered a tiny silver watch.

"Uh-oh, I'm sorry, but I really have to run or I'll miss my plane." She made another face. "And I locked the damned door. I'm sorry, I'd usually have a key, but I left it on the kitchen table just to give him something to think about."

"No problem. It's a nice day. I'll wait here on the porch."

"If I know Ward, he'll be up there till dark. Why don't you drive on up? You won't have any trouble at all in your pickup. Just follow the driveway down around the barn to your left. You can't miss it." She flashed me a smile and left the veranda, angling across the short dry grass toward the Ferrari. "I hope I see you again, Mr. Roman," she called gaily over her shoulder.

"You bet," I said loudly, lighting a cigarette and following her at a more sedate pace. I sucked on the cigarette and tried to think of one of those witty things I used to say; nothing came readily to mind.

4

I LEANED AGAINST THE PICKUP FOR A WHILE, LISTENING, but if Ward Bannion and the runty salesman were playing with guns they were doing it quietly.

I drove down the curving gravel lane toward the barn, edging carefully around a medium sized motor home parked carelessly half-on and half-off the narrow road. Bug-spattered and grimy, the darkly tinted side windows of the vehicle were rimmed with gaily colored decals from what appeared to be every state in the union. It had Texas license plates and a small foreign car riding on a trailer hitched to the rear.

Must be the salesman's, I thought, wondering what a man might sell that would take him into every nook and cranny of the country. Saragache County, Texas certainly qualified as a nook, if not a cranny, with more than two-thirds of its original territory having been swallowed by a man-made lake that stretched from its northern boundary to the border of its neighboring county below.

But maybe he and Ward were friends, fellow gun lovers perhaps, part of that strange breed who love guns above and beyond their necessary function in their lives, men who can spend hours stroking cold blue steel the way other men lavish adoration on satiny female flesh. I owned guns because sometimes in my business the need arose, but I didn't have to like them any more than I did a hammer when I needed to drive a nail. I had discovered a long time ago that worshiping inanimate objects had a built-in frustration quotient: they gave so little in return.

As mountains go in Texas, the mound of earth and rocks and trees behind Bannion's house was only a hill. A tall hill, to be sure, with steep slopes and sharp ridges, cedar and hardwoods and a sheer fifty-foot cliff along its trailing flank.

I crossed a barnyard littered with the rusting relics of a time when the mule was king: hayrakes and cultivators, cotton drills and harrows, all with warped and rotting tongues, doubletrees, and rusty chains. Through the gaping barn doors I glimpsed a gleaming new tractor and a parade of shiny new implements with three-point hitches.

Once again I tried to fit the Ward Bannion I remembered into the alien realm of plowing, planting, and reaping; once again, I could not.

On the outer edge of the barnyard a long aluminum gate blocked my way. I stopped the pickup and got out. Two horses in a small corral hooked to the north end of the barn watched me over the fence as I unlatched the gate and swung it back against its stop.

One of the horses nickered softly. I nickered back, a poor imitation, and the larger one, a mare, I thought, tossed her head in disdain and trotted around the perimeter of her small circular world. The other one watched her, then turned back to me, pumping its head up and down as if in approval of my performance.

I laughed and lit a cigarette; I was climbing back into my pickup when I heard the unmistakable sound of a working car motor in low gear, a protesting whine that ended in a backfire as the engine down-shifted one more time.

I searched the side of the hill with my eyes, following the road to where it disappeared into a thicket of young oak, continuing up the hill along the most likely trajectory, shifting back again as a vehicle, almost hidden in a bubble of dust, broke out of the oak thicket and raced along a field of milo stubble toward me.

I walked back to the gate and waited, feeling a warm rush of anticipation. Twelve years is a hell of a long time, and Ward Bannion was not just another wartime friend. He was the man who had saved my life and for a short but meaningful time we had been closer than most brothers I knew. But maybe that had meant more to me than it had to him: I was an only child and he had had an older brother and had grown up in the middle of more relatives than he could count.

A firm handclasp, a quick slam on the shoulder, and smiles so wide they hurt. That's all we allowed ourselves, all the mores of our generation and background would allow. The masculine customs were sharp and clear, the rituals binding: men shook hands and pounded each other on the back; women hugged and kissed.

Except for the fact that his hair had turned silver, he hadn't changed as much as I had anticipated, his broad face a tad fuller, the square jaw a little more pronounced. His dark gray eyes seemed set deeper beneath shaggy eyebrows, cheekbones a bit more prominent.

We shuffled around awkwardly for a while, grinning at each other, talking nonsense about my trip from Dallas, the weather, finding it difficult to span twelve years. Finally, he seemed to remember his companion, a slender compact man who had been leaning against the door of the van, watching us and smiling, idly scratching his leg above his boot.

"Hey, Nate, come here. Want you to meet a friend of mine, Dan Roman. Dan, this is Nathan Barr, another friend, and the best damn farrier west of the Mississippi. I think I mentioned Dan to you a couple of times, Nate."

"Yeah, you did," Barr said, the smile widening. "A couple of times."

His head seemed too large for his body, a thick tangle of blond hair curling inward just above his collar heightening the leonine effect. His eyes were pale blue, set deep, guarded by heavy sandy brows at least three shades lighter than the Kenny Rogers beard and mustache that covered the lower portion of

17

his face. His handclasp was firm and dry, his movements quick and graceful, as economical as those of a cat.

"No more than a couple of dozen times," he said, "give or take one." He grinned at me and released my hand. "Golly, I sure hope I get to see your blue leotards with the big S and the red cape before I—" He broke off into a mock death rattle as Bannion's big hand encircled his neck from behind.

"Don't mind Nate," Bannion said. "He's uncomfortable around grownups. He tends to prattle." He ruffled the smaller man's cap of windblown hair. "But don't you think he makes a nice pet?"

Barr's gusty barking laugh was genuine, delighted. He backed away from the heavy hand. He looked at me and shook his head. "I know he looks tame, but for God sakes don't get too close when you're feeding him."

They both laughed and I joined in. It was the easy raillery of a long standing friendship, and for a second I felt a faint twinge of jealousy, a sense of loss. Time had diluted my memory of Ward Bannion's easy humor and quick wit, the same time that had given me an exaggerated recollection of his size, had added scope and dimension to create a larger-than-life image in my mind. The reality was not a disappointment exactly, but he was no longer an invincible giant either. He was only a man three inches taller than me, a little thinner, and a hell of a lot more handsome. But I couldn't fault him for that, almost everybody was.

"Nate," Ward was saying, "if you'll drive the van, I'll ride on up to the house with Dan. Maybe if we act nice, Carol Anne will dig us up a beer or two."

"Don't count on it," I said. "Depending on how far she had to drive, Carol Anne may be winging off into the wild blue yonder right this minute."

"Oh, shit! Dammit, Nate, I thought you were gonna remind me we had to be back by five o'clock. Now she'll be pissed when she gets off her run and come storming in here in the middle of the night."

"I wouldn't count on that, either," I said. "Unless 'tell

18

Ward to kiss my ass' is a quaint term of endearment in these parts.''

Nathan Barr pounded the side panel of the dusty van, bellowing with laughter. He climbed inside and lay forward across the steering wheel, his mouth gaping at us through the dirt-coated windshield, his body shaking.

Ward watched him, smiling wryly. ''Don't take much to tear him up,'' he said, then turned his smile on me. ''Well, what did you think of sweet Carol Anne?''

We walked to my pickup. ''Pretty lady,'' I said, sliding behind the wheel. ''A lot prettier than most stews I've come across.''

He chuckled quietly and dug a pack of cigarettes out of his khaki shirt pocket. ''Not a stewardess,'' he said. ''She's a co-pilot.''

''Well, she's damn sure the prettiest pilot I've ever seen.''

IIe lit the cigarette and let the smoke spurt out with a sigh that came all the way from his boot tops.

''She's that, all right, but she's also a damn strong minded woman. I don't know. Maybe it's the difference in our ages.'' He was silent for a moment, puffing smoke. Then he gave me a sidelong glance. ''Sixteen years.''

''That much,'' I said, deciding it wasn't the right time to mention Susie, the fact that she was twenty-four. ''That would make her twenty-six? Isn't that a little young for a pilot?''

''Not when you graduate college at twenty with an Aeronautical Engineering degree,'' he said glumly. ''She may not show it, but Carol Anne is pretty smart.'' He rolled down his window as I rounded the barn and squeezed past the motor home. He reached out a big hand and let his fingers make grooves in the grime on the metal side of Barr's well-worn rig.

''Nate's home nine months out of the year,'' he said. ''I don't think I could handle being cooped up like that.''

''You said he was a farrier?''

''A damn good one, too. But shoeing horses is more his avocation. He mostly sells guns and uniforms. He's a jobber. Cop uniforms and cop guns. Thirty-eights, forty-fives, and

.357s. Any brand you want, and his prices are right." He wiped his fingers on the side of his boot. "He's not in it for the money. Nate and his daddy Moser own a string of motels all across the country and half the bars in St. Louis, Missouri. Nate always wanted to be a cop but he couldn't hack the physical, a heart murmur, high cholesterol, or some damn thing. I guess maybe this is as close as he could get."

"He looks fit enough now," I said, drifting to a stop near my original parking place. "You known him a long time?"

Ward nodded. "I guess five years now. He's older than he looks. He's only twelve years younger than me." He tossed the cigarette butt out into the driveway and opened his door, giving me a lopsided, inquisitive smile. "You still private eyeing, I guess."

"When I can't get out of it." We climbed out of the truck.

"Damned good one, too, from what I hear."

"Don't believe everything you hear."

He smiled. "Believe it or not we have all the modern communications systems down here in Jerico Falls now. Things like TV and radio and newspapers. I even have a satellite dish out there behind the house. You forget you've made the news a couple of times the last few years?"

I walked around the truck feeling a little foolish. "Local stuff," I said. "Small potatoes in the scheme of things."

"There's no such thing anymore, buddy. A Baptist minister in Alabama gets caught lollygagging with one of his parishioners and the next morning everyone in Saginaw, Michigan, chuckles about it over their morning coffee. The world is not just shrinking, it has shrunk, and we all live in glass houses." The lopsided smile was back. "You don't watch a lot of TV, do you?"

"None that I can get out of."

We moved away from the pickup as Nathan Barr zipped past his motor home without slowing and headed straight for us, zigzagging the front wheels of the van, his cherubic face glowing like a murky sunset through the dirty windshield.

"He's crazy," Ward said, "but he grows on you."

5

WE HAD TEXAS BARBECUE FOR DINNER. THIN SLICES OF lean brisket immersed in a tangy sauce and brought to a boil. The sandwiches were thick and messy and delicious washed down by copious amounts of beer. I ate two and thought seriously about a third, then changed my mind when Ward and Nate only had one each.

"This is great stuff," Nate said.

Ward shoved the bowl across the table to me. "Clean it out, Dan."

"I'm fine," I said. "Any more and I'd give Texans a bad name."

"No way, man," Nate said. "Great state, Texas. I'm not a native but I'm beginning to feel like one. Lots of horses in Texas. Fat Stock Show in Fort Worth. I never miss it. If I wanted, I could keep busy six months a year on the contacts I make at the Fat Stock Show alone. And rodeos. Man, you have some fine rodeos in Texas. Great horses. Trouble is lots of the cowboys shoe their own. Can't say I blame them a whole lot. Not many farriers around nowadays and half of them don't know what they're doing." He bunched a scrap of rye bread into a ball and popped it into his mouth, chewing slowly, his hairy face pensive. "I don't know why the hell

21

I'm complaining. I get five times more work than I want to do the way it is.''

Ward grunted and fished a cigarette from his shirt pocket. "Fascinating job. Standing in horse shit all day cuddling a horse's leg between your balls. That's what I call kinky stuff.''

"Don't knock it," Barr said. "Only thing bad about it is the fleas, and the fleas here in Texas are the worst there is. Big as horseflies.''

Ward snorted. "Texas fleas are no bigger'n anywhere else.''

"Oh, yeah.'' Barr bounced to his feet and yanked up his pants leg, pointed triumphantly to eight or ten tiny red bumps between his boot top and his knee. "Flea bites. Takes a mighty big flea to bite like that. Five of them suckers could carry a man off.'' He scratched tenderly with a short slender forefinger.

"Look more like chigger bites to me," I said.

"No chiggers around here," Ward said. "Too hot and dry. He must have picked them up back in Missouri . . .''

"Fleas,'' Barr said, dismissing the subject with an imperious wave. He snaked his pants leg down over his boots and went to the cabinet where he had left a bottle of Wild Turkey he had brought in from the motor home. "I'm buying. How do you guys take your booze?''

"No thanks," I said. "Maybe a beer later.''

Ward shook his head. "Nothing for me, Nate.''

Barr turned with the bottle in his hand. "Well, I won't tempt you. Hey, look, I've gotta big date tomorrow with some mean horses. I know you guys got a lot to talk about, so I'm gonna take off.'' He put down the whiskey and came over and held out his hand. "Good meeting you, Dan. See you later, okay?''

I shook his hand. "Same here, Nate. Watch them hind legs, they're killers.''

He laughed and went through the door onto the rear wooden porch, boot heels popping a rapid tattoo.

"Back in a minute, Dan.'' Ward followed him. "Hey, wait up, numbnuts.''

I lit a cigarette and cleaned off the table. I scraped and rinsed the dishes and stacked them neatly in the sink. No dishwasher that I could see. No blenders, no mixers. No microwave oven. Not even a toaster. None of the accoutrements of a well-kept kitchen. No feminine touches at all. The room was neat but no attempt had been made to prettify it, to make it home.

I wondered where his wife and kids were, where pretty Carol Anne fit into his life. Judging by her overnight bag and her astringent words, she had spent the night and had probably counted on spending another. So obviously he and his wife were no longer together.

I opened a can of beer from the refrigerator and went back to the table and sat down in Barr's former chair, searching the night outside the window for the answer. I couldn't find it.

6

"I GOT YOUR LETTER," I SAID. "AND I GOT MY SORRY NO-good ass right on down here."

Ward chuckled, then worked his face into a grimace. "Dumb idea. I get a lot of them when I'm half sloshed." He sat down at the table, blinked his eyes, then stroked them lightly with a thumb and forefinger.

"You mean I read it wrong? I thought you were asking for help of one kind or other."

He nodded, looking into the darkness outside the window. "I was. I still am. We have a situation here that—" He broke off and took a drink of beer. "But before I get into that, did I ever tell you about the Caulders and the Bannions?"

"You told me a little about the Bannions. I don't remember the name Caulders."

"Caulder. Roy Bannion and Abel Caulder. Young men, good friends. They came here from Indiana around a hundred years ago. Partners. Apparently they had quite a bit of money between them. Nobody knows for sure and family history's pretty vague about where they got it. Anyhow, they bought up most of this valley, twenty thousand acres more or less. Went into the cattle business. Did right well, too. They had to kill an Indian now and then and hang a rustler

24

or two for stealing their cows, but all in all they prospered, had their ups and downs the way the cattle business has always been. Jerico Falls started along about then on land they donated, and I guess that's when the snowball started rolling. People came in. The town grew. More people came in, among them a woman named Nellie Radcliffe." He finished off his beer.

"Aha," I said. "The plot thickens. Or is this a history lesson? Should I be taking notes?"

"Just try to stay awake. This won't take long." He folded one big square hand around his pack of cigarettes on the table and shook one loose. "You've probably already guessed it. Both our young heroes fell for the lady, my great grandmama, so you know who won out. But men in those days didn't take defeat lightly, and the old partnership went bust right down the middle. They divided the land equally, and Roy Bannion bought up Caulder's half of the livestock. Caulder took off in a huff, went on out west somewheres, California some say, then showed up one day about five years later with a herd of sheep. That didn't set well with old Roy, particularly since he'd been grazing his cattle on Caulder land all that time. Anyhow, one thing led to another and they had themselves a pretty good little range war going here for a while. Nobody much got killed, a couple of cowboys and a sheepherder or two, but neither old Roy or old Abel ever shed a drop of blood. Finally, the Army sent in a company of soldiers and the whole thing just sort of petered out. It did and it didn't. That was the end of the shooting war, but the Caulders and the Bannions have been enemies ever since. Only a few of us, the ones who cared to dig back and find out, ever knew exactly why. All over a woman. Empires have toppled for less, I guess. It's never amounted to much over the years, at least not in my time, a flare-up now and then, somebody gets cut up a little, a few fistfights. A lot of loud talk in the tonks out on the highway. But that's usually all it is, a lot of talk." He stubbed out the half-smoked cigarette, his broad face morose.

"Let me guess," I said. "The range war's flared up and you want to hire me as a gunslinger."

He made a half-hearted attempt at a smile. "I almost wish it was as simple as that."

"Okay. How complex is it?"

He sighed, a look of pain crossing his face, as fleeting as a bird's shadow on a rock. "As complex as murder. Or maybe as simple as murder. Two murders, actually. Two kids, eighteen, a boy and a girl. Two kids in love I've since found out. They were planning on eloping during the Christmas break and getting married."

"Break? College?"

He nodded. "He went to Baylor in Austin. She went to UTA in Arlington. The only time they got to see each other was on a weekend trip home. Nobody knew about them, you see, except for one or two of their closest friends. And they were sworn to secrecy."

"Secrecy? Why?" And then the fog lifted. "A Bannion and a Caulder."

He nodded again, the pain back on his face. "Cody's boy. I told you about Cody."

"Yes. Your brother."

"Stephen Bannion and Lisa Caulder. She was Abel Caulder's daughter. Abel's about forty-nine, Cody's age. He was named after his great granddaddy. He's a hard arrogant man and he's part of the reason I sent you the letter."

"You'll have to explain that."

"It isn't complicated. The murders occurred two weeks ago yesterday—Saturday night, somewhere between eight o'clock and ten according to the county coroner's office. And so far we've got zip. No clues, no motives, nothing. We've had some county help from the Sheriff's department and some from the state. They also came up empty. Abel—and Cody, too—is understandably upset. Particularly, I think, since I'm a Bannion and in charge of the investigation. Abel hasn't said it right out, at least not to me, but he probably thinks I've got shit for brains. And maybe he's not far wrong. I haven't been able to put two coherent thoughts together since this damn thing happened.''

"Too close to it, maybe.''

He shrugged and shook loose another Winston. "Don't make excuses for me, Dan.''

"It's not an excuse. Your nephew and a girl you probably knew well. If you were on a big city force they wouldn't let you near the case. Don't you have someone else you could assign?''

He grimaced. "I've got an old fart a year away from pension who forgets his gun half the time, and won't wear his upper plate except when he's eating. I've got an eager beaver recruit who'll hang a ticket on anything that moves, and throw your ass in jail for saying shit in front of a lady.'' He stopped and sighed. "And then there's Lonnie Caulder. I inherited him and old Clint Doolittle. Lonnie's a ladies' man. He spends ninety percent of his time chasing other men's wives, spends the other ten sulking because he never catches any. He hates my guts because they hired me as Chief instead of promoting him, or maybe it's because I'm a Bannion. He told Ace Macon he believes Steve killed Lisa and then turned the gun on himself. That would have been a very neat trick since they both had their hands tied behind their backs, and were both blindfolded.''

"Blindfolded. What do you make of that?''

"I'm not sure,'' he said, drawling the words. "It could be for the obvious reason, to hide the killer's identity. But why bother if he meant to kill them, anyway? I think maybe there was another reason, a very human reason: it's a lot harder to kill someone when they're looking at you, staring into your face, asking why.'' He rubbed a thumb along the bridge of his nose. "One thing I remember they taught at the FBI school in Quantico. It concerned profiling a killer by analyzing the murder scene. There are a lot of factors involved, but in this particular case the instructor was illustrating a 'gentle' murder as opposed to a brutal violent one, a case where the victim was killed as quickly and as efficiently as possible, no mutilation, no violations, the body left where it would be

27

found quickly; even carefully covered to protect it from predators and the elements. In other words, treated in an almost loving manner, with respect, at least.'' He stood up and went to the refrigerator, pulled the tabs on two more cans of beer.

"See," I said brightly, "you haven't forgotten everything."

He nodded absently, took a small sip of beer. "It's odd, but that's the first thing that went through my mind when I first saw the bodies. They were lying side by side near a picnic table, one shot each in the head, and he had covered them with an old Indian blanket we later discovered came from the back seat of Steve's car. It's as if he wanted to . . . to care for them, protect them. Christ, I know it's weird, but that's the feeling I had."

"You keep saying 'he.' "

"Habit. It could be a woman just as well, I guess, except it didn't seem to be a woman's type of crime. It was a large caliber gun, at least a .38, maybe larger. Then there's the fact that the bodies were brought there—the rodeo picnic grounds out at the south edge of town. The girl was small, maybe a hundred and ten, but Steve would have gone one-sixty easy. So it would have taken a little muscle."

"Maybe there were two of them."

"It's possible. The kids were driven there in Steve's car, so the killer either walked away or was driven by someone else. Steve's car was parked a few yards from the bodies."

"You *know* they were brought there, or are you guessing?"

"We know. There were stains on the rear floorboard and back seat of Steve's car, and there was almost no blood on the ground beneath the . . . heads. Not nearly enough according to the coroner and, besides, it was pretty obvious. There was no . . . gore."

"Physical evidence?"

"Very little. Both bullets exited, so all we have to go on are the entry holes. Common nylon twine used to tie their hands, and balled up Kleenex and strips of cloth used on their eyes. The Kleenex came out of a box in Steve's car. Everything checked for prints. Nothing.''

"That's it?''

"There are some packets of weed seed and whatnot they got out of the kids' hair and clothing and shoes, a triangular wedge of dried mud that may or may not have come off the killer's boot heel at the angle where it meets the sole. A man's boot, by the way. It's too wide to be a woman's. Just plain old dirt like you'd find anywhere in this county, and the bad part is, it hasn't rained in so long it could have been lying there for a month.'' He sucked in a balloon of air. "Zip. Just like I said before.''

I lit a Carlton and drank the last of my beer, warm and flat and unpleasant. Ward was staring out the window again, the morose expression back on his face.

I didn't mind the silence. In a manner of speaking it was a reprieve. So I smoked my cigarette and helped him search the darkness, wondering what his face would look like when I told him I didn't do murders.

7

HE STARED AT ME BLANKLY, SHOCK PROPELLING HIS BUSY
eyebrows upwards. "What the hell you mean, *you don't do
murders*?"

"A bad choice of words," I said, wincing. "You know,
like the maids who don't *do windows*—"

"I know what you mean, dammit! But . . . but what the
hell do you *mean*?"

I sighed. "It's just a rule, Ward. A rule I made a long time
ago. I quit being a cop partly because I didn't like being
around dead people, or people who make them that way. I
just decided I wouldn't get involved in murders. That's all."

"Shit!" He slapped the table and expelled his breath in a
gusty explosive laugh. "Damn, you had me going there for
a minute. I was really beginning to believe you."

"Believe it," I said mildly.

He stared at me, uncertain again. "Come on. What are
you telling me? It hasn't been a year ago that I read about
that—what was it—that rich kid who killed his grandpa—hey,
come on, man, don't shit an old shitter. And that's the third,
fourth time I've read about you cracking some big case up
there in the big city. You think we don't get newspapers down
here? Come on, Dan. I've seen you on TV—and who do you

think it was who brought up your name in the meeting the other night? It wasn't me. It was Tony Caulder, that's who. Tony Caulder, one of Abel's boys. He used to write for the *Dallas Times Herald*, up until about May I think it was when his daddy bought the old Saragache County *Gazette* and turned it over to him to run. It was Tony who suggested we bring in someone from the outside, Tony who brought up your name—'' He broke off, his face brightening. ''Hey, if you're worried about your fee, don't. Abel Caulder said he'd take care of—'' He broke off again, looking nonplussed.

I realized my face was changing color; I could feel the heat. ''If I wouldn't do it for you, I damned sure wouldn't do it for a stranger!''

''Oh, hell,'' he said contritely. ''I didn't mean—I wasn't trying to insult you. I just wanted you to know that you didn't have to work for nothing. Abel can sure as hell afford it, and come to think about it, it would probably look funny if you didn't take it. I didn't tell them we were old friends. I figured they might change their minds if they knew that—''

''I met a man named Theron Alldyce at the Plaza. I told him I knew you years ago. And how about your buddy Nate?''

''Okay. No problem. So we met back during Nam. Once. No big deal, right.'' He was smiling broadly, the first real smile since I'd met him at the gate. ''Don't worry about Nate.''

I dug around in my eyes with a thumb and forefinger, mainly to blot out his beaming face. Christ. I was getting ready to do it again, leap willy-nilly into the middle of someone else's misery, the worst nightmare of all, cold-blooded murder. And to be honest, I couldn't blame it all on Ward. From the moment Alldyce had mentioned murder at the Plaza I had felt a stir of unbidden excitement, instantly squelched and allowed to resurface only as repugnance. But the more Ward talked and explained, the more the secret feeling grew, nosing its way into my consciousness, undeniable and transcendent. In my book murder equaled madness, a darkness of the soul, transgressors who have gone beyond shame and pity and compassion. Killers frightened me, cold-blooded killers frightened me the most; the fact that I found the whole thing fascinating frightened me most of all.

"I'll call Abel and Cody," Ward said casually. "They both want to meet you. Nine o'clock in my office sound about right?"

"What for? An audition?"

"Oh, hell no, nothing like that. I figured you might want to ask them some questions or something, find out some of the things about the kids that I can't tell you."

I studied his face, back to its normal sun-baked hue. "You spent six or seven years in the FBI, Ward. I'd think you'd be better at this kind of thing than I am."

"No, I had an accounting degree, remember, and except for the last year I spent my time hunched over a set of damned books. I was never an investigator. Particularly the kind of investigator required for this kind of work. You are. You're exactly what we need, an unbiased outsider. You have to remember I'm a Bannion and I'm lucky to get a civil hello from a lot of the Caulders. Some of them have never talked to me at all and a lot of others would probably lie. This county is still divided, buddy. I know it's stupid, but there it is." His face tightened. "You said it yourself, Dan. I'm too close to it. After all Steve was my nephew and I thought the world of him. Time is running out and I'm catching flak from the Sheriff, the state, not to mention the Caulders, and I'm getting nowhere. But most of all I want the son-of-a-bitch myself and I'm afraid he's slipping away from me."

There was a note of desperation in his voice that made me want to look away. I busied myself with a drink of beer and stubbed out my cigarette. He stared through the window, a knot of muscle bunching in his jaw and when he spoke again he sounded almost detached, his voice a dry, monotonous drone.

"I know you are wondering about Jean, Jackie . . . and Ellen." He brought his eyes back to mine, his face suddenly contorted. "I lost them, Dan, and I've been haunted by the knowledge that it was my fault." His eyes gripped mine for a long burning sixty seconds. "The last year in the FBI. I got tired of my job and demanded duty in the field. They obliged me finally. My second case I was assigned to a team of agents on a case that was already two years old going nowhere fast. A serial killer, a man roaming a wide area through the South. Tennessee, Alabama, Kentucky, and Georgia. He was killing families, almost always four people. A man, wife with two children. A boy and a girl. After almost two years of investigation we knew almost nothing about him.'' He paused and took a deep sighing breath, his face almost back to normal. ''We lived in a small town, Rincon, Tennessee, and an enterprising young reporter on a Memphis tabloid somehow found out about my new assignment to the Roadrunner case—that's the name the media had hung on the son-of-a-bitch—and decided it would make an interesting story for his dinky little paper. Anyhow, nobody knows why the story was picked up by a major Memphis paper and the madman evidently decided that my family would make excellent victims for his next project. Rincon had less than two thousand people so you can imagine how long it took to find out where we lived and everything about us.'' His eyes were on the cigarette trapped between long slender fingers, most of the color back in his face.

''He was a furnace salesman from Atlanta, Georgia. A little man, wife and two children of his own and as far as I know none of the shrinks he has been examined by over the years have ever been able to figure out why he did what he did. He made one mistake in my case. The night he picked to fulfill his compulsion to kill was the wrong one. I was called out around midnight on another case we were working on. When he arrived at my house there was only Jean, Jackie and Ellen.'' He stopped, swallowing audibly. A shudder rippled through him and he reached for another cigarette.

''Look, Ward, there's no need—''

He stopped me with a look and a humorless smile. ''You're right. There's no need to fill in the details.''

''Look, man, I'm sorry.''

He nodded, lit the cigarette, and blew a blue-gray puff of smoke toward the ceiling. When he spoke his voice was low and dull, almost pedantic. "I lost something that night as well. I've never recovered it. I'm not sure what it was but I was lost for a long time."

There was nothing I could say that would matter to him, so we sat for a while watching the smoke curl from his cigarette.

Then he shook himself like a wet dog on a riverbank, a ghost of his natural smile creeping across his face. "How about it, Dan? If you say no deal . . . well, it's been damn good seeing you again, anyhow."

I stared across the table for a long moment then nodded and pushed to my feet. "Okay? I'll be at your office in the morning. If your brother and Abel Caulder want to cooperate, I'll give it a whirl. If they don't, I'll go home. Fair enough?"

"Fair enough. But, hey, where do you think you're going? I got an extra room—"

"That wouldn't be smart, Ward. We're not old friends, remember? I saw a motel out on the highway that looked pretty decent. I'll stay there."

"One night," he said dubiously. "I don't think it would matter."

But I was already on my way through the door into the dining room, the wooden floors of the old house popping and creaking under my feet. I felt a need to leave. I was vaguely dissatisfied: with myself, with Bannion, or maybe with the situation; I wasn't sure why. I wanted to be by myself to think, to be conversant with myself, as they say. I needed to reconcile this Ward Bannion with the one I had known in Vietnam, this descent from a confident fearless fighting man to a middle-aged doubter. It wouldn't be a pleasant trip, but to do what I had to do I would have to go back.

8

I MET WARD BANNION ON A FRIENDLY HILL IN VIETNAM. A secured hill in the Army lexicon, which meant that at some point in the recent past all available intelligence indicated a lack of enemy presence.

I'd seen him a time or two before—once in a bar in Saigon, in dirty jungle fatigues, drinking silently in a corner of the smoky noisy room, dark eyes surly and defiant under the black beret that identified him as an Airborne Ranger—and again in another noisy smoky room, a briefing room at Pleiku, a mix of helicopter pilots and Ranger brass. I was only peripherally aware of him—just another badass Ranger, bigger than most, a granite Irish face that exuded confidence instead of sweat, dark gray eyes that roamed ceaselessly, made assessments, moved on. A career soldier, I would have guessed, a lifer.

I was flying a slick—a Huey 204 troop carrier—and the mission was considered a pussy run, a ten minute flight along a narrow valley already secured by South Vietnamese troops, a two minute low-level pass up the side of the friendly hill, a one minute hover to dump my cargo, then home again in time for evening chow. Simple.

My cargo was a four man reconnaissance team of Airborne Rangers, my only crew member Sergeant Max Conroe, crew chief and door gunner. Somewhere behind us other Hueys were bringing in squads of Rangers to join with ARVN's in a planned assault on the object of the recon team's surveillance, a tall brooding hill immediately to the north, a sinister, denuded, useless-looking bit of real estate that had been secured twice before only to be relinquished to overwhelming Viet Cong counterattack.

The flight went pretty much according to plan, the ten minute pull along the valley uneventful, flying the treetops just in case all the dark faces below were not on our side. The hill was taller than reported, but I still made it in two minutes flat, sliding up and over the lip of a small sloping plateau, catching my breath as the injured earth came into view, scorched and shriveled and blackened, clotted with the tortured remnants of trees, bomb craters, and tadpole-shaped napalm tracks.

I automatically searched for a landing zone, feeling my insides pull tight as I eased the Huey forward and down, nosing into a small burned-out clearing near the bottom of the slope.

I hovered a foot above the torn and pitted soil, keeping one eye on the rim of the hill, the tight muscles in my stomach forming a knot. This was the time if there was going to be one, the big bird hanging like a balloon on a string, perfect target from the ragged line of jungle.

I felt vibration and lift as the recon team debarked—almost all. I heard voices behind me and risked a backward glance.

Conroe was out from behind his gun, out of his belts and chest armor, tugging at the harness on the fourth man's rucksack.

The team leader, already a half-dozen yards up the slope, stopped and looked back. He took a step toward the Huey, his right hand going into the air, his mouth wide open, a look of surprise crossing his face as his chest suddenly jetted blood, whatever he was yelling lost forever in a gout of obscene red as another bullet went into the back of his head and blew away the bottom half of his mouth. Behind him the rim of the hill was abruptly alive with Viet Cong, popping out of holes everywhere, AK47's and pith helmets, black pajamas and bandannaed heads.

Instant hell. The two Rangers on the ground back-pedaled toward the Huey, crouched low and firing. But the answering fire was overwhelming and they fell before they had covered half the distance.

Behind me Conroe cursed and scrambled for his machine gun. The fourth Ranger dropped to one knee and returned fire—one short burst—before he toppled slowly forward, dove headfirst through the cargo door into the blackened stubble to join his dead teammates.

It was my first brush with the totality of instant death, of systematic war close up, and for one eternal moment I hung frozen over my controls, caught in a rigor of absurd disbelief, feeling the Huey resonating like a drum, shuddering, seeing before me a surreal landscape peopled with stick figures, celluloid images that would go away when the lights came up. I was swept with the sudden paralyzing thought that Conroe and I were all alone, that we were fighting the Vietnam war all by ourselves, stranded on top of a goddamned nothing hill waiting to die.

Conroe's machine gun clattered; adrenaline blasted in my veins, surged up into my throat. A million nerve cells fired in my brain and instinct took over. I began the automatic moves that would get us the hell out of there.

The helicopter rose, trembling, engine whining—six, ten, twenty feet—then dipped sickeningly, lurching sideways and fell, a deadly *whap whap* overhead as the main rotor blade disintegrated, one large whirling segment skipping up the slope like an ineptly thrown knife, interrupting, for a few precious seconds, Charlie's murderous fire as they scrambled for safety.

The Huey slapped the earth like a stomped foot, bounced, skidded, came to rest balanced precariously on the lower lip of the slope. I slammed downward into the armor-plated seat, feeling something important let go in my head, my vision filled with black flying insects, sparkling stars.

The next few seconds were forever a blank. Somehow I got out of the helmet and harness, crawling around the seat toward the cargo bay, raising to my knees once to see Conroe lying behind his gun, his head propped against a bulkhead, everything gone above his eyes.

That was when the cockpit exploded behind me, impossible sound and a giant hand cupping my torso, slamming me forward across the blood-slick metal deck, headfirst into the bulkhead just to the left of Conroe's body.

I woke up looking into the top of Conroe's open skull, a gray and red shimmering mass that had no literal meaning. I found myself wondering groggily if it hurt, then almost giggled when I realized the absurdity of a dead man hurting.

Dead, I understood dead. They were all dead. All the soldiers were dead and there was only me to dispose of. And I would be easy. I wasn't a fighter, I was a flyer, a people mover, a goddamned bus driver for Christ sakes!

I turned my head and looked out the cargo bay door toward the upper slope. They were on their way, walking cautiously but confidently now, jabbering in that Godless clatter they called a language.

Little men no bigger than average well-fed American twelve year olds. Goddamn kids coming to kill me.

My head ached. Streaks of fire radiated from the crown of my skull. My eyes blurred with moisture. I blinked them free.

Little bastards coming to kill me!

And with that thought sizzling in my brain, I crawled around Conroe's body into the gunner's pocket, manned his pylon-mounted machine gun at the door, killing, in the very next instant my first human being, watching him tumble and roll with a savage primal glee, swinging the gun on to the next, and the next, seeing the now crouched, dodging, darting figures crumple and counting methodically, as if my eventual worth would be measured only by the number of fallen Viet Cong.

My breath whistled through my teeth. I spat adrenaline, my very existence crystallized around this pristine moment in time, screaming men and the whisper and snap of bullets in the air around me, the scaring stench of cordite and the cloying smell of death clotting my nostrils, invading my soul.

I fought the bucking gun and waited for death, wondering with a kind of dismal detachment why it was taking so long. A line of dark-suited men already lay sprawled grotesquely along the upper reaches of the slope, and others stumbled blindly among the blackened stubs of vegetation, holding themselves together with blood-red hands, their faces a ludicrous mixture of shock, fear, and something else that could have been embarrassment at their own vulnerability.

And still I fired—untouched—a warm stream of some primal fluid oozing down across my stomach and into my groin, my left ankle shrilling a steady message of scalding pain.

Short vicious bursts at specific targets. Conserving ammo, making the rounds count, only vaguely aware that men were falling outside my line of fire, both to my left and to my right, sometimes seconds before I reached them with my gunsight.

I pondered this anomaly, dimly wondering if I could be hallucinating, and all the while the volume of sound around me swelled to sickening proportions, a dissonant crescendo blotting out light and reason, the physical world outside my metal nest going crazy, the very earth itself whirling upward in vast upheaval, sights and sounds I would have recognized had it not been for my obsession with the gun and my enemies moving inexorably forward.

I hunched my shoulders and kept on firing, stoic to the end, accepting my coming annihilation with ponderous aplomb, recognizing the moral necessity and judicial correctness of it, understanding that the time of foolish notions and protean joys was at an end, that only a generous allotment of sheer arrogance had brought me this far.

The gun bucked and snarled. Men died. I felt immortal—Zeus slinging thunderbolts, Zorro slashing Z's.

It was then, at the zenith of my maniacal frenzy, that I heard the bellowing voice behind me and turned to look across the belly of the bird to see the red, angry face of

Lieutenant Ward Bannion, wide shoulders filling the opening, black beret cocked on close-cropped yellow curls. Beyond him I could see the skids of another Huey rocking a few feet off the ground, two men in jungle fatigues kneeling, automatic rifles stuttering at their shoulders.

Bannion gestured wildly; I stared at him blankly for a second, then made a little wave and yelled, "Welcome," and turned back to my gun. A dark bandannaed head popped out of a bomb crater. I blew it away, the head inside coming apart in a shower of marbleized spray.

I heard a curse behind me. The Huey rocked some more, and seconds later I felt rough hands slide under my arms, yank me loose from the gun.

"Goddammit, Lieutenant! Who the hell you think you are? Audie Murphy?" He slid me across the metal deck to the door, leaped down. "You stoned, or what?" He peered at my eyes.

"I have a broken ankle, I think, and I may be concussed."

"Figures." He slung his M-16 across his shoulder and picked me up like a baby, then loped down the slope to the waiting Huey, rolled me expertly into its gaping side. Without pause, he whirled and began cover fire for his two men. The Huey's door gunner joined in, showering me with hot brass.

I scooted back against the swing seat and watched the battle with a kind of amused tolerance. It no longer had anything to do with me. The professionals had taken over the stage. I had had my walk-on, spoken my lines, and there was a kind of contentment in that. I wanted nothing more to do with killing my fellow man. I craved peace, solitude, intellectual pursuits, love. I suddenly realized I was thinking in terms of the future again, of life beyond this arena of death.

Bullets drummed into the Huey, sending tiny shock waves through the metal into my hands propped on the deck. The helicopter rose petulantly, rolled, swayed, returned to its previous position. I could hear the drone of the pilot's voice, cursing.

I saw the three Rangers grouped at the door, heard a yell,

and saw Bannion's face disappear. Seconds later it reappeared as his two men threw him unceremoniously in beside me. He clutched his left leg a few inches above his knee. A jagged exit hole pumped blood in lazy spurts. He winced and looked away as one of the Rangers applied a tourniquet.

The helicopter slipped sideways along the side of the ridge, whipping foliage, gaining altitude as we reached ARVN territory in the valley, swinging wide and well away from the baldheaded, friendly hill.

Bannion's gaze met mine. We stared at each other silently for a moment. His eyes were strangely hot, hostile, his wide mouth twisted in pain. My head throbbed, my ankle screamed, and I felt an unreasonable spurt of anger.

"That little black hat," I said. "I always thought they looked damn silly."

His man applied a pressure bandage to the seeping wound. Bannion tried to hide a grimace of pain. He wet his lips, making no headway with the caked red dust.

"I just goddamn hope you're worth it," he said.

That was how we met. Not an auspicious beginning. We became friends later, during the two months we spent in the hospital, recovering from our battle wounds, my broken ankle and his splintered thigh bone both in casts. The fact that we were both from Texas helped, as did the discovery that we both were on a first name basis with demon rum. He loved to talk and most times I didn't mind listening. We had read the same books and listened to the same kinds of music. He had a wife and two kids. I had a wife and a kid on the way. We argued about politics and agreed that religion was for Christians, kindly well-meaning folks maybe, but not inclined to have much fun.

We built the friendship from scratch. Out of knowing some of the same truths, out of the certain knowledge that ours was the sorriest war yet, close to Korea maybe, but still the meanest, most useless. Out of a certainty that we would not survive and, perhaps most of all, out of a quiet unspoken pride that we had each done what we had to do. It was our war, after all, however meaningless, and we had done what our country asked of us. Nobody could fault us for that. At least that was what we thought at the time.

We never once talked about that day on the nameless hill, and when a brace of starched REMF's from Saigon came around looking for a hot body to pin a ribbon on, I told them to pin it on Conroe and the four Rangers. I was just along for the ride. I sent them down to therapy to see Ward Bannion. I never found out what he told them; we never talked about that day, either.

It wasn't always easy to make connections, but after we got out of the hospital we managed eight to ten more weekends together before his tour was over and he returned to the world.

For thirty dollars I bought a rectangular room with a double bed, TV, one chair, and a sanitized toilet. The bathroom tile was chipped and pitted, but the water was hot and the bed was middling good, so I had no complaints.

I went to sleep easily, then woke up in the early morning hours, dreaming, something I didn't often do. I sat on the edge of the bed and smoked a cigarette and thought about the decaying town of Jerico Falls, about human frailty and senseless murder. But mostly I thought about Ward. Nothing had been resolved during my few hours of dream-laden sleep. I still wasn't sure if he was less than I remembered him to be, or if what I remembered was more than he ever really was.

9

ABEL CAULDER WAS A TALL, THIN MAN WITH LONG ARMS and big work hardened hands. He had a long weatherbeaten face, beginning to seam, wispy brown hair that thickened perceptibly over his ears and on the back of his neck. A thin nose with a delicate flair, a square thrusting jaw. He wore frayed Levi's, a wrinkled work shirt, and two days' beard stubble. His boots were impeccable, made from some exotic animal skin. His expression seemed frozen, cast along permanent lines of intense irascibility; a no nonsense man who had apparently decided a long time ago that life was no joke, and had cast aside humor and frivolity along with the other foolish accoutrements of youth.

His voice, however, was soft and clear as he stood to shake my hand when I walked into Ward Bannion's spartan office.

"Mr. Roman. Nice to meet you. Ward here tells me you're from Dallas."

"Midway City, but he's close." He squeezed my hand gingerly, then let it drop, his palm rough but surprisingly warm.

"Dan." Ward was standing behind his desk. "I'd like you to meet my brother Cody. Cody, this is Dan Roman, the detective Tony was talking about the other night."

Cody Bannion stood up, a slender compact man of medium height. He nodded without smiling and extended his hand. "Glad you could come, Mr. Roman." He had pale blue eyes and a thick swatch of gray-streaked blond hair, a round pleasant face that bore not the slightest resemblance to his younger brother's.

I nodded silently and shook his hand, unwilling to say that I was glad to be there, unwilling to admit, even to myself, that I had awakened with a heightened sense of purpose, an acceleration of awareness, a low grade high.

Ward cleared his throat. "Take a seat there, Dan. I thought a meeting between the three of you might be beneficial here at the beginning, get the details of your contract ironed out—"

"No contract," I said. "Not until I decide if I'll take the case."

"Okay," Ward said quickly, cheerfully. "No hurry about that. I figured you would have some questions for Cody and Mr. Caulder here." He hesitated as if he'd forgotten something. "Uh, I understand your fee is three hundred a day. Well, we have no quarrel with that." He paused, his head swinging back and forth between the two men flanking his desk at either end. "Do we?"

Caulder dismissed the subject with a wave of his hand, his expression unchanged. "I was under the impression that it was settled, that you were going to take the case."

"So was I," Cody said, a perplexed look on his face.

I turned to Caulder. "Chief Bannion told me a little about the situation here in Jerico Falls, the Caulders and the Bannions. A detective is only as good as the information he collects. Most of that information comes from people, relatives of the victims, friends. Sometimes he lucks out and there's physical evidence at the scene of the crime. We don't seem to have much of that here. If the people of this town won't talk to me I'm not going to find out who killed your daughter." I turned and looked at Cody. "Or your son. I may not anyhow, but without your full cooperation, I won't have a fighting chance."

"You don't have to worry about the Caulders," Abel said in his soft clear voice. "We've got nothing to hide."

Cody shot him a quick annoyed glance. "What the hell do you mean by that, Abel?"

"It means what it said. That's what it means." Something that may have been a grimace or a fleeting smile quirked the edges of his mouth.

"Are you implying that the Bannions *do* have something to hide? Are you forgetting that my son was found with your daughter? He's just as dead as your girl."

"I ain't forgetting anything. I ain't forgetting they was together when they shouldn't have been, either."

"You think I liked that any better than you do? By God, if I'da known about it, I'da kept his ass chained to the snubbing ring every night of his life. That girl—" Cody broke off, breathing hard, his round face florid.

"What about that girl?" Abel asked softly.

"All right, goddammit!" Ward slammed a huge clubbed hand into the metal desktop. "Dammit, that's just what Dan's talking about. If you two can't be in the same room for five minutes without snarling at each other like a couple of stray dogs, what do you think the rest of them are gonna do if they hear you're fighting again? They'll clam up like . . . like clams, is what they'll do. Now, Dan needs to talk to both of you but I think he'd better do it one at a time. Come on, Cody, let's go down to Dixie's and get a cup of coffee." He walked around the desk and stood beside his brother, a semi-belligerent look on his face, a look that said "I'll carry your sorry ass if I have to."

Cody studied his brother's face for a moment, then got up and meekly left the room. Ward looked at me over his shoulder, rolled his eyes, and grinned. He quietly closed the door behind him.

Abel Caulder made a smothered, choking sound. I looked at him. He still looked the same except his adam's apple was bobbing up and down and I finally decided he was chuckling.

"Old Cody. He'll never change. Easiest man in the world to rile up. Always was. Even when we was kids back in school I could get his goat just by looking at him and kinda grinning like I knew something he didn't, like I knew about the brown streaks in his drawers. Even in high school when we was almost sorta like friends I could set him off easy as pie. I even took center away from him on the basketball team. Even though he's shorter than me he could jump higher, but when we went for tryouts, I'd say or do something to make him mad and he'd screw up every time. He hated to be called Bunion worse than anything, I guess, or Shorty. And he never seemed to catch on to what I was doing. He just wore his Bannion pride like it was some kind of halo and you'd better not stand between him and the light. It's a funny thing, though, we never had a fistfight in all them years, just cussed and fussed at each other a lot.''

"You had no idea Steve and Lisa were seeing each other?"

He sighed. ''Yes, as a matter of fact, I did. Back in early summer, I guess, was when it started. She began acting mighty strange, quit going out with boys, started spending a lot of evenings over at her girlfriends' houses, acting secretive, that kind of thing. I decided I'd better find out what was going on and I followed her a few times. It didn't take long to find out she was meeting that Bannion boy. I'll admit that I followed them too, a time or two. I had no real objections to the Bannion boy. He was a good-looking kid, smart, and seemed to be ambitious. Lot better than most around here. My only worry was that he might be trifling with her, you know, out for what he could get, then bye-bye, off to college and something to laugh about with his buddies.''

"It's a problem," I said.

"Well, I thought about it some. She was turning eighteen and I'da bet money she was still a virgin, and that's some kind of accomplishment in itself. But how long can you keep them under your thumb? She was going off to college this fall and could damn well do anything she wanted to with a boy, so I couldn't see that breaking it up would do much good. We had close feelings between us and I didn't want to ruin that. Her mother's been dead four years now and I tried to make up for it, but I suppose you can never do that. I've found out from one of her friends that they were planning on getting married Christmas, so I guess I did the right thing.'' He ran a hand across his head. ''Maybe not, the way things happened.''

''It's hard to know sometimes. Other paths, other dragons.''

He shook his head. ''I know there are no easy answers nowadays, no guarantees. They're killing girls everywhere, Dallas, Houston, Denver, Seattle. At least she wasn't . . . wasn't violated.'' It was only a slight break in his voice, but somehow I was suddenly aware of pain, a palpable wave that flowed between us like magnetic flux. There were furrows in his face I hadn't noticed before, a cloudiness in the washed out gray eyes.

''Were there any boys, any one boy in particular she used to go with, who might have been upset about being dropped?''

''None that I know of. She went out with several boys during her senior year but usually not for very long. She said most of the boys her age weren't ready to grow up, that all they wanted to do was drive fast, drink, do dope, and have sex.''

''Same old music,'' I said. ''A different tempo and a few new notes.''

He nodded again, lips quirking. This time I was almost certain it was a smile.

''The times you followed the kids, did they go to the same place? Did they seem to have a favorite place to park?''

''Yes,'' he said, without hesitation. ''Out at that small lake behind Ward Bannion's place, around on the north side of that big hill behind his house. It used to be a stock tank actually, three or four acres. But it has trees and it's a secluded private spot.''

''Any enemies that you know about?''

''None. She was a sweet lively girl. Everybody loved her.''

Not everybody, I thought.

We talked for a few minutes longer, but there was nothing more he could tell me that had a bearing on the murders. He gave me the names of two of Lisa's closest friends, the two who weren't away at college. He told me where I could find his son Tony, his other son Ralph who worked with him on the ranch and lived in the small town of Twigg, ten miles to the east.

He unfolded his lean body out of the chair; we shook hands again. He moved to the door with a noticeable limp in his left leg. He stood for a moment with his hand on the knob, looking at me, his expression unchanged from its mode of perpetual anger.

"Find him, Mr. Roman. Just give me a name, I'll handle it from there."

"Frontier justice, Mr. Caulder? And what if I make a mistake?"

His gaze didn't waver, gray eyes suddenly bright and shiny. "I trust you. You won't do that."

He turned and went out.

"And what if I don't find him at all?" I said to the empty room, an old familiar feeling comprised of futility and resentment stealing over me. People who paid you money wanted results, expected miracles if need be. I could have told him that family-oriented killings aside, pitifully few murders were solved in this country, that murder is fast replacing baseball as the national pastime, the game of choice. I could have told him also that I was no super sleuth, not James Bond or Ellery Queen, not even a heavy-handed, quick-triggered Mike Hammer. I was simply an average man with a knack, closing fast on middle age, a survivor of one big war and countless small ones, a cynic with nothing to guide me except a shaky set of principles long out of style.

I sat back down and lit a cigarette and waited for Ward and Cody Bannion.

No miracles today, Mr. Caulder. That's somebody else's job.

10

Murder scenes sometimes have an eerie ambiance, giving off unpleasant vibrations, exuding an essence of evil that is very real but usually has its origins in the mind of the observer, three parts imagination, one part the visible residue of the act itself, the traces of violence that are an almost inescapable consequence of death by misadventure.

But the spot where Lisa Caulder and Steve Bannion's bodies had been found gave off no emanations, provided no traces of the violence that had ended their young lives.

Maybe that's because they weren't killed here, I thought, staring at the spot where Ward's finger was pointing, seeing nothing but short, curling bermuda grass, a thin yellow covering on the dry, hard-packed earth. A few feet off to our left, a concrete picnic table huddled under an oak tree, a hammered metal barbecue brazier a few feet beyond that. Cody Bannion waited at the car parked a discreet distance from the crime-scene tape still looped around several nearby trees. Pipe jetting smoke, he studiously avoided looking in our direction.

Ward dropped to one knee, carefully poked around in the spiky fingers of grass. "A few little brown spots here. See?

That's all we found. Not nearly enough for them to have been killed here.''

I nodded and lit a cigarette. "You have any idea where they went? To park, I mean. They must have had a favorite place.''

He stood up and brushed at his knee, scowling. ''No. Steve and me got along real well, we were buddies in fact. He'd come to me a lot of times when he had things on his mind he couldn't talk to his dad about. You know, sex stuff sometimes, how to deal with people, ask me to get his daddy off his back, things like that. But this one thing, he never talked about. Maybe he was afraid because she was a Caulder.'' He lifted his sweat-stained, flat-crowned hat and ran a hand through his hair. "I don't know why, though. He knew I never put much stock in that old feud. Me and him used to laugh about it sometimes.'' He turned and looked toward the car. "But he knew his daddy didn't feel like that, so maybe he was afraid I'd let something slip.''

"Cody take it seriously?''

He slapped the hat against his leg, replaced it on his head. "Yeah, he does, I'm sorry to say. Old Abel owns about two-thirds of the land the Bannions used to own. Cody's been having a pretty hard time of it the last couple of years, the cattle business being what it is. And now with the oil prices going to hell and gone, they're shutting down a lot of old stripper wells and marginal stuff that isn't profitable any-more. He's hurting and the more he hurts the more convinced he becomes that we've been cheated somehow by the Cauld-ers. Cody's usually a methodical, logical guy, but he's got tunnel vision bad when it comes to the Caulders.''

"You don't think it's possible then that he knew about Lisa and Steve?''

"Oh, hell no. Nothing devious about Cody. He'd have gone right through the roof. He was set on Steve getting his degree same as the rest of us, and he's been scraping some to get him in school, but I think he'd have cut him off quick as a wink if he had known. Abel Caulder's daughter? No-siree. He blames Abel for most of his problems. I think he's

50

wrong.'' He looked toward his brother again. ''Maybe that's easier than blaming yourself. He's too damn bullheaded to run sheep and goats the way every other rancher around here does. He's a cattleman, by God, and cattlemen don't run woolies.''

''Sounds like a dozen western movies I've seen.''

He snorted and looked around, making a sweeping gesture of resignation, dismissing the subject.

''You seen all you want to see here? Wasn't much.''

I nodded and we moved toward his car. He stopped at the tape and took out his pocketknife. ''Might as well take this down. Nobody pays any attention to it, anyway.''

I walked on to the car.

Cody had moved into the back seat, the door open, watching a group of boys playing baseball near the side of the rodeo arena.

He took the pipe out of his mouth and pointed at the game. ''Baseball. We played basketball back in my day.''

''My game was football.''

''Well, here in Jerico Falls we didn't really have enough boys to make up a good football squad and, besides, it cost too much money for the equipment. Another thing, the school didn't have enough land for a football field and they did have an old auditorium we used as a basketball court. Didn't take much for equipment. They furnished the balls, we bought our own T-shirts and shorts and shoes. Did right well too, our senior year. Won the county tournament. Only had nine boys on the whole danged team.''

''Abel Caulder was telling me you played ball together.''

His pleasant expression vanished. ''That's right, we did,'' he said flatly. He looked up, eyes squinted. ''What else did he say about me?''

''Nothing really. He just mentioned the basketball in passing.''

''Don't guess he told you he stole the center position out from under me.'' His voice had turned harsh and grating, the words spewing around the pipestem.

"No, he didn't." I resisted an urge to prod him with the truth, mainly because Ward was walking toward us.

We climbed into the car. Ward lit a cigarette before he switched on the motor.

"The seeds they found in their hair," I said. "Did the lab identify them for you?"

Ward waited until he finished his turn onto the highway. He cleared his throat. "Not yet. They're still at the lab in Abilene."

"Two weeks? Isn't that a little long for seed identification?"

Ward gave me a disgruntled look. "Well, uh, to tell you the truth, Doolittle—that's that old geezer I was telling you about—didn't leave them when he took the clothes and the other stuff. The package fell off the back seat on the floorboard and we didn't know it until we went over to pick the stuff up about a week ago. I made him hotfoot it back over there and drop them off. They should be about ready."

"You should fire the man," Cody said.

Ward shrugged. "It coulda happened to anyone." He flashed another look at me. "What brought that to mind?"

"Might help to identify the area where they were killed."

"Might," he conceded after a moment, "but we got weeds growing all over this valley. More weeds than grass seems like sometimes."

"Could have been one of those serial killer psychos," Cody said heavily. "Or some devil-worshiping cult. There's something mighty odd about them blindfolds, and the way they was laid out there so neat and everything. Like it was some kind of ritual—" He broke off, his voice thick, raw with undisguised pain.

"Cody reads a lot," Ward said into the silence that followed. "Like about that guy Son of Sam and that Bundy feller they got set up to die. They say he mighta killed thirty-six or thirty-seven women. Can you beat that?"

"What does that have to do with this?" Cody's voice was dry and under control again. "You'd be better off if you read a little more and quit chasing women and playing poker every Saturday night of your life. Save money, too.''

Ward flashed me a quick sidewise grin. "Reckon you're right about that, big brother.'' He lifted his foot off the accelerator in anticipation of an upcoming red light. "But like I always say, to each his own. You like to read about life, I like to live it.'' The old Chrysler eased to a halt, sat quietly rumbling under the pull of the air conditioner.

"I'll need the names of Steve's friends,'' I said. "And maybe a couple of his latest girlfriends before Lisa.'' I pushed in the dash lighter and took out a cigarette. "And I need to know if he's had any trouble with anyone lately. That means anyone, no matter how insignificant it may have seemed at the time.''

He was silent while I lit the cigarette. I punched the lighter into the dash.

"I can tell you about his girlfriend,'' Ward said. "He only had one during his senior year, a girl named Patti Dunright. I can give you the names of his friends, but I don't remember any kind of trouble at all, do you, Cody?''

"No,'' he said shortly. "Not unless he got some bullshit from some of the Caulder boys that he didn't mention.''

Ward made an exasperated sound. "Come on, Cody. All that old crap about the Caulders and Bannions is forgotten. The younger generations don't care a hoot about that nonsense. If you and Abel would leave it alone, just let it die, everybody in town would be better off.''

"I know what I know,'' Cody muttered stubbornly. "Caulders are a sorry bunch of thieves.''

Ward swore under his breath and gunned the Chrysler through the intersection, hitting thirty-five in less than half a block. I glimpsed a twenty-mph sign and poked him in the ribs. "Better watch it, that eager beaver cop of yours might give you a ticket.''

Behind us, Cody cackled; an unexpected sound.

"He'd do it, too,'' Ward said, smiling. He slowed to make the turn onto the square, allowed the big car to drift halfway down the block to the reserved area. He parked two spaces away from my truck, between a plain vanilla Ford with a whip antenna and a set of light bars and a Chevy Blazer outfitted in much the same way.

We got out and started up the walk. Down the block a car door slammed. A voice called out: "Hey, Ward, hold it a second!"

Nathan Barr trotted up the sidewalk, then abruptly changed course and cut across the threadbare, yellow lawn. Cody walked on. I waited with Ward.

Barr was puffing when he reached us, cheeks pink above the beard. "Jesus, man, I'm really outta shape." He coughed and breathed deeply. "Hey, man, I just came by to tell you I moved my motor home out of your back yard. Moved it down to Nash's Service Center. Got some problems with them damn diesel jets, or the fuel pump, or something. Anyway, I just wanted you to know so you wouldn't maybe think somebody come along and pinched it."

"Thanks," Ward said dryly. "I'da been up all night worrying."

Barr laughed. "Right." He stepped around Ward and held out his hand. "How you doing, Dan?"

"Fine. And you?"

He grimaced. "Not so great. I gotta run back up to St. Louis. I'd rather take a beating with a hot poker."

"Jesus, Nate, you just spent more'n two weeks back there. Your daddy worse?"

He nodded solemnly, then turned back to me. "Hey, man, I saw your Ramcharger out there at that Roundtree Motel early this morning. You're not staying there?"

I nodded. "Yes, I am."

He looked at Ward. "What the hell's going on? I thought he was a buddy of yours. You making him pay good money to stay at that roachtrap? I thought he was gonna stay with you."

Ward slipped his arm around the smaller man's shoulder. "I need to talk to you about that. You're the only one in town knows me and Dan are old friends. We want to keep it that way."

He nodded slowly, looking puzzled. "Okay by me, but that don't mean you have to stay out there in wetback heaven." He shoved a hand into the pocket of his well-worn jeans. "Use my motor home. It's all cleaned up spic and span and it's got everything you need. I'll stop by and tell Nash to hook it up to his electricity on my way out of town."

"I couldn't do that," I said half-heartedly, automatically closing my hand on the keys he shoved at me.

"Sure you can. Got clean sheets on the bed and everything. I don't know when I'll get back and you can look after it for me. I'd really appreciate it. I'll tell Nash to wait'll I get back to worry about the motor."

"There you go," Ward said. "I told you he was crazy, but he's goodhearted along with it."

Barr made a deprecatory gesture. "Goodhearted don't get it. It's a quid quo pro. He watches my motor home, and he's got a base of operations."

"Good enough," I said, "but I think it's a little light on my side. I'm getting all the best of it."

"No, you ain't," Barr said. "Just enjoy. I'll park it around out in the back away from the noise and everything. It'll be pretty private if you decide you might want to do a little entertaining or something. There's liquor in the cabinets and beer in the fridge, so help yourself." He grinned broadly and winked.

Ward reached out and cuffed him lightly behind the head. "Dan's a married man. He don't go for that hot-zipper crap like you do."

"Look who's talking," Barr said and faked a swift one two into the big man's midriff. He whirled away, lifting a hand. "Hey, I've gotta cut out. I gotta long drive ahead of me. See you guys in a few days maybe, if I'm lucky." He poked Ward in the stomach with a stiffened forefinger. "Don't forget, big fella. You promised to take me fishing for some of them big Texas catfish you've been bragging about."

"Sure," Ward said. "I'll take you back to my little lake. It's chock full of catfish."

"Your lake? You gotta lake?"

"I told you about it. Over on the north side of that mountain we were on the other day. Pretty little place. Full of catfish." He looked at me and grinned. "Pollywogs."

"Gee whiz," I said. "Pollywogs."

"Sounds great," Barr said. "We'll do it. Look, I gotta make tracks." He bounced down the sidewalk. "See you later."

"Take it easy," Ward called after him.

"Thanks," I said.

He lifted his hand again, trotting out to the small tan sports car I had last seen on the trailer behind his motor home. He folded his compact body inside the car, fastened the seat belt, and drove off down the street.

"Nice guy," I said.

"Better'n most I've met," Ward agreed. "Don't know a lot about catfish, though."

We turned and followed Cody's tracks through the Spanish doors.

11

PATTI DUNRIGHT WAS SHORT AND TRIM AND BOUNCY. SHE had an attractive face, pug nose and freckles notwithstanding, and a heavy mass of auburn hair that rivaled Susie's in density. The daughter of the only orthodonist in town, she also served as his receptionist, secretary, sometimes helper, and gofer, according to Ward. She and Steve Bannion had dated all through their senior year, an enduring case of puppy love that had lasted into the early weeks after their graduation, then abruptly came to an end; no one seemed to know why.

I watched her stand up from her typewriter and come around the small metal desk. I admired Steve's taste. Cheerleader type, I thought, limber and daring, the top girl on the pyramid, the last one off the field. She had round hazel eyes, a well-shaped mouth that wore a set, friendly smile. Her skirt was full and colorful, her blouse white and crisp, a smattering of lace at her throat. She wore a small, thin-banded silver watch, no other jewelry. I would love to have a daughter just like her, I thought, and wondered how in the world Steve Bannion could have let her go.

"Yes, sir, may I help you?" Her voice was as crisp as her blouse, as bright as her smile.

"Ms. Patti Dunright?"

"Yes."

"My name is Dan Roman. I'm working with Chief Bannion on the murders of Lisa Caulder and Steve Bannion." I left it there, expecting some kind of reaction, not sure what it would be—pain, sorrow, regret . . . something.

Her full lips thinned a little. "Yes, I've been expecting you. Chief Bannion called a while ago."

I stared at her, a little nonplussed. Ward hadn't said anything about calling. I cleared my throat unnecessarily, hawking up irritation.

"I'd like to talk to you about Steve . . . and Lisa too if you knew her."

She smiled faintly. "Of course I knew her. We have a small school, Mr. Roman."

"And Steve?"

"Steve and I were . . . friends for almost a year."

"Sweethearts. That kind of friend?"

Her smile broadened perceptibly. "Sweethearts? Dad's the only person I've heard use that term. Years ago he used to call Mom sweetheart."

"I guess that sorta dates me. At any rate, you were boyfriend and girlfriend, right? Are those the right terms?" My voice was heavy, more combative than it had a right to be. Dealing with self-assured young ladies had never been my long suit.

"Yes, we were." Her chin quivered suddenly. "I'm sorry, Mr. Roman, I'm not trying to be a smart aleck . . . I'm . . . I'm trying to keep from crying."

"Look," I said, instantly contrite, turning to indicate the empty waiting room. "Would it be better if you came out here and we sat down—"

"No, no, this is all right. I'll be fine, really." She plucked Kleenex from a hidden box behind the counter, dabbed at the corners of her eyes. "Go ahead, ask me anything you want to know, Mr. Roman."

"Why did you and Steve split up?"

Her head lifted, eyes wide. "I don't see what that has to do with—"

"All right, scratch that for the moment. Did Lisa Caulder split you up?"

"No," she said emphatically. "He didn't start up with Lisa for over a—well, for a couple of weeks after we broke up." She bit her lower lip and looked over my shoulder, hands tormenting the wad of Kleenex. She looked back at me and sighed.

"What you asked, maybe it does have something . . . I don't know how . . . but we broke up because I wouldn't do the things that Stevie wanted me to do."

"What sort of things?"

She hesitated a moment longer, color washing into her face. "Not sex. I—we did our share of that. It was other—things—drugs mostly. Drug parties and sex parties, everybody changing partners and things like that."

"What kind of drugs?"

"What kind of drugs? Marijuana in the beginning. I tried to smoke it a couple of times, but it just made me sick. But Stevie loved it, he always had a bag or two hidden around in his car. But that wasn't so bad. It was the other things, the pills, the stuff they called hash, coke . . ." Her voice faded.

"Heroin? They may have called it horse, smack, snow, skag . . ."

Her head bobbed. "Yes. Heroin. That's smack, isn't it? And coke is cocaine? They called it blow sometimes, too, but—" She broke off and shook her head. "It scared me to death."

"Did Steve have a habit? I mean, did he have to have it, get sick if he didn't."

"Yes," she said, her voice low, sad. "He would get sick and vomit, shiver and shake almost to pieces. He'd be nervous, irritable and couldn't sleep hardly at all. That was near the end, though, just before we broke up. He was beginning to scare me with the things he said, about things he and Bobby did to get money for drugs, stealing, rolling qu—homosexuals."

"And Lisa, was she a part of it?"

Her mouth tightened again. "Yes, she was. She was going with Doyd Slater. I heard Doyd call her the biggest head around one time when he was mad at her. I'm not exactly sure what that means, but I think it meant she did a lot of dope. Doyd and her did something they called free . . . something—"

"Freebasing."

"That's it. Freebasing. That was the same thing they all did a lot, I think."

"Did you tell Chief Bannion any of this?"

"No, lord no. Anyhow, he's never talked to me about . . . about Stevie."

"Did you tell your father—anybody?"

She shook her head, eyes downcast. "No. I didn't want anyone to know I was going out with a . . . a druggie." She went back to gnawing on her lower lip. "But—but I loved Stevie. I really did, Mr. Roman, and I thought I could get him to stop."

The eternal vision of womankind, I thought: If he loves me and if I love him enough, he'll change. They never seemed to learn that we rarely ever did.

I took out my cigarettes, then looked around and found no ashtrays and put them away again, acutely aware that the turn the conversation had taken had left me with a feeling of uneasiness, a faint creeping chill.

How could Ward Bannion not know about this, as close as he and Steve had been? But maybe he did. If he did, why hadn't he told me?

How could the coroner have missed it in his autopsy? But maybe he hadn't, maybe it was there for the reading. If not, why not? And again, why hadn't Ward mentioned it?

"Where did Steve get his drugs?"

"I don't know. They never talked about that. They just seemed to have them."

"You never saw Steve give one of the others money?"

She shook her head. "No. Stevie didn't have a lot of money. His father is a rancher and the ranchers around here

60

are having a hard time. Stevie used to do some work on Saturdays at the Shoprite supermarket, but I know he didn't make much. We used to do things that didn't cost a lot, and sometimes I paid for a movie or sandwiches. A lot of time we just drove around in his car with some of the other kids." Her eyes were brimming again—tender memories of better times. But maybe they were more for Stevie than for herself. Whatever their origin, they added authenticity to a story that was giving me problems.

I took a notebook and pen out of my pocket. "Doyd Slater you said. Who were the other kids involved in taking drugs?"

She hesitated, took a small half-step away from the counter. "I—I don't want to get anyone in trouble. Doyd left for California a couple of months ago. That's why I told you about him. Most of the other kids are still around here. I'm not a . . . snitch, Mr. Roman."

"I never thought you were. But some of your friends are into hard drugs; they need a friend very badly. A friend with guts enough to make a hard choice and help them get help while there's still time. They obviously have their parents fooled as strange as that seems to me." The words sounded pompous and false even as I said them. My fourteen year old son Tommy had died under the influence of drugs, a stolen car, and two strung-out buddies following hallucinogenic visions down a lonely country road to oblivion. And I, perceptive cop that I was at the time, had had no inkling that he had ever taken anything stronger than a headache pill.

She smiled faintly. "Kids can fool their parents, Mr. Roman. A lot easier than they can fool other people." She rubbed a coffee ring on the counter with one slender finger, then looked up at me. "Is this in connection with . . . with Stevie's murder? If I tell you . . ." She let her voice fade again, an invitation for another lie.

But I'd had enough of lying. "I can't promise you, Patti."

She shook her head, sighed, then slowly began to call out their names. I wrote them down, six in all. She went on, haltingly, to tell me what she knew about their current whereabouts. Two of the boys had left town. She had heard they had gone into the merchant marines. Bobby Radcross worked with his father on a surveying team, and two of the girls had jobs in Jerico Falls. The third girl she wasn't sure about. She'd heard rumors that the girl had gotten pregnant and had been sent to relatives in Louisiana to have the baby. They didn't believe in abortion. Donna Gilcrest worked as a secretary at a local real estate office, and Norma Dew sold cosmetics at Spartan's Department Store.

"Bobby Radcross is mean," she said somberly. "I'd be careful with him if I were you. He probably won't talk to you, and if he does, he'll lie. He's big and he's got a bad temper. When he gets mad he goes a little crazy. He'll hit you when you aren't looking. Not even Stevie would mess with Bobby when he was mad." She smiled suddenly. "But tough as he is, even Bobby isn't invincible. He and Steve went down to Houston back in—oh, July, I think it was. They came back all boogered up from a fight. Bobby was the worst. Somebody had really worked him over good." The smile widened a fraction. "Everyone has a weak spot, something that scares them to death. Bobby's is snakes. Even the little grass snakes. He freaks out."

"Do you know why he and Steve were in a fight?"

"No. Steve and I had already broken off and none of the others seemed to know anything about it. I don't talk to any of them very often anymore."

"Are they still going around together?"

"I think so. I see them around town. Sometimes they're all together, sometimes not. Norma Dew is still going with Bobby Radcross, but the other girls have new boyfriends."

"You don't know if they're still taking drugs?"

She made a small unhappy face. "I don't know for sure. I hear things, you know, from other kids. I guess they are."

The outer door behind me opened. A young woman and a boy about seven came in. I turned back to Patti in time to watch an amazing transformation: woebegone to vivacious in the rise and fall of an eyelid.

"Hi, Mrs. Diddle." She leaned over the counter.

"Denny! My goodness, how handsome you look today! I've been hoping you'd come back to see me!"

The boy stared up at her solemnly, buck teeth shining.

I smiled at Patti and nodded my thanks and escaped in the furor of her enthusiastic greeting. A very resourceful young lady, a definite asset to her father's business.

I lit a cigarette and climbed into my truck.

Denny Diddle. That poor kid. He'd need more than a set of braces to get him through this life.

12

WARD BANNION WAS SEATED BEHIND HIS DESK WHEN I pushed through his office door. One thick leg slanted across a corner of his desk, a phone receiver trapped between his jaw and his shoulder, he was trying to light a smoke with hands that wouldn't stay still, a cigarette that jiggled and bobbed in the center of his mouth. It took a second for me to realize that he was giggling uncontrollably, broad face dark with collecting blood, white pressure streaks radiating from the edges of his lips. He flipped the burning match to the floor and snatched the cigarette out of his mouth, allowing his mirth to become audible, a rasping, rattling chortle that did nothing to soften the knot of anger in my stomach.

He waved me toward one of his visitor's chairs. I drew up in front of his desk; stood.

"Carol Anne," he wheezed. "Danged if you ain't the funniest—" He broke off, staring at my finger on the disconnect bar, merriment still holding his features captive while he absorbed this unexpected development, a lugubrious mix of shock and consternation taking root as several silent, bloated seconds ticked away.

"The autopsy reports, Ward," I said evenly, coldly. "Where are they?"

He blinked. "Why, they're—" He cleared his throat. "Why, what's the problem?"

"Did you read them?"

"Course I read them." A note of belligerence, edged with caution.

"Tell me what they said."

"Well . . . well, all they said was . . . to put it in my own words, they said both victims died of massive trauma to the brain caused by gunshot wounds fired at fairly close range."

"What else?"

"What else? What else could there be—"

"Don't jack me around, Ward, goddammit! Don't even try it. I'll go out there and get in my damn truck and haul my sorry ass back where it belongs."

"Hey, Dan, man, I'm not lying to you. It ain't on the autopsy reports." He paused, wet his lips, the color gone behind the sun-bronzed skin, leaving an unhealthy yellowish hue. "I know where you're coming from. I knew you'd find out sooner or later. They—we decided there wasn't any good reason to write it down on a public document like that. Ruin the name of two decent kids just because they had some traces of barbiturates."

"Barbiturates? How about blow, smack—"

"Nosiree! None of that hard stuff. Hell, all the kids nowadays try it sooner or later. But you know how stories like that grow. First thing you know they'd have been dopeheads, druggies, regular dope fiends. Since it didn't have anything to do with their murders—"

"How in hell do you *know* that?"

"Come on, Dan. This is Jerico Falls. This ain't Dallas or Houston. We're just a little wide spot in the road. We don't have any of that drug craziness going on down here. Man, I wouldn't stand for it. I saw too much of that shit in Nam, what it does to people's minds."

"You said 'they' a while ago. They who?"

He scrubbed a heavy hand through his silver mop of hair, brought it down to finger his chin. "They . . . well, that was Cody and Abel . . . and me, I guess. I went along with it."

"Who was the doctor?"

He combined a facial grimace and a lopsided smile. "Marvin Bannion. He's a cousin—"

I barked a sound not meant to be a laugh. "You are un-goddamn-believable, Ward! Don't you know that all of you are guilty of felony obstruction in a murder case? Cousin doctor could lose his license and the rest of you could end up in the pokey." I wasn't sure what I said was true, but I doubted he would know the difference, anyway.

"Naw," he said, the color rushing back to his face. "Marvin went beyond what he had to in the autopsies. Hell, it was obvious what killed them. If he hadn't seen the tracks—" He bit off the words, trying to cover his slip with action, whirling the swivel chair to a small filing cabinet behind him. "Hell, here let me show you."

"Whoa, buddy," I said softly. "Tracks? Since when do pills leave tracks?"

"Huh?" he said over his shoulder. "Oh, they call it skin-popping, I think. They dissolve the pills—"

"Bullshit, Ward. That's not the story I heard. I told you not to lie to me, dammit!"

"I'm not," he said earnestly, turning back from the cab-inet with two single sheets of paper in his hands. "Here are the autopsy reports. See for yourself."

"Shit!" I turned and walked toward the door.

"Hey, Dan, wait a minute. You've been talking to Patti Dunright, right? You got to consider something here. Stevie dropped her for Lisa Caulder back in early summer. She was all tore up about it, still is from what I hear. She's not a bad kid, but you know about a woman scorned and all that, and she said some mean hateful things about Stevie after the split. You can't take everything she tells you as gospel. I hope you know that."

I turned. "I know that. I'm also finding out I can't take everything you say as gospel either. I didn't expect that. I'm sorry as hell about it."

Our eyes met across ten feet of empty space, locked, held, the space suddenly alive, charged with unknown meaning.

His face was sorrowful; mine felt tight and dry and hard. The silence grew, and I understood that something had changed. We were no longer what we had been; what we were now remained to be seen.

I turned and left.

A tall lean man wearing a sky-blue jumpsuit and highly glossed boots was waiting for me when I got back to my Ramcharger. He pushed away from the fender he was leaning on and gave me a wide smile as I approached, his hand outstretched.

"About ready to give up and go looking for you," he said. "Although I wanted to speak to you alone. My name's Tony Caulder and unless I'm very badly mistaken, you're Dan Roman."

"Yes," I said, returning the smile, gripping the long slender fingers that responded with surprising strength. "Ward Bannion mentioned you."

"Nothing derogatory, I hope," he said wryly, then laughed, a smothered chortling sound reminiscent of his father's. "I don't know if he told you but I'm the one who suggested you be brought in to help with our little murder investigation. You won't remember me, of course, but I know quite a bit about you. I wrote an article for the *Times Herald* about a year ago—the Kincade-LeClair murder thing. That was an impressive bit of detective work, Mr. Roman." He smiled again, an easy rearrangement of narrow lips around a mouthful of long white teeth. Thin brown hair combed straight down the sides of his head with a swath curving across his forehead gave him a slightly rakish look; large gray-tinted glasses masked his eyes. Twenty-eight, I judged.

"An impressive bit of luck," I said. "But go right ahead. I don't have all that many admirers that I can afford to discourage one."

He laughed again and took a pack of long thin brown cigarettes out of his shirt pocket. "I thought I might do a little piece on you, Mr. Roman. A public service announcement, perhaps, advising the citizens of Jerico Falls of your expertise in matters of this kind, and urging that they give you all possible cooperation in your investigation.''

I thought about it for a moment, adopting a studious expression suitable for a fan. ''I'm not sure that would be in the best interest of the investigation, Mr. Caulder.''

''Tony, please. There are so many Caulders around here mister gets to be confusing. Why not?''

''Everyone involved, even peripherally, would be waiting for me to come around and question them. It would give them time to prepare, practice what they mean to say, lie or fact. It's always better to contact people without warning. That's going to be difficult enough in this case as it is.''

He nodded reluctantly, clearly disappointed. ''All right. I'll buy that for the time being. But word travels fast in a town this size. I doubt there are many people in Jerico Falls who don't already know who and what you are and why you're here.''

''If they do, then they know a lot more than I do.''

His thin eyebrows lifted quizzically, but he let it go, applying a paper match to the end of his brown cigarette, holding it to his mouth between two yellow stained fingers.

''Did you know about your sister and Steve Bannion, Tony?''

''Know about them?'' Smoke gusted around the words. ''Oh, you mean their dating. No, I didn't. I've been living in Dallas the last couple of years and busy as a pack rat ever since I came back here to run the paper. I live here in town and very seldom find the time to go out to the ranch. I've taken on a seven day week, I'm afraid, in running the *Gazette*.''

''It's a nice little town,'' I said.

''Yes, it is. I like it. After Dallas, it seems so laid back it's sorta like dozing.''

''Not much crime, I wouldn't think.''

''Very little. What there is, is mostly petty stuff. A little stealing, a fistfight now and then—''

''Any problems with drugs?''

''Not to speak of. Oh, hell, I know some of the kids puff

a little grass now and then, and I've seen a little snorting at some parties and like that. But mostly we're cool when it comes to drugs."

"You don't know if Lisa ever did any drugs?"

He frowned, his lips forming a negative curve. "I can't swear she never tried any, you understand, but I don't believe she was into them, as they say. She was an extremely healthy vital girl. She used to help me on the paper some. I never saw any signs of it, highs or lows, sniffing, drowsiness, like that. But then, I wasn't looking for them, either."

"No rumors about Steve and drugs?"

The frown deepened. He bit his lip, his eyes, indistinguishable spheres behind the glasses, searching my face. "No. But I haven't been back all that long, remember. Are drugs involved in this, Mr. Roman?"

"Dan, please. It's too soon to tell, but drugs are involved in so many things today, they can't be overlooked."

"That's true," he said soberly. "I just did a piece last Sunday on a big bust over in Eastland County. Mexican black tar heroin, something over twenty-five pounds. Twenty-two million street value, can you imagine? Pretty potent stuff. They're bringing it up from Mexico by the bushel. We're running a close second behind Florida now, I understand. But, hell, what do we have, eight or nine hundred miles of border? You can't plug all the holes. Even if you could, it wouldn't matter a whole lot. They fly it up in small, fast, low-level planes and drop it off in somebody's back pasture."

"It's a problem."

He pursed thin lips and we watched a small knot of old men crossing the street to the park, grouped closely together for safety, hunched shoulders and faltering steps, rheumy eyes searching the ground ahead for the pitfalls they had come to expect.

"How did you feel about Steve and Lisa going out together?"

His smile was bleak; I wished he'd take off the damned glasses so I could see his eyes.

He shrugged. "I didn't know it, of course, but I suppose Steve Bannion was about as good a catch as she could find around here. At least he had some ambition. He wanted to be a vet, I understand."

"A Bannion and a Caulder. That didn't bother you?"

He let out another of his father's chortles. "Oh, hell no! That wouldn't matter to anyone except Dad and Cody Bannion. And sometimes I think even they are fakes. They had some trouble once, that much I know. A long time ago, back when they were in school together. But I don't think it had anything to do with that old half-assed feud, that Hatfield and McCoy stuff that people love to talk about around here. I know a lot of Bannions and I like most of them. I like a lot of Caulders and don't like some, so it all evens out."

"No idea what happened between them?"

"I've heard a lot of stories. Everything from a fight over a girl to a knife fight out at the Rodeo Grounds. And there was something about a basketball team, fighting over a starting spot on the team or some such foolishness. But I've never heard Dad say anything. He just flat won't talk about it." He shifted his feet and patted the thin cap of hair which was rapidly being disarranged by the wind. He ducked his head below the level of my truck and asked the question he had probably come to ask.

"Have you made any progress, Dan?"

Before I could answer, a feminine voice trilled his name. He raised on his toes to look. Halfway down the block, a young woman with blond hair stood outside the open door of a narrow red brick building under a sign that read: Saragache County *Gazette*. She gestured wildly, bouncing up and down on her toes.

He shook his head and sighed. "Another damn crisis. These old presses—" He broke off and quickly shook my hand. "Good to meet you, Dan. I'll catch you later, okay?"

"Sure," I replied automatically, and watched him lope easily across the street and down the sidewalk toward the girl. A smart young man, I thought, perceptive, knows talent when he sees it. I lit a cigarette and wondered how in the world Susie and I had missed his article in the *Times Herald*. Between us, we usually read every headline, if not each article, in the Dallas paper. But maybe it had come out at one of those times when we were both out of town, when my next door neighbor, Hector Johnson, gathered up the tell-tale newspapers from my lawn and dumped them in the trash.

Instead of climbing into my truck, I wheeled and walked south along the square. I had spotted Spartan's Department Store on my way to see Ward, and maybe I could catch Norma Dew with her guard down, before someone came along and told her to watch out for the tall, handsome stranger from the north.

13

NORMA DEW WAS WILLOWY AND TALL. SHE HAD COOL BLUE eyes and hair the color of sand. Parted in the center of her head, it fell in rippling waves to her shoulders, bunched there in gleaming loops and coils, forming a perfect backdrop for her face, small neat features faultlessly formed, fine-textured skin luminous, free of imperfections. She had a sassy smile, a low throbbing laugh. She didn't fit my mind's eye image of a drug addict.

I loafed along the counter while she waited on a customer, a middle-aged man in rough range clothing and a sweat-stained hat. She was flirting outrageously and he was eating it up, a silly grin on his weather-stained face, run-over boots doing a little stag dance as long forgotten juices flowed in crusty, stagnant veins. She handed him his package and patted his hand, telling him what a lucky woman his wife was to have such a thoughtful man. He went out beaming, obviously a well-satisfied customer. I decided that maybe it was some kind of new sales technique.

"May I help you, sir?" Her voice was firm, all business. No hint of flirtation, not even much friendliness in the cool blue eyes. She wore dark slacks and a pale yellow sweater with the cuffs pushed up to mid-forearm, a strand of pearls. If she used makeup at all, I couldn't detect it.

"My name is Dan Roman, Ms. Dew. I'm working with Chief Bannion on the murders of Lisa Caulder and Steve Bannion. I understand you were a good friend of theirs."

She nodded calmly, no surprise, no apprehension that I could see. "Yes, Lisa was my very good friend. I didn't know Steve as well, but I liked him." She brought slender fingers together on the glass countertop, clasped them loosely. "Lisa and I went all the way through school together. We became really good friends in high school. It was such an awful thing to have happen." Pale, silky-looking lashes shuttered the blue eyes for a moment, clenched tightly, then fluttered wide again, a gleam of moisture brimming the lids, quickly blinked away.

"It was," I agreed. "And we intend to find out why. Most importantly who. And maybe you can help. Do you know of anyone with a grudge against either of them? Someone who had eyes for Lisa, maybe, and blamed Steve for his lack of success? Or it could just as easily work the other way, some girl who thought Lisa had beaten her time with Steve?"

She looked faintly startled, a little amused. "Do you think one of the kids did this?"

I shook my head. "First of all, you call yourselves kids. You're not kids anymore. You're young men and women. Not grownups yet, but certainly not kids, either. Youth is no barrier to murder. Kids, real kids, twelve, thirteen, have been known to commit murders; sometimes their own families are the victims."

If I had intended to shock her, I failed. She gazed back at me quietly, unimpressed, a product of the times. Inundated with daily inoculations of make-believe TV violence, three minute encapsulations of a murderous, hostile world on the five, six, and ten o'clock news, she had undoubtedly become inured to violence in all its various manifestations.

"Well," I asked. "Do you know of anyone?"

She lifted shoulders. "No. Dating wasn't that big a thing. No one took it very seriously."

"Steve and Lisa must have. They were going to get married."

She shrugged again, meticulously tailored eyebrows lifting in an obviously practiced look of cynical indifference. "Perhaps."

"You don't believe they were going to get married?"

"I don't know, Mr. Roman. Possibly."

I looked around. A few people, mostly women, drifted along the aisles of the moderately sized store. We were along the left wall, out of the main line of traffic to the cash register, isolated to some extent. As far as I could tell no one was paying any attention to us. Her composure was beginning to prickle under my skin. I decided on another direction.

I leaned an elbow on the counter. "I understand Steve and Lisa were into drugs, that you and Bobby Radcross and a few others were into some pretty heavy shit." I watched her eyes, watched them change from cool and mocking to clear and shining, tiny pinpoints of ice-blue flame flickering in their depths.

Her lips curled involuntarily, a smile that was no longer sassy. "You've been talking to Patti Dunright," she said bitterly.

"Why do you say that?"

"Because she's the only one who—because she's been telling stories around town that aren't true, that's why."

"Are you saying they didn't do drugs?"

"Not that I know about."

"You were her best friend, you'd know, wouldn't you?"

She started a shrug, then let her shoulders slump instead. "I—I think so. I don't know anything about drugs."

"You've never smoked grass?"

"No."

"Never snorted a line of coke?"

"No. Please . . . I wish you'd leave. People are watching us."

"Never stuck a needle in your arm?"

"No, I told you, no! Please, leave me alone."

74

"All right, Ms. Dew, I'll leave. But first, I'd like you to push the sleeves of your sweater above your elbows. The left one first, please."

She stared at me, anger and horror warring in her face, the brittle composure shattered, gone, eyes brimming with tears again.

"I—I will . . . not! You have no right to—" She broke off and whirled away down the counter. She darted through an opening at the other end, made a right turn near a towering display of auto tires, and disappeared from sight.

I drifted away from the jewelry counter. Nobody seemed to be watching. I browsed a moment at a sporting goods display, tossing a football into the air, fingering the stocks of a row of shotguns mounted on a board.

I left the store a few minutes later, discomfited by the way I had handled the Norma Dew interview. Somehow I had the feeling that she had been expecting me, had recognized me instantly and trotted out her pose of sophisticated disdain especially to deal with me. It had served her well but had not been able to withstand a direct frontal assault against her personally.

I lit a much-needed cigarette and strolled up the square toward my Ramcharger. But maybe it hadn't been a total loss, I thought, maybe I had come away a little wiser, after all.

There was a note tucked under my windshield wiper, a message from Ward:

Come on in the office. I got some good news for you.

He wasn't there, but the woman behind the communications console waved me over and gave me a slip of paper.

"The Chief said you could use the phone in his office," she said, wrinkling her plump face at me in a knowing smile.

I unfolded the paper, found more of Ward's neat precise writing. Only this one wasn't a message from him.

I'm home, you big lunk. What in the world are you doing down there in Jerico Falls? Tearing down the walls? Call me—quickly.

Susan

I felt a stirring deep inside, a warm furry kitten uncoiling, stretching, a familiar agitation in my vitals that never failed to make me feel foolish, never failed to make me feel good all over.

I went into Ward's office and picked up his old-fashioned phone, feeling the dispatcher's eyes on me through the glass partition. I dialed, hoping my grin didn't look as silly as it felt.

14

WE WENT THROUGH A FEW MINUTES OF WHO MISSED WHO the most, who loved who the most, and what a terrible inconvenience these separations were. That was always necessary to Susie, and I had come to find that I didn't mind it much myself—excellent reinforcement for a shaky ego.

"What in the world are you doing down there? And just exactly where is down there? I never heard of Jerico Falls, Texas."

"First," I said. "What are you doing home? The old goat decide to give up, or what?"

She laughed, a low throaty sound she used when she was pleased. "The old goat, as you put it, came down with a case of laryngitis. Isn't that lovely?"

"Terrific. What's the prognosis?"

She fairly yelped with pleasure. "Two full days, probably three. How long will it take you to get home?"

"Well," I said, pausing to light a cigarette, clicking the lighter near the phone so she would know, using the brief respite to scan for alternatives. "Well, I'm not at a backing away place right now, Susie. A better idea would be for you to hightail it down here."

"Hmmmmm." There was disappointment in the sound,

but she handled it well. When she spoke again, her tone was cheerfully noncommittal. "You haven't said what you're doing down there, Danny. Who are you looking for?"

"I'm not exactly looking for anyone. Well, in a way I am, I guess. Do you remember me talking about a man named Ward Bannion?"

"I think so. You knew him in Vietnam?"

"That's the one. He's the Chief of Police here in Jerico Falls. It's his nephew who's been killed—"

"Killed? Murder, Danny? I thought you said—"

"Yeah, I know what I said." I heaved a sigh. "But this is a special case, Susie. Ward saved my life. I owe him whatever my life is worth."

"It's worth everything to me," she said warmly. "But that can be dangerous. You know I worry about you enough the way it is—"

"I suppose you think I don't worry about you? Prancing around all over the state with a bunch of old lecherous politicians—"

"Not all of them are old," she said, the throaty sound back in her voice. "And don't try to act like you're jealous. You don't have a jealous bone in your body."

"Maybe not, but I've got a special kind of hell reserved for anybody who messes around with my woman. Nobody messes with my woman but me."

"Lordy," she said breathlessly. "How do I get down there again?" She went off into a peal of laughter. I held the receiver away from my ear and grinned at the woman sitting behind her console, glumly watching me spend the taxpayers' money.

"Hey," I said. "This is a city phone. We'd better get off. If you'll catch the six o'clock shuttle to Abilene I'll pick you—"

"Oh, honey, I'll never make it. I have to fix my hair, bathe—and I'm completely pooped. Why don't I come down first thing in the morning? All right? I'll get a good solid night's sleep and see you bright and early in the morning. Will that be okay? About nine?"

"Sure," I said, and paused for a second. "Hey, Suse, this is really great, you know that?"

"I know it," she said, and made a kissing sound into the phone. "Goodbye, darling." She made the kissing sound again.

"Goodbye," I said and hung up quietly. I have my limits.

Ward Bannion was coming up the sidewalk as I pushed through the heavy Spanish doors. He slowed, stopped, a wide grin spreading across his face. "You got your message, I see."

"That I did, thanks."

"How come you didn't tell me she was a celebrity? Shucks, I've seen her on the TV news a lot of times. I made the connection with the names, but I knew you didn't have a daughter and I didn't dream such a young pretty gal would go for the likes of you."

"Women are unpredictable creatures. They have a great capacity for overlooking a man's inadequacies. Take sweet Carol Anne, for instance."

The grin widened. "Touché. You're a lucky sucker, nevertheless. She seemed right anxious to get in touch with you."

"She's flying down in the morning. I'm going to pick her up in Abilene. And that reminds me, did you send someone over to pick up the evidence from the lab?"

He shifted uncomfortably, made a long face. "Naw, as a matter of fact, I didn't. Old Clint Doolittle didn't come in this morning and Ace Macon had to run his Pa up to the hospital in Eastland. I'll get somebody over there tomorrow for sure—"

"Never mind. I'll stop by and pick it up. You just give them a call and tell them I'm coming."

"Well . . . yeah, sure, I can do that. What time do you think?"

"I don't know for sure. Probably ten, ten thirty, around there. What difference does it make?"

"None, no difference. I just want to be sure they have it ready for you."

"Okay, I'll see you later." We exchanged nods and smiles, the residue of our earlier encounter still there between us, unseen, but palpable. I climbed into my truck with an uneasy gnawing at my insides. Where had he gone, the quick, sure fighting man I had known? Out of what crucible of dreams and hopes and fears had this Ward Bannion evolved? From what I could determine he had done little or nothing to solve the murder of his nephew and his nephew's girlfriend.

Sheer incompetence? Or something else? No wonder the Caulders had demanded outside help. Abel Caulder appeared to be a perceptive, sensitive man, and over and above his probable distrust of a Bannion there would be a father's grief tearing at him, a father's anger calling out for vengeance.

I glanced at my watch. Five minutes before five o'clock. I had no idea what time surveying crews quit work, but twilight wasn't too far away, and I knew they couldn't work beyond that.

I got out of the truck and crossed the street to a phone box on the corner. I found a battered book attached to a chain, a thin hardbound book with no more than ten yellow pages. It took only a moment to find Radcross Surveyors, to fix their location on the abbreviated map in the corner of their ad.

I lit a cigarette and crossed back to my truck. The square was rapidly becoming deserted again, a few city employees filtering out of One Century Plaza, old men leaving the park benches, another empty, aimless day whittled away.

Theron Alldyce, the first living person I had encountered in Jerico Falls, was bouncing down the sidewalk between two women, a tall, hump-shouldered brunette in rimless glasses and a short lady in a rumpled seersucker dress. She was as fat as Theron himself, a round expressionless face that stared at me woodenly as Theron spotted me and slapped his thigh, fired at me with a make-believe gun in his fist.

"Who's he gonna kill!" I heard before the firing of the Ramcharger's engine drowned him out.

Town must be in a bad way humor-wise, I thought, and

drove out of the square wondering what the friendly little man did for the citizens of Jerico Falls. If anything.

"You just missed him, sir." The young brown-haired girl in the front office of Radcross Surveyors was obviously on her way home. She fitted a cover on her typewriter and gave me a tired smile. "You must have met him on the street. It hasn't been more than a minute or so. He drives a red Cougar."

I nodded. "Thanks."

I got into my truck and drove back the way I had come. The only red car I had met on the narrow gravel street had almost run me into the ditch, taking his half right down the middle, riding his horn, rear wheels spitting gravel and raising a cloud of dust so thick I had pulled over and stopped. I had heard him take the turn at the corner, hitting the paved street with screaming tires and popping exhaust. Across an open field, I watched him accelerate, motor blasting, then brake suddenly and swerve into the parking lot of a small convenience store.

I gunned the Dodge. With any kind of luck at all he might still be there.

A hundred yards away from the store I saw a splash of red through the sumac bushes lining the road. I eased up on the gas, allowed momentum and engine idle to take me the rest of the way. The Cougar was parked near the rear corner of the store, slanted the wrong way across the better part of two spaces.

Without giving it much thought, I eased the Ramcharger to a stop on the left side of the Cougar. Close. So close I expected to hear the scrape of metal. When I didn't, I got out and walked around the car and looked inside. The keys dangled; an unexpected bit of luck. I opened the passenger door and locked it, slammed it shut. I stepped back and surveyed my handiwork. The driver's window was open but he couldn't reach it. Unless he was smart enough to carry an extra set of keys, or dumb enough to smash a window, he would be there when I was ready to talk. I went back and locked up my truck, lit a cigarette, then strolled down the sidewalk to the front door and went in.

There were several customers in the store. More than I expected, judging from the number of cars outside. I located the drink cooler, popped the tab on a can of Pepsi, and drifted around looking for him.

He wasn't hard to find. I'd caught a glimpse of yellow and black through the windshield as we passed, a big head with dark windblown hair and a gaping mouth that could have been cursing or laughing, so I had some idea of what I was looking for.

I found the head, with its mop of tangled black hair, bent over an electronic game off in one corner of the store, a big solid-looking body encased in dirty jeans, a yellow T-shirt, and a frayed black denim jacket. His mouth was crimped in a little round O, an intense malevolent expression on his dark square face as his fingers manipulated levers, squeezed the pistol grips of futuristic laser guns in a frenzy of fighting mania, blasting little crab-like airships peopled with creatures called Zargonats. A low-pitched computer voice taunted him when he missed, promised annihilation, a sneering voice, sibilant and ugly.

I leaned a shoulder against a nearby wall, sipped Pepsi, and watched. He seemed to take his game seriously, stomping run-over, mud-spattered boots when he missed, muttering "all right!" and "right on!" when the tiny enemy ships exploded into electronic limbo. He looked fully as mean as Patti Dunright had said, and I was seriously considering hurrying back outside and moving my truck when the game ended with a clamor of bells, a nasty insulting laugh from the Prince of the Zargonats defying him to try again. But Bobby Radcross had had enough. He stared up at his total of enemy dead, muttered a satisfied oath, and slammed the machine's bumprail with the palm of his hand. "Gotcher ass," he snarled.

He whirled, grabbed a bag of groceries from the end of the counter, and brushed right by me, dismissing me with one fleeting glance from dark eyes still shining with the thrill of victory. He swaggered to the door and went out.

I sighed. The die, as they say, was cast.

I tried to remember what else Patti Dunright had told me. He looked big and mean, all right. How bad he was—well, that remained to be seen.

15

HE WAS STANDING IN FRONT OF HIS CAR, ARMS AKIMBO, thick legs widespread, a picture of violence barely contained, the part of his face that I could see as dark as a West Texas thundercloud. The bag of groceries lay overturned on the hood of the Cougar.

I dumped the unfinished portion of my Pepsi in a container by the door, paused to light a cigarette, then stared off into the west as if enraptured by the splendor of the setting sun. It *was* a delightful sight, streaks of crimson, purple, and orange—

"Hey! Hey, you fancypants!"

The heads of two departing customers swiveled, turned away again hastily as they beat a retreat to their cars. I continued to gaze at the sunset, enthralled.

"Hey, goddammit! You! You in the brown coat."

I turned slowly, allowing my face to go slack with surprise. I pointed a timid finger at my chest.

"Yeah, you, asshole! Is this your goddamned truck?"

"I don't know," I trilled, pitching my voice as high as it would go. "Is it black, and does it have a cute little hood ornament?"

He cursed and slung his arms, did a little two-step dance

and lashed out a foot at my truck. The hood ornament vanished.

"Not anymore, you sonuvabitch! Now get your goddamned ass down here and get this pile of junk away from my car before I trash it!"

I trotted down the thirty feet of sidewalk, drew up in front of his car, puffing a little for effect. I bent to look between the vehicles. "Goodness, how did I manage to do that? They *are* close!" I straightened and looked into his fiery eyes. "Well, after all, you could have just opened your other door—"

He poked me in the chest with a stiffened forefinger. "Move your goddamned car, asshole! I'm not telling you again."

"You mean my truck," I said, giving him an ingratiating smile. "The car is yours." I considered wringing my hands, decided it would be too much. "I simply don't understand why you're so upset," I said petulantly, crossing behind the vehicles, listening for his boot heels behind me. "I didn't *hurt* your silly little car."

"You damned well better not, either," he said, his voice curiously stilled, something there that hadn't been there before, a kind of breathlessness that brought a tiny tingling chill to the hollows behind my ears. I could hear a smile in his voice and I couldn't think of any good reason why it should be there. Maybe one good reason—and I began to wonder if once again I had let impulsiveness and overconfidence overload my ass. He was bigger than me, twenty years younger, and the smashing drive of his leg at my hood ornament had revealed a dexterity I wouldn't have thought possible in someone his size. I thought fleetingly of the .38 in the pocket of the truck. It seemed a long way away.

I pulled up at the door of the truck, turned casually, my inane smile still intact, jaw muscles trying to cramp. He was three feet away, staring at me with cold unblinking eyes. We had gone beyond burr under the saddle and thorn in the flesh. I was simply prey to be evaluated, a stranger who had no respect for other people's property.

I worked the door handle, then snatched my hand away, my smile slipping. "I—I guess it's locked," I said, and patted my pockets, noting that the big hands were already clubbed, the wide mouth pursing to an O, the same O that had accompanied his killing frenzy with the electronic game. I backed a step away from the door, still patting pockets, fashioning the look of horror he would expect from a dumbassed stranger asshole who had finally realized he was going to get a lesson he well deserved.

"Jesus," I said, stressing the sibilants, "I—I guess the key's . . . inside."

He nodded as if it mattered little, took a half-step sideways and craned his neck to look inside the pickup, a casual look as if to verify blame. "You poor dumb shit," he said conversationally, pressing his nose to the glass.

I hit him. Powered a right into his solar plexus with just about everything I had. I was convinced he was all that Patti had said he was and this was not a good day to die, not with Susie coming.

I did it right, but the angle was wrong and he was still on his feet. Stupefied and gasping, all bent over and spitting vomit, but not as enervated as I would have liked, not beyond a relatively quick recovery depending on what he had inside. Already he was trying to straighten up, sucking for oxygen like an overheated engine, big legs widespread for stability, left shoulder pressed against the truck. I looked him over, wondering where to hit him again.

His midriff was out of the question a second time, his hands were locked there in place. His jaw jutted invitingly, but that way lay misery, broken knuckles, pain, months of working little round balls. Widespread legs left his groin unprotected, but that was a cheap shot, a last resort, not a cool thing to do to a man at your mercy. I'd had a few of those and it wasn't any fun. Not for weeks, months sometimes.

That left his head and his neck. I could see thick rolls of muscle on his neck, I probably couldn't find the carotid if I tried. So that left his head.

I grabbed a handful of hair in my left hand, dug my fingers

into the back hand of his jeans. I felt him tense, gulping strength by the mouthful, felt resistance come into his body.

Grunting with the strain, I yanked him half-erect, turned him around, and ran him headfirst into the doorpost of my truck.

He was still out when I reached the Rodeo Grounds. I stopped near the edge of the park, as far from the rodeo arena as I could get. The sun had set but it was still light enough to see what I wanted to see.

I opened the passenger door and hauled Bobby Radcross out onto the ground. I rolled him over on his stomach and stripped the black denim jacket over his shoulders and down his arms to the handcuffs at the middle of his back.

He had thick bulging biceps, heavily corded forearms. But no tracks. No needle marks anywhere on his arms or hands. I felt a little thrill of apprehension. What if Patti Dunright had lied?

I replaced the jacket, then squatted on my heels beside the inert body and lit a cigarette, unmindful of the rapidly fading light. Assault. Kidnaping. Unlawful restraint. Twenty years hard labor, or what passed for hard labor nowadays. And I couldn't get on a witness stand and swear that he had done anything except cuss a little. What could I truthfully say? That he had frightened me?

Radcross moaned and stirred. I tossed away the cigarette and inspected the jeans. Skin tight; old, faded, and ripped in several places. No way was I going to pull them down and add attempted sodomy to my rash of crimes.

I took out my pocketknife and made a small slit in his pants at the bend in the back of his leg. I carefully parted the material and tilted the opening to the remaining light.

My breath whooshed outward in a gusty sigh. They were there; what some junkies call the trail of tears and others call the tracks of joy. An irregular line three inches long. Some new, some old, some almost too faint to be seen. But there. Irrefutable proof. Brother Bobby was a doper, a head. Or more accurately, a leg.

I quickly slit the other pants leg, feeling the body stirring under my hands. Darkness had finally come and I had to use my cigarette lighter, but the misery line was also there, not quite so long, not quite so many puncture marks, in all likelihood the spot he currently used.

I tugged and lifted and shoved Radcross back into the truck. His head lolled limply. He muttered obscenities. Slobbered a little.

I went around and slipped in behind the wheel. I lit a cigarette to replace the one I hadn't finished. I watched his face as he struggled up out of oblivion into the darkness rapidly engulfing the land. I turned on the inside lights, trying to decide how best to handle this explosive young man. Without the cruelty and belligerence, his features looked almost child-like, handsome to a degree. He had long, black eyelashes I hadn't noticed before, a well-crafted nose, thin walls flaring gently as he breathed. He looked healthy, vital, a splendid specimen of vigorous American youth. I wondered how long it would be before the drugs exacted their price. Years? Months? I had no idea. Most of the junkies I had come in contact with as a police officer had been there for a while, already into stealing, mugging, and robbery to support their habits. They wore their addiction like a hair shirt, their only concern the next fix, the ravages of their ongoing war clearly discernible in both their attitudes and their physical symptoms. If Bobby boy was that far along he didn't show it. Not yet. Not to my inexperienced eye.

I listened to his snuffles and groans, finished my cigarette, and waited.

16

"YOU BASTARD," HE SAID SULLENLY, SNIFFING WETLY. "You hit me when I wasn't looking."

I dug a handkerchief out of my back pocket, unfolded it, balled it into a wad of cloth, and shoved it against his nose. "Blow. You're making me sick."

He blew. I wadded the cloth some more, dropped it into his lap. "You can keep it."

"Thanks," he said automatically, then curled his lip. "You bastard, you hit me—"

"Right, I did. You scare me, Bobby. All that strength and a brain the size of a walnut. You were going to bust me up and I'm fond of me the way I am, thanks."

He closed his eyes and rolled his head. "Jesus, my head hurts."

"Yeah, I'm sorry about that, Bobby. I didn't plan it this way. Survival is the father of ingenuity, as they say. If it's any consolation to you, you left a pretty neat little dent in my door panel."

He ran his tongue around the edges of a mean little grin. "You got a right to be scared now, you cock—"

I reached across and squeezed his jaws together. "You've got a dirty mouth, too. Did anybody ever tell you that? Didn't

89

your Mama and Daddy ever wash your mouth out with soap?'' I tightened my hand against the resistance of lumpy jaw muscles, feeling his cheeks slowly giving way, seeing tears of pain start in his eyes. I let go. He immediately spat a curse, seeing nothing but weakness in my retreat.

"You're a real hardass, Bobby. I'll concede that, okay? You can go on cussing, and I can go on hurting you, and it won't prove anything either way. That isn't what I want from you.''

"What the hell are you, some kind of freaky queer, or something?'' He seemed to notice for the first time that we weren't still at the store. "Where the hell are we, anyway?'' I thought I detected a faint rill of alarm in his voice. Maybe he was afraid of the dark.

I didn't answer. I reached across in front of him and opened the dash pocket. I took out the Smith & Wesson Airweight.

He snorted a shaky laugh. "Whatta you gonna do, shoot me? I know where we're at. Them lights over there is the rodeo arena. That means some guys are working, probably on the chutes or something. Am I right?''

"You're right,'' I said. "Over there a few yards to our left is where your friends Steve and Lisa were found.''

"Hey, man, I don't know nothin—''

I held up my hand, a cartridge between my thumb and forefinger. He stared at it.

"You know what this is, Bobby? I'll tell you anyway. It's a .38 caliber unjacketed bullet. A hollowpoint. You have any idea what a bullet like this does to the human head when fired at a fairly close range? Maybe not, if you're lucky. But I'll tell you anyway. It explodes—the head, I mean. Hydro-static pressure. The eyeballs pop out onto the cheeks. The cheeks balloon and burst wide open like faulty racing slicks. Blood and brains spout out of the nose, the mouth, the eye sockets, the skin ruptures in a hundred places—''

"Shit, man!'' No doubt about it. I'd touched a tender spot.

"That's what happened to your friends. There's bits and pieces of them on the ground somewhere, sticking to bushes, grass, weeds, whatever was there where they were killed.

Two weeks, it's dry and shriveled and crusty now—what's left after the birds and the insects—"

"Shit, man, I don't know nothing. I'd tell you if I did. I swear. They were my friends. Steve was my buddy. Don't you think I'd turn the asshole over if I knew? But I don't know anything about that night, not anything."

"Maybe you know more than you think you do. Will you talk to me, answer my questions?"

The dark eyes burned at me. He wet his lips again, most of the belligerence gone from his expression, replaced by something I read as caution. "You're that guy everybody's been talking about. That cop from Dallas they said was coming."

"Not a cop, Bobby. Private cop. I'm working with your police, though. My name's Dan Roman."

He nodded. "That's it. Old numbnuts Ward Bannion hired you, huh?"

"Will you talk to me?"

He squirmed. "These damn handcuffs are hurting. You wanna take them off?"

"Not just yet."

He smiled a thin mirthless smile. "Still afraid of old Bob, huh?"

"I'm tired. If I shot you, I'd be up all night."

He stared at me silently. "You'd do that, you'd shoot me?"

"Quick as a goddamned wink," I said savagely, feeling a sudden urgency as I saw my edge slipping away. "Right in that lump of stone you call a head, just to see your eyeballs pop out on your cheeks."

"Jesus." He shivered, tried to cover it with a shrug. "You ask your damn questions, maybe I'll answer, maybe I won't."

"Where did you and Steve get your drugs?"

His eyebrows flickered like hairy worms. "Drugs? Shit, man, I don't know—"

I leaned over and slipped my hand beneath his knee, gripped the slit in his pants leg and yanked. The old material gave up with very little sound. Bobby stared blankly at his exposed knee.

"I found your tracks, stupid! Did you think that was clever, unique, that nobody ever thought of it before? Come on, Bobby, let's cut out all the bullflop. Maybe you've been smart enough and lucky enough to keep your family from finding out that you're a druggie, but you're not smart enough or lucky enough to keep me from telling them. Maybe they already know and it doesn't matter. Okay, so I've lost my edge. Which is it, jerkoff, do they know or don't they?"

"None of your goddamned business."

"Okay, so they don't know. Now, back to the subject. Where did you get your drug supply?"

"Man, I don't know. Steve handled that end of it. He got the goods and we passed them out to our gang."

"Pushed them, you mean?"

"Naw, man. We all hung around together like. We were a club like."

"You gave them the drugs?"

"Well, they had to pay for their share—"

"Then you were pushing, stupid. Where did Steve get them?"

"I said I don't know. Just somebody he knew. He called him Big Bwana."

"Big what?"

"Big Bwana. You know, like the blacks used to call the white hunters in them old African movies. We saw one on TV one time, me and Steve. He cracked up over the name, went around calling everybody Bwana for weeks. Then it kinda faded, but he still called some people that. Like the teachers were Bwana and the principal was Big Bwana, and like the cops were Bwana and his uncle Chief Bannion was Big Bwana and the mayor and governor was Big Bwana—like that. It didn't mean nothing. It coulda been anybody."

"You never asked him?"

"Hell yes, I asked him. He'd just give me a shitty little smile and shake his head and say, 'Big Bwana, like I told you.'"

"Did Steve sell drugs to anyone outside your group?"

He shrugged. "I didn't know it if he did. I don't know

what he did when I wasn't around. I didn't give a shit, it wasn't any of my business."

"What kind of drugs? Other than grass and barbiturates, I mean."

His face turned sullen. "What're you doing, man? Setting me up for the local fuzz? They hassle me too damn much the way it is over my driving. I don't want 'em shaking down my car every time I hit the streets."

"I thought we understood each other. I don't give a rat's ass, Bobby, how much dope you do, or how you do it. I'm working on Lisa and Steve's murder. Maybe this is the way to go, maybe not. I don't know yet. But right now it's the path I'm on and you happen to be walking it with me. Maybe that makes it tough on you, but that's the way it is in this life. Sometimes the path is smooth, sometimes it's rocky. You happen to be in a rocky patch right now and I'm the mean sorry bastard who can make it a hell of a lot rockier. So, talk, goddammit!"

"Well," he said, after a face-saving few seconds. "Up till last December it was mostly grass and some speed, uppers and downers, you know, a little coke once in a while but coke was hard to come by in this little hick town."

"How about heroin?"

"Not then, man. No smack until . . . well April, somewhere along in there. First came the coke. Steve came prancin in one day with a full ounce, said he'd found the mother lode. There was always more, man. Then like I said, along about April he come in with some Mexican black—powerful damn stuff, man."

"How much?"

He scowled and gave me a quick hard look. "I don't know how much he had. A lot, I guess. He was practically giving the shit away, hell, he did give us some, our bunch, you know."

"Did he say where he got it?"

"Shit no, man. I told you he never said nothing about his source."

I lit a cigarette and thought for a moment, leaving him to

gaze moodily at the lights in the arena. So far, in a general way, what he had told me corroborated Patti Dunright's story. I felt an undeniable sense of relief. Patti Dunright had passed my interior polygraph with flying colors and it was good to know that I could still sometimes depend on hunches, rely on my instincts when it came to people.

"My arms are hurtin bad, man."

"Okay," I said. I fired up the engine and drove out of the park. We talked desultorily on the way to the convenience store, but he could not, or would not, tell me anything more of substance.

At the store, I pulled in beside his Cougar. Not quite so close this time. I reached across and shoved open the passenger door, motioned for him to turn around. I unlocked the handcuffs and watched his hunched shoulders as he rubbed his wrists, still sitting on the edge of the seat, one foot dangling.

After a time, a long time it seemed, he turned suddenly around, only to find himself staring into the bore of the .38.

A sneering grin came to his face, the dark eyes as cold and deadly as they had ever been.

"You're still scared, asshole," he said.

"You're right, Bobby. I'm scared. I think you're a little bit nuts, maybe more than a little bit. Maybe it's the drugs burning out your brain, but, whatever, don't ever come up on my blind side. Remember hydrostatic pressure."

He grinned, slipped out of the truck, and slammed the door. He swaggered over to his Cougar and pondered how to get in. The sack of groceries was gone.

17

Nathan Barr's motor home lived up to its advance billing. Still grimy on the outside, encrusted with bird droppings and road film, It was as neat as an old maid's hope chest on the inside. Pleasantly surprised, I poked around in the stunted refrigerator. I found bacon and eggs, unopened packages of cheese, bologna, ham, and a bloody-looking roll of hamburger meat, more beer than I could drink in a week. In a pullout cabinet bin, I found a reasonably fresh loaf of bread, a package of uncooked sesame rolls, and an open box of Oreo cookies. I located cooking utensils wedged into especially designed racks under the tiny double sink, cutlery in a spill-proof drawer next to the miniature stove. Plastic plates and plastic glasses, each stored in its own special niche. Everything had its place, a safe refuge designed to withstand life on the open road, the sudden twists and turns, the hard stops. I even found a gun, a .45 Colt automatic, fully loaded. I wondered if it was his traveling gun and if he had forgotten to take it with him to Missouri. More and more we were getting to be a nation of guns, defensive as well as offensive. Even when I wasn't working I never traveled without one. The highways were simply too damn dangerous, too many crazies cruising, looking for victims.

I ate fried bacon and scrambled eggs. Not my favorite dinner fare, but it was quick and easy and filling and very little cleanup. An after-dinner cigarette, and I went prowling again, checking out the pint-sized toilet that I could barely squeeze into, the coffin-sized shower. I let the water run for a while—still cold—and decided to forgo a shower.

I found the bed behind a privacy sliding door in the rear of the motor home. Not quite full size, but close enough if you happened to like your sleeping companion. I thought about that for a while and felt a warm expansive glow. I began to feel good about my new temporary living quarters for the first time. That bed made up for a lot.

I ended up sitting outside in one of two folding aluminum chairs that Barr—or somebody—had thoughtfully provided. A rollout awning protected my head from an occasional pecan giving up its war with gravity and a heavy canvas groundcover kept my feet away from such wee critters as ants and wood ticks.

True to his word, Barr had parked the motor home at the rear of the garage, a long low building of white block and aluminum trim, quiet now behind a six-foot cedar fence designed to protect the sensibilities of passing motorists from a welter of quietly rusting auto parts, cannibalized transmissions and rear ends, gutless engine blocks.

The motor home faced outward away from the garage, my view a barbwire fence gleaming dully in the moonlight, a limitless expanse of darkness and somebody's pasture, a gently rising swell of land faintly discernible, ending in a dark jagged line of trees on the horizon.

The air was clear and crisp, not yet uncomfortably cool. I sat and smoked and thought, the only two things I can do reasonably well at the same time.

Bobby Radcross had been trying to dominate my mind all evening, lurking in the shadowy edges of my consciousness like a dark flower trying to bloom. I opened up and let him in, acknowledging to myself that I had handled Bobby badly, clumsily, motivated by both anger and a kind of irrational fear. But, even now, calmly, coolly, I could think of no better way it could have been done. Radcross was a loose cannon, a rampaging spark in a fireworks factory. He could only be contained, never controlled. He lived by raw impulse, the desire of the moment. I had met too many like him to be fooled, had helped send my share of them to jail. Maybe, as the bleeding hearts will tell you, it's not the answer, but, right now, it's the only one we've got.

I moved on to think about Jerico Falls, to puzzle over Ward again, the subtle changes I couldn't define. I went over my conversations with Abel Caulder and Cody Bannion, Patti Dunright and Norma Dew, turned finally to Lisa and Steve. I thought about senseless murder and head wounds—and hydrostatic pressure—and that brought me full circle to Bobby Radcross again.

I snorted him away, shook my head like an old wet hound— and that was when I saw the shadowy apparition coming around the end of the motor home. Marching confidently, almost silent in the ankle deep grass, looming out of darkness into the light.

I recognized him almost instantly, looking bigger than he should in a ten gallon cowboy hat, different than he had before in old range clothes, a pair of gaudy, wrinkled boots.

But Bobby Radcross had been on my mind, a dark menacing presence, and my hand snapped instinctively toward my left armpit, to the gun that wasn't there.

He stopped abruptly. "Goodness! Mr. Roman! I hope I didn't startle you."

"Not a bit," I said, flicking limp fingers at my shoulder. "Pesky bug."

"Yes," he said portentously, as if I had just made some grave, esoteric revelation. "I must say *I* was a little startled— to see you, I mean. I thought you were Nathan sitting there." He trundled onto the canvas patio and stuck out a plump hand.

"He had to go to . . . to St. Louis, I think, Mr. Alldyce. Somewhere in Missouri, at least."

"Ah, I see. His poor father again, I suppose. Nathan is

so devoted to his father. That's so unusual today, don't you think? Especially for one of the baby-boomers."

"Well, it's great, all right, but I don't know if you could call him a baby-boomer or not. He looked a little young for that."

"He's thirty, I think. Oh, well, perhaps I have the wrong term. What's the other one, the groupies?"

"I think you mean the yuppies, but even then I'm not sure Nate—"

"Oh, well." He made a dismissive gesture and sank into the other chair. It squeaked and popped alarmingly. "I can't keep up with all the changes in this fast lane world of ours, Mr. Roman. We're simply burning ourselves out. One of these days—poof." He made an explosive gesture with both round hands, let them sink to his paunch, wriggle together like small fat worms. A diamond pinkie ring caught the overhead light and exploded in my eye. "Oh, well," he said again. "I might have known Nathan would have a very good reason for not keeping his appointment. He was supposed to shoe Starfire and Molly B today. He's very good, you know. The animals seem to trust him implicitly. Starfire can be worrisome when he wants to be, but Nathan has absolutely no problems with him."

"Tricks of the trade, maybe," I said, lighting the last Carlton in my pack.

"Speaking of trade, Mr. Roman. How are you doing? Any leads or suspects or . . . or whatever it is you look for?"

He caught me completely off guard. I gained a few seconds by busily crushing the empty cigarette box, looking around for some place to put it, finally shoving it into my jacket pocket, clearing my throat, and looking squarely into his little round eyes.

"Mr. Alldyce, I think it would be better if you asked Chief Bannion that question—"

"Why?"

I shrugged. "He's my boss. At any rate, it's not good practice to go around talking about an ongoing case."

"Balderdash," he said testily. "You may answer to Chief Bannion, young man, but Chief Bannion answers to me."

"Really?" My disbelief must have shown in my face.

"Yes. Really. I'm the mayor of this town, Mr. Roman, as much as that will undoubtedly amuse you. I have been for twelve years." He reached up and took off the ten gallon hat. "Now I'm the mayor. When I wear that hat, I'm a rancher. I have another hat, a silly little white hat I wear when I'm the specialty chef at Alldyce's Fine Food and French Cuisine out on the highway."

I must have looked as disgruntled as I felt; he laughed and slapped his thigh.

"Really, Mr. Roman, if you have some reason for not telling me, then that's quite all right. I understand the necessity for prudence in your profession. Wouldn't do at all for the culprit to know how close you are on his tail, eh?"

"Not at all," I said. "He might do something desperate, like give himself up."

He erupted into laughter again, slapped the hat back on his head, looking for all the world like the sappy, bumbling sidekick of some 1940s cowboy star.

He struggled up out of the chair. "I'll just be getting on now, Mr. Roman. I do hope I haven't made a total nuisance of myself. If I sounded a little short back there, I hope you won't take it personally. It's just that I sometimes have trouble making people take me seriously." He made a wry, self-deprecating grimace. "That's what comes of looking like Buddy Hackett, and sometimes acting like Bobo the clown." He laughed and I cautiously joined in, unable to think of anything to say that would be contradictory and reassuring at the same time.

We shook hands. I walked with him to the front of the motor home. "There isn't anything concrete to report, Mr. Mayor," I said. "I've talked to some of their close friends, and none of them could shed any light on the murders. We'll be getting what little physical evidence we have back from the lab tomorrow. Maybe it'll give us some kind of fix on where the killings took place."

He stopped short, a lugubrious expression on his rubbery features under the ridiculous hat. "You think they weren't killed out at the Rodeo Grounds, then?"

"No chance," I said, wondering what kind of report Ward had given him, if any. "Not where they were found. Killings that violent leave tracks. There weren't any there."

He shook his head, looking a little sick. "Terrible thing, Mr. Roman. Just children, really. Two of the nicest kids we had in this town . . . in this county. I don't see how anyone could—" He broke off and made a short fierce gesture. "But someone did, didn't they?" He tilted his head to look up at me. "Why?"

"That's what we have to find out, Mr. Mayor."

"Do it," he said, his voice low and scratchy. "Do it, Mr. Roman. Find out why, and most of all find out who."

I nodded. "I intend to."

18

I GOT AN EARLY START THE NEXT MORNING, ALLOWING something over two hours for the eighty mile trek to Abilene. More than half the distance would be farm-to-market roads and state highways, a lot of turning and twisting, some ups and downs that would provide excellent hiding places for county mounties and state patrol. With the closing of the spigot in Washington, money was tight in rural Texas, and every little fifty dollar speeding ticket helped. Out-of-county license plates made you the fairest game of all. Some traveling salesman called it a toll tax, others used less complimentary terms. Yankee tourists were mostly ignored as long as they didn't try to hog the road and minded their manners at the rest stops.

So, having no desire to add to the Saragache County coffers, I locked my speed control at fifty-five, lit a cigarette, and settled back with Dean Martin and "Welcome to My World," feeling one step ahead of life for a change, the concrete highway twinkling in the brilliant morning sun like Chinese sparklers, urging me on. For the first time in a long time I was exactly where I wanted to be, on my way to meet the woman I loved. Everything paled before that fact, faded to the nether regions of my mind, unpleasant memories to be resurrected another day.

I had spent a restless, uneasy night, a new bed and old familiar feelings of futility and vague primal fears combining to plague my mind, to keep me staring into the darkness of the dead hours, the time when life is at its lowest ebb.

But this was a new day, a new direction. I had awakened leaden and listless, unfit for social discourse with human or beast. A cold shower and the pleasant shock of remembrance had cured all that, left me fired with the uplifting vigor of a zealot. I was riding the crest of a swelling high, a natural high that wove its own warm rich cocoon of isolation, effectively blocking sights and sounds—the thick green countryside about me, an occasional motorist sharing the lonely road—almost blocking the flashing whirling lights and wailing siren of the car that was coming up fast behind me.

I checked my speed before I kicked the brake to release the cruise control. I was on the downside of a hill and the needle had ticked over a couple of notches to fifty-seven. Two lousy miles over the limit. Chickenshit behavior, even for a county cop. I wondered how long the greedy bastard had been hanging back there, awaiting the inevitable moment when momentum and grade combined to roll me over the top into fair-game country.

The lights flashed—one light actually, a gum ball machine slanted lazily on the top of the car—the siren whooped to a clucking halt, Spike Jones shrieked and chattered on the golden-oldie station, and I cursed half-heartedly and let the truck coast to a stop, grimly determined not to let some half-assed clown cop spoil my day.

I watched in the rearview mirror while he got out, a short stocky figure with shoulder-length black hair and wide shoulders. He wore some kind of jogging shoes, chinos, and a heavily studded black leather jacket. He looked like no cop I had ever seen, not out on the highway in the middle of cattle country. I reached across and took the .38 out of the dash pocket.

He saw the action and understood what it meant. He

stopped abruptly near the end of my rear bumper. He held his hands up chest high, palms out, then gripped the edges of the jacket, lifted them out and up, and slowly turned around.

"Hey, man. No hassle, okay? Just a little talk. No guns or nothing like that. I'm DEA, man, I got some ID here if you want to see it."

Drug Enforcement Agency. I studied his stubbled smiling face in the mirror and lost a little more faith in my government. I dropped the gun into my coat pocket and eased out of the truck, faced him.

"I'd like to see it, if you don't mind."

His head bobbed. "Sure." His hand slipped inside his jacket.

I showed him the gun. "You pull anything out of there I can't fold, spindle, or mutilate, mister, and I'll—" I let it drop. I wasn't scaring him much, anyway.

He laughed and pulled back the jacket with his left hand, showing me the flat pocket, the two stubby fingers probing inside. He brought out a thin leather case, let it flip open. I saw some kind of a badge and an ID card. I held out my hand.

The picture matched—no big surprise. The name, Leonard Newton Nueboldt, was unfamiliar—again, no big surprise. The only person I knew who worked for the government was the nephew of a friend of mine. The ID card was ornate and looked authentic, the badge a little fancier than it had to be. Typical government over-frill. Maybe they had made up for it by cutting the clothing allowance.

I flipped the case at him and pocketed the gun. "Is this what the well-dressed DEA agent is wearing this fall?"

He nodded amiably and laughed, then looked up and down the highway and took a sack of tobacco and papers out of his shirt pocket and began rolling a cigarette. Real tobacco as far as I could tell. "Maybe you ought to be showing me some identification," he said. There was a hint of command in his voice, a touch of the arrogance that all cops adopt sooner or later, protective coloration that acknowledges their own vulnerability, and is, essentially, an attempt to negate it.

It was my turn to laugh. "You stopped me, friend. If you don't know who I am then you're a hell of a lot stupider than I think you are."

He smiled and tugged the drawstring tight on the sack with long white teeth, ran a tongue along the seam of the humpbacked cigarette. He twisted one end and stuck it between his lips, lit it with a kitchen match scraped across the sole of his boot. By the time he finished I was getting a little tired of the cowboy show.

"You said you wanted to talk, so talk. I've got a plane to meet."

He nodded soberly and took one more deep drag on the homemade cigarette, then flipped it into the middle of the road. "As you might have guessed, I'm not advertising that I'm DEA. Not exactly deep cover, but I'm maintaining a low profile. My face is too well known in this part of the state for anything—"

"I'm sure that's a problem," I said. "But what brings you to me? If you're planning on shaking down my vehicle, then you'd damn well better get started. I'm leaving here in ten minutes flat, or sooner. And one other thing, you'll have to show me some paper before I'll let you touch a door handle."

He squinted one eye and looked up at me, a little color coming into his pale face, dark brown eyes gleaming. "You're a hard man to deal with, Mr. Roman."

"Not ordinarily. But right now I'm a tad rushed and a little outta sorts. I was feeling great five minutes ago, but you've screwed that up for me. Now, what did you want with me, Agent Nueboldt?"

"Okay," he said tersely, striking his chest with a balled fist, as if it was some kind of starting signal. "You've been going around talking to a lot of people about drugs. Drugs happen to interest me very much. I hate drugs. I hate the scum who deal the shit. It occurred to me that these people may have told you things they wouldn't tell me, knowing who

I am and all. It occurred to me that you seem *very* interested in drugs, Mr. Roman. More so, say, than your average private cop peeking in keyholes. In my simple fashion I decided that I should perhaps talk to you, ask you about your unseemly interest in drugs, ask you perhaps exactly what kind of drugs it is that you're trying to find.''

I recognized the technique. He wasn't even particularly good at it. I was neither angry nor intimidated. But maybe that was because he had puffed up as he talked, inflating his chest, flexing the muscles in his jaws, biting off key words in an acid-edged voice, looking more like a ruffled bantam rooster than a dreaded government man.

"Aspirin," I said. "I'll admit it. I've been hooked since I had my first headache as a kid—"

"I could take your ass in," he said coldly. "On a concealed weapon charge, if nothing else."

"Yeah. I guess you could if I'd lay down and let you tie me up."

He snorted and walked around in a tight little circle, kicking aimlessly at bits of dried armadillo on the highway, pale skin blotched with red. He clearly didn't like what was happening and just as clearly didn't know what to do about it short of calling in state or county reinforcement. He obviously didn't want to do that. I was just a fishing trip. He wanted information he thought I might have, but so far I had refused to allow him the high ground necessary to acquire dominance. He stopped abruptly and whirled to face me, hands on hips, dark eyes faintly menacing.

"The Caulder and Bannion kids," he said harshly. "Were they users? Is that your tie-in to drugs?"

I shrugged. "Not according to the autopsy reports." I was being deliberately evasive and I wasn't sure why except that he seemed to be operating from a very low level of intelligence, a barroom gossip level, and so far I hadn't been able to figure out where he was coming from, or where he was heading. "Look, Agent Nueboldt, I'm involved in a murder investigation. That's priority one. I don't give a damn about your drug operation, if there is one, about how you hate drugs and the turdballs who deal it. You think you're the only one who hates pushers? Well, you're wrong, pal. The thing is, I was hired to find a killer not a pusher, and there damn sure wasn't anything in my contract that said I had to pimp for the DEA in the meantime.''

He puffed up again, a not unexpected reaction. "You got a bad attitude, Mr. Roman. You ought to work on that. You can't work without a license, you know—''

"Five minutes," I said.

He threw up his hands and whirled toward his car. After a few feet, he stopped and turned. His voice was low, level, and hard: "If you find it, Roman, you goddamned well better come to me.''

"You got it," I said. "If I find it, I come to you." I opened the truck door. He was still standing there. "Maybe *it* will find me first," I said.

"Don't let your mouth overload your ass, Mr. Roman.''

"Okay, let's see if I got it all. If I find it, I come to you— and don't let my mouth overload my ass. I think I've got it now." I gave him a little wave and a big smile, got into the truck and drove off.

A half mile down the road, I checked my rearview mirror. He was still standing there, head down as if he might be rolling another cigarette, or, more likely, plotting my imminent incarceration.

Stupid, stupid! When would I ever learn?

19

I WAS LATE. ONLY A FEW MINUTES, BUT SUSIE HAD AL-
ready deplaned, gathered her luggage together, one small
suitcase and an overnight bag, and was sitting in the general
waiting room talking to a blue-haired lady with diamond
studded fingers and a makeup encrusted face. The woman's
mouth was going sixty miles a minute and judging by Susie's
strained smile each minute had been an hour.

One of her fans, no doubt, I thought, and smiled inwardly.
She had not yet become accustomed to people recognizing
her when she was not on camera, had not yet come to grips
with the combined realities of constant statewide exposure
and a very memorable face.

For a time I had assumed that her discomfiture was a modest maidenly pose designed primarily to counter my sometimes caustic gibes about video stars and queens of the
airwaves. But somewhere along the way I came to realize
that she was truly embarrassed. Not so much at the recog-
nition, she understood the inevitability of that, but at the
effusive compliments that had more to do with her beauty
than her delivery, more to do with a kind of slavish devotion
than respect for a job well done. A disproportionate number
of her fans seemed to be adult males, eighteen to eighty,

their letters salted with thinly veiled sexual innuendo, return addresses and telephone numbers, sometimes little gifts, offers of no-strings-attached larger gifts ranging from French blenders to a new Mercedes. Sometimes, depending on my mood, I thought it was funny; other times I thought it was damn sick. She was amused or revolted, depending on the letter. But she was always amazed, and sometimes I watched her and wondered if what she saw in the mirror even remotely resembled what I saw when I looked at her.

She looked up and saw me standing there, and an almost ludicrous expression of relief overwhelmed the frozen smile. She came out of the seat as if propelled by exaltation, threw wide her arms and uttered a little scream, then hurled herself at me like a lioness protecting her young, chortles and squeals, a hug worthy of Schwarzenegger, lifting, actually *lifting* me up on my toes, planting a noisy wet kiss on my disapproving lips, letting her mouth trail across my cheek to my ear, hot breath puffing around a husky whisper:

"This'll teach you, you dirty rat, not to be late!"

"Consider me taught," I said, marveling at this unseemly display of public affection that I couldn't have beat out of her with a stick. An affectionate smile, a decorous peck on the lips was her standard airport greeting; on better days, a friendly hug.

I grinned down at her; blushing furiously now that her moment of impulsive mania had passed, she turned to the blue-haired woman. "Excuse me, Mrs. Warden, this is my husband, Dan Roman."

"Pleasedtomeetcha, I'm sure." She held out a plump hand, gave me a fleeting glance, and turned adoring eyes back to Susie. "Oh, Arthur just isn't going to believe I've been talking to Susan Roman in person! You're his very favorite, you know, he wouldn't miss your broadcast for anything!"

"Why, thank you," Susie said. "It's good to know I have one loyal fan."

I finished with Mrs. Warden's hand and let it go; she didn't seem to notice.

"Oh, I love you, too," she gushed. "We all do. My sister Flo will simply be green, and my other sister—"

"Yes," I said, and patted Susie's cheek. "We all do. She's just . . . just so lovable." I picked up the cases. "Come along, darling. We're brunching with the Perots this morning. You know how frumpy he gets when we're late."

"Oh, my!" Mrs. Warden trotted along behind us. "You mean the H. Ross Perots? You tell him I just loved his movie! And you tell him we're behind him a hundred percent—"

I looked over my shoulder and winked. "I surely will. Old Harry will be pleased no end."

"Bye-bye, Mrs. Warden," Susie said, giving me a menacing look. "Nice talking to you."

"Bye-bye, Susan. You be careful now, you hear me? We'll be watching you every night, and I'm so pleased I finally got to meet a celebrity! Thank you very much for your autograph!"

Susie waved at her from the door and I turned to look. She was standing where we left her in the middle of the aisle, looking somehow woebegone, splinters of icy blue light flashing when she waved.

"Golly," I said. "Her big chance to mingle with the beautiful people and we just up and walk right out of her life."

She squeezed my arm—harder than necessary, I thought.

"You weren't very nice back there," she said, and smothered a giggle. "H. Ross Perot, my left foot! Anyway, I don't think his name is Harry. I think it's Henry."

"Henry or Harry," I said. "It doesn't matter. What I want to know is what brought on your little Sheena of the Jungle act. You know how I deplore such vulgar public displays of affection."

The giggle became a full-fledged laugh as we reached the Ramcharger. She leaned on my shoulder as I unlocked the door. "Lordy. She rode down from Dallas with me. She talked some nice man into changing seats with her so we could chat, as she called it. I learned more about her and her family in the last hour than I'll ever know about you. My eyes were glazing over when I looked up and saw you standing there grinning like an ape. I guess I just freaked out. Did I embarrass you?'' She rose on tiptoe and kissed my cheek. "If I did, then I'm glad. That was the point, you know.''

"Not me. I'm used to beautiful women throwing themselves at me. Happens all the time.''

"I'm not surprised,'' she said darkly, giving me a sidelong glance that had lost much of its humor.

I handed her into the truck and put her luggage in the rear compartment, marveling, as I often found myself doing lately, at her intriguing combination of naiveté and sophistication. At twenty-four she had been to a good many countries of the world, the hotspots, witnessed enough man-made and natural disasters for ten lifetimes, dealt with paupers and with kings, heroes and despots, men who killed for fun and those who killed for profit. It touched her deeply at times, filled her dreams with horror, and yet she awoke each morning with a clear-eyed vision of the world as a wondrous place. She still believed in the basic goodness of Homo sapiens, in honesty and integrity and love. She firmly believed that all other women found me irresistible, a preponderance of evidence to the contrary notwithstanding. And feeling thusly, still trusted me, which made it damn well impossible for me to cheat on those rare occasions when the rising tide of male hormones and opportunity coincided.

But it was not at all one-sided. I loved her, obsessively at times, my heart seized at unexpected moments, pierced with an intensity so fierce it took away my breath, left me feeling puerile and foolish, as cautious as a scorched dog before an open hearth. I had lost two women I loved to death, I had no desire to lose one to life. There were sixteen long years between us, a mere pittance from her end, a yawning eternity from mine. I was wise enough to know that all things change with time, and not always for the best. That scared me sometimes, brought an icy chill to my heart, overlaid my life with a dark surly cloud of foreboding.

I climbed into the truck and sat looking at her. She looked back. We exchanged fond smiles, then met halfway for a kiss. I fired up the engine.

"One little errand, my love, then it's home to our little aluminum castle overlooking Thunderbolt Creek."

"That sounds nice."

"Well, not exactly overlooking. It's over the hill and down a ways, but if you watch close you can see the doves coming in to water at sunset."

"Who wants a slurping, gurgling creek underfoot, anyway?"

"Right. It'd just keep us awake at night."

"And we need our rest."

"You got it," I said, driving off the parking lot and heading for the Abilene police station. "That's what you came down here for."

"Yeah."

As good as his word, Ward had called and made arrangements for me to pick up the physical evidence from the police laboratory. I presented identification, signed a property release form, and five minutes later climbed in beside Susie with a plastic bag the size of a Ziploc freezer bag. A number of other, smaller bags were visible through the clear plastic, each, apparently, with its own identification label. The bag was sealed with a bright red label that read: CRIME SCENE EVIDENCE, DO NOT TAMPER.

I handed the bag to Susie and dug out my pocketknife. "Tamper," I said. "Let's see what we've got." I started the truck's engine and drove off the lot, working my way into the surprisingly heavy traffic. The last time I had been there, Abilene had been a friendly, laid-back country city, nobody in much of a hurry, oil and cattle setting the pace for living, easygoing people, slow and courteous. But things had changed. Horns blasted. I saw red, angry faces, jutting fingers. I heard shrill invective, invitations to battle. I wondered what had wrought such a startling transformation: tight money, low cattle prices, market fluctuation in oil, an invasion of Fundamentalists? We might well have been in downtown Dallas at the changing of the yuppie guard.

Susie gave me a dubious look. "This is sealed, Danny.

The fine print says not to open without proper authorization or you'll destroy the integrity of the evidence—"

"This evidence lost its integrity riding around in the back seat of a police car for a week. No judge in his right mind would allow it into a courtroom. Go ahead, open it."

"Okay, if you say so." She opened the knife and slit the tape. "There's a lot of smaller packages inside." She dipped a hand into the bag, came out with several flat plastic packets of varying sizes. She selected one and held it up to the light, read the inscription, and tapped it against her hand to gather the contents into one corner.

"Seed," she said. "Tiny little seed." She turned it over and read the back half of the label. "Item #8. Fleabane seed taken from the head of Lisa—" She broke off. Out of the corner of my eye I saw her head whip in my direction. "Head? My God, Danny!"

"Hair actually. All of this is stuff they found on the bodies, Susie. They weren't killed where they were found, so maybe what we have here will help us find where they were killed." I went on to give her a brief rundown, leaving out things like head shots and hydrostatic pressure. When I finished she stared down at the packets now lying on the seat between us. She nodded mutely.

"It's okay. We can wait until we get to the motor home."

"No," she said, and picked up another plastic bag. She studied it for a moment, turned it over, and cleared her throat. "Item #4. There's only a few of these, Danny. Sunflower seeds. They're pretty big. They were found—"

"No need for that," I said. "Just tell me what you have."

She nodded, hair spilling down across olive cheeks as she bent to her task. As usual, she looked resplendent in a wine-colored, long-sleeved sweater and navy blue slacks, a white and blue checkered neckerchief knotted around her firm smooth throat. She wore no jewelry except for a wedding band and a small, leather-banded watch. Her skin was fine-textured, unmarred by the usual pits and craters of adolescent excesses. She wore very little makeup, needed none. But it was her eyes that brought her face alive, gave it the critical balance of beauty; velvety brown, they could be as warm as a lover's caress, or as penetrating as twin lasers directed at the soul. I could lie to her, or look at her; I couldn't do both.

20

"BERMUDA SEED," SUSIE SAID, TAPPING ANOTHER PACKET against her finger. "These are really tiny, Danny, but there are quite a few of them." She put it back in the pouch.

"More fleabane seed. These came from the . . . him, Steve." She put the packet back in the big bag and selected another, a larger bag, its sides bulging with a larger amount of seed. "What's milo, Danny? There's two of these, also, and they have a lot of seed."

"It's a sorghum grain crop," I said, calling on my childhood ranching experience. "I don't remember much about it except it's a dry land crop and makes for good dove hunting in the fall."

"I don't see how you can shoot those beautiful little birds."

"They were never in much danger from me."

I punched in the dash cigarette lighter. "What else do we have?"

"Let's see." She gathered up the remaining packets. "There's nothing in Item #1 but some chunks of dried mud. Item #7 is four or five cockleburs, and Item #3 looks like a nail."

"A nail?"

"Yes. A funny-looking little curved nail. It says here that it came out of Item #1."

I scratched around in my brain while I lit a cigarette. Then I remembered. "The nail must have been embedded in a chunk of mud they found at the Rodeo Grounds," I said. "Close to where they found the bodies."

She nodded. "That's what it says. The nail was found in a triangular wedge of dried dirt approximately two and a half inches long."

"What does it say about the mud itself. Anything?"

"Clay base, with thirty percent sandstone, four percent limestone, two percent coarse gravel, small rocks—"

"That about covers the whole county I would think. What do they say about the nail?"

"Nothing. They just say 'nail found embedded in Item #1.' It's bright and shiny like it's never been used, but it looks bent a little." She held it out. I took it and examined it through the clear plastic as well as I could and still keep one eye on the highway. Just as she had said, a nail, bright and shiny, probably an inch and a half long, slightly curved as if it had been struck off center and kicked away from the work. A special-use nail, I thought, with a rectangular head considerably thicker than normal, one edge extending off center from the shank. Something fluttered in my brain, peeked at me out of a murky morass of faulty memory cells, mocked and jeered, then slipped away without a trace.

I grunted and dropped the bag into Susie's waiting hand. She slipped it into the larger container with the others. "So, what do we have? Sunflower seed, milo, a lot of milo, and bermuda."

"And fleabane seed," Susie said. "I think fleabane is a little white and yellow flower. But we still have one more. This one just has little bits and pieces of . . . well it looks like little bits of tree bark to me." She grinned at me and turned it over. "Let's see how close I am."

"You probably already looked," I said.

"No, I haven't . . . there, I was right. Oak tree bark and some flaky stuff they call horsetails. The bark came from both of them, and the horsetail stuff came from Steve's sweater.'' She leaned forward and looked into my face, a shine in her eyes. ''Does any of this mean anything to you, Danny?''

''Horsetails grow around water. In water or at the edge.'' I looked at her smiling face and felt a stir of excitement that had nothing to do with love or lust or even appreciation of beauty. I was remembering what Abel Caulder had said about Ward Bannion's little lake, the kids' favorite spot on Saturday nights when Ward was gone. An old stock tank, he had said. There would undoubtedly be horsetails growing there. I knew there was milo nearby. Bermuda grass grew everywhere, as did fleabane. There would have to be an oak tree or trees to shade the cattle from the sun, and cockleburs grew all over the country.

I could still feel Susie watching me. ''What's the matter, Danny, are you having a brainstorm or a pain?''

''Yeah, a pain, I'm hungry as all get-out. How about you?''

She nodded, not satisfied with my answer, but knowing from experience that was probably all she'd get. ''I could eat a salad, I guess.''

''Next restaurant we see,'' I said, suddenly exhilarated. ''You can give the Perots a jingle and tell them to get their butts on over here.''

She smiled, but her heart wasn't in it. She had taken a peek into my world for a change, and after her initial revulsion, had found it intriguing. The shine in her eyes told me that. Murder in the abstract can do that for you. Everybody loves a puzzle and most people way down deep believe they could be a detective.

The simple truth was I didn't want her looking too hard at what I did for a living, the seaminess, the sleaze, the occasional danger. She tended to romanticize my job a bit, confusing it to some degree with the weekly feats of derring-do by handsome actors masquerading as private eyes. And that was fine with me. My armor could stand a little shine. My job was looking for people, runaways mostly, people who left where they were to go somewhere else for all kinds of reasons. There was little excitement involved, almost no brainwork, and absolutely no glamour. A thankless job and tasteless work, too much time rubbing elbows with the products of misery and sloth, that great network of humanity teeming just below the first rung of the ladder.

There's a good reason for that: you go where the runner goes, and nobody runs away to hide at the top.

"This is really nice, Danny," Susie said, stepping down out of the motor home to where I waited in one of the aluminum chairs.

I studied her face for a moment. "Now, look. There's a Ramada Inn out on the Interstate. It's less than an hour's drive—"

"No, no, really. I was disappointed when I saw the outside—you'll have to admit it's a little dirty but it's neat as a pin on the inside, and everything's so *clean*." She turned to look across the wire fence, at the rolling pastureland. She swung an arm in a wide expansive gesture. "And we have a view . . . and there's the creek down there you told me about—what was it, Thunderbird?"

"I don't remember. I made it up."

She laughed and sat in the other chair. "The bed looks comfy."

"Uh-huh, it is."

"Well," she said, then added brightly, without looking at me. "I noticed some beer in the fridge. You want me to get you one?"

"Hmmmm. No, I don't think so, not right now. Thanks, anyway."

"You're welcome."

We drifted into a companionable silence. I lit a cigarette and watched an occasional meadowlark bolt out of the yellow-brown grass ahead of a lazily drifting white-faced cow. A flock of blackbirds swarmed the tree line along the creek, gathered in disorderly ranks and swooped low across the hill and disappeared. Behind us, on the other side of the six foot fence, a hammer clanged on metal; a power lug wrench dismantled a tire.

We talked a little, desultorily, about nothing important, still not looking at each other, but acutely aware.

Building tension, anticipation.

We fell silent again, ignoring each other. An old familiar game.

Then, after a while, we got up and went inside.

21

"I'LL BE BACK LATER THIS AFTERNOON," I SAID, BENDING to kiss puffy lips pursed in a moue of half-hearted disappointment. "I'll stop and pick up some rib eyes and potatoes and the making of a salad and we'll have a Roman Special for dinner. That sound okay?"

She extended round tanned arms and snagged my neck before I could rise. "I may just lie here all afternoon and . . . regenerate."

"I could use a little of that myself," I said, "but there's something I need to do. It won't take too long. If you decide to take a little walk or anything, be sure to lock up and take the keys. I'll leave them on the kitchen cabinet." I ran a finger along her jawline to the dimple in her chin and pressed. "And don't go wandering off too far. This big city, you'd get lost for sure."

She chuckled lazily, eyelids drooping. "I may be right here."

I kissed her again and pried loose her arms, stood up. She already looked asleep, but as I turned to go, she opened one eye. "Since we don't have a TV, you might pick up something to read, magazines, *People*, *Us*—anything. All Mr.

Barr seems to have is a stack of *Horse and Rider* and an old Bible.''

''I'll do it. In the meantime you could read the Bible, and I'll explain anything you don't understand when I get back.''

I waited a couple of seconds, but this time she appeared to be genuinely asleep. From past experience I knew she could come out of a thirty minute nap completely rejuvenated, clear-eyed and ready for what came next, be it more love-making or dinner and dancing until dawn. She had remarkable recuperative powers, even for a twenty-four year old, and that worried me a little. There were times when I felt each and every one of my forty years individually, like rusty old chains clanking along the ground behind me. And at such times I wondered if maybe I wasn't cheating her, that the best part of my years had come and gone, that what I had to offer was only a facsimile of what I once had been, that all that remained was a walking, talking, reasonably active husk of a man.

I locked the door quietly, climbed into the Ramcharger, and drove across town to the police station, my high feelings of a few minutes before washed out by a dark and brooding sense of foreboding.

Ward Bannion wasn't in. Another black spot in my suddenly darkening day. I went back out to my truck.

To hell with him. I'd check it out myself.

I found the lake by simply following the tracks through Ward's barnyard, around the edge of the milo field and along the base of the hill. It was on the north side of the hill, out of sight of Ward's house. Three acres, I guessed, long and narrow and not very deep judging by the color and the normal water marks along the shore. Hardwood trees and a thick tangle of brush and vines lined the bank nearest the hill. The other, lower, shore grew nothing but weeds and a number of deeply rutted cow trails leading down to the old water line.

I found the small clearing at the upper end, near the low-level dam; an ancient powder-gray picnic table and a rusted out barbecue grill mutely testified to better, happier times.

The table was stippled with bird droppings, the legs beginning to rot; the grill lay on its side, surrendering to time and the elements. Above it all a giant red oak tree spread multi-colored limbs. The area was littered with fallen leaves, chunks of dead oak limbs, pieces of bark; yellow bermuda tendrils peeked through in random places. Fleabane formed a threadbare carpet of sorts.

Even before I got out of the truck I saw drooping sunflowers and horsetails here and there. Neat rows of milo stubble grew right up to the edge of the clearing and, no more than five or six feet away, I could see a tangled mass of sawbriers and cocklebur bushes.

I felt a chill, a small surge of adrenaline, a harder chill.

It was the killing place. I knew it as surely as I knew that stone was hard and flesh died.

Here. In the darkness where the black flowers bloom their fullest.

They had come to make love and stayed to die. Hands tied, eyes blinded by strips of cloth. I looked around the rustic peaceful spot and for the first time felt the full horror of it, of young lives wasted for no good reason, no reason good enough.

I backed the truck up a few yards and got out. All that remained was to find the exact spot. The tracks of violent death. There would still be some, two weeks and three days of insects and predators notwithstanding. I lit a cigarette, took a deep breath, and began my search.

I found the first of it not more than five minutes later: several strands of fine silky blond hair attached to a piece of scalp and a chip of bone. It was stuck to the inside leg of the picnic table with a mucilage of blood and brain. I left it there.

I stood up and guessed the most likely trajectory, then dropped back to my hands and knees and worked my way outward from the table. I found another piece almost immediately, a chip of bone the size of a quarter, very little scalp with only three or four hairs still intact, the bone dappled with dried blood. I shoved a stick into the ground and lined up with the table leg. Now I had a more or less true trajectory.

I stood up again. I was less than two paces from the milo field, close enough to see an area the size of a king-sized bed that had been scuffed and marked by human feet, the grain stubble bent and broken and trampled to the ground.

Strangely reluctant, I took the two paces and saw it immediately, a brown, crusty spot the size of a dinner plate, swarming with fire ants, the dome of their winter home only a few inches from where the head had lain. From there blood-streaked grooves and indentations led back into the upper edge of the clearing, as if the body had been dragged.

I found the other blood spot two rows away from the first. The second body also appeared to have been dragged back into the clearing, maybe to get it away from the fire ants or to make it easier to load into Steve's car.

I studied the footprints between the rows of milo stubble, but the impressions in the dry hard soil were useless for purposes of identification, too shallow to cast and, as far as I could see, revealed no tell-tale markings or unusual wear patterns. At least one person involved had worn boots of the high-heeled variety; the deeper indentations here and there were clearly visible. But there again, I could find nothing to distinguish them from thousands of other similar boot heels worn daily throughout Saragache County, so they meant little.

I was climbing to my feet for the last time when I felt the first stinging bite, high on my lower leg, above my boot top and below my knee. I slapped a hand against the cloth, found a tiny wriggling lump, and squeezed, feeling in that same instant another bite, higher on my thigh, and then another. Fire ants!

I shucked my boots and pants. Danced around slapping beastly little red critters darting around my legs like soldiers in enemy territory, a good dozen of them, all unerringly hellbent for my groin area, as if they knew by instinct man's most tender spot.

It was a short war and I won. The tally was eight bites and

ten of the enemy vanquished, tiny splashes of alien blood from my lightning smashes that hurt far more than the bites ever would. I wiped off the traces of blood and tried not to shudder. I hated insect bites and stings with an abiding passion, feared them with an irrational fear completely out of proportion to the damage they could inflict. Snakes had never been a problem, but bees, wasps, hornets, and yellow jackets curdled my blood, sent me dancing and flailing like a punk-rocker gone mad.

I stripped down and shook out all my clothing, examined the insides of my boots. I left the clearing a few minutes later, bites stinging, grateful there weren't more. Fire ants are known for their aggressiveness, their dedication to defending the colony. I had obviously incited the ire of a small scouting party, and even now the survivors might well be rallying the colony for a massive counterattack.

I shuddered again and drove a little faster.

Avoiding them. Another image.

I took a drag on the cigarette. "Silicone tar or talc, that sort of thing.

22

THIS TIME WARD BANNION WAS IN. HE GREETED ME WITH a grin and waved me to a seat. "Don't know that I expected to see you today, what with your lady coming down and all." There was a hint of lasciviousness both in his grin and in his tone, but it wasn't something I could take offense at.

"She's here," I said. "I left her out at Barr's motor home."

"She's a pretty woman. Since them CNN jaybirds are scrambling their signal, I been watching TNS for their twenty-four hour news. I've seen her a lot, but like I said, I didn't connect her with you. Boy, you must be a lousy card player, your first wife was a good looker too. How do you do it?"

"They like my imitation of Yasir Arafat." I took out a cigarette, delaying the moment a bit, hating to destroy his high spirits.

He laughed and lit a cigarette of his own; monkey see, monkey do.

"I picked up the evidence," I said. "Everything ready for me, no problems."

"Good. Just wish there was something there that meant something, do us some good."

"Seed mostly, but that's no surprise. All kinds of seed."

I took a drag on the cigarette. "Milo—a lot of milo—bermuda, fleabane, a few sunflower seed, some cockleburs, and bits and pieces of oak bark, particles from horsetails." I leaned forward and dusted ash into the wastebasket at the end of his desk. "Give you any ideas?"

He leaned back in his chair, one hand dragging through his hair, pursed lips funneling smoke toward the overhead light. He slowly shook his head. "Hell, them things grow all over this county, wouldn't know where to begin looking."

"Lots of milo fields?"

He frowned in concentration. "Not a whole lot, no. Ain't all that much land for crop farming around here. Best land is sandy bottomland and they grow peanuts on it. Easier to grow, better cash crop. Milo fields. I guess I could take you to three or four around here if I had to. That many, besides the one out behind my place."

I stubbed out my cigarette, crossed my legs, and gently scratched one of my ant bites. "You won't have to, Ward."

"Won't have to what?" He slowly came forward in the swivel chair.

"Take me anywhere. I found the place where they were killed."

"Are you sure—" He broke off and waved a heavy hand. "Of course you're sure or you wouldn't say it. My God, where?" He stared at me, eyes wide, fixed.

"There's a tank there," I said. "Oak trees at the upper end, an old picnic table, a charcoal grill, and the milo field comes right up to—"

"Jesus," he said softly, hollowly, color washing out of his face. "Cody's field."

"Cody's!" It was my turn to stare. "Not yours?"

His hand moved again, a gesture of impatience. "Mine, yes, but Cody plants it. I've got no use for farming—Jesus Christ, Dan, are you certain?"

"I wasn't there to see it happen, but that's the only way I could be more certain."

"My God, that's right out there behind my house!"

"On a Saturday night," I said. "Would it matter? From what I've heard, you're gone on Saturday night."

He nodded slowly, some of the color returning to his face. "Nearly all. I play poker a lot, take Carol Anne down to Austin, get drunk once in a while with Nate or somebody. I can't do that around here. People expect more out of their public officials." He made a wry, derisive expression and rubbed his jaw. "I was gone the night it happened, all right. I was—"

"I know where you were," I said, smiling a little at his quick sharp look. "So the fact that it happened out behind your house didn't mean anything if you weren't there to hear or see any of it."

"That's one way to put it," he said morosely. "If I had of been home where I belonged—"

"Dead-end thinking, Ward. It doesn't lead anywhere. Did you have any idea that the kids were using your lake back there as a trysting spot?"

"Hell, no! If I had—" He broke off and brought back the wry look. "Hell, if I had, I wouldn't have done a damn thing about it." His broad face took on a thoughtful look. "Except maybe to tell them to be careful Cody didn't see them."

"You really think Cody would have cared enough to do anything . . . rash."

He crushed his cigarette butt, thinking it over. "I honestly don't know. I know a lot of what he says about the Caulders is just blow. Like a lot of little guys, old Cody's a little cocky, too cocky for his own good sometimes. Basically, he's a pretty good guy, but he does carry a grudge a little too far at times. He blames the Caulders for everything bad that's ever happened to him and that's nonsense, of course, but maybe he does hate old Abel as much as he says he does. Whether he'd let it carry over to Abel's daughter—hell, I just don't know." He looked at me, frowning. "What're you leading up to?"

"Nothing. It's just that Abel doesn't have all that many hard feelings toward your brother. That's what he seemed to be saying to me."

"Don't believe everything you hear." He pushed back from the desk. "You want to take me out there and show me—?"

I shook my head. "You won't have any trouble finding it. Just park back away from the little clearing under the oak tree. You'll find a piece of skull stuck to the leg of the picnic table, another piece where I have a stick stuck in the ground. About three paces from the stick, out in the edge of the milo field, you'll see the scuffed-up area, see where they dragged the bodies back into the clearing. That's probably where they loaded the bodies in Steve's car."

He looked disgruntled. "Why don't you want to come?"

"I've been there, Ward. Besides, I have a date with my wife. Take one of your men. Do any of them have crime-scene training? I'm sure there's a lot more evidence if you look for it."

"I've had a little training my last year in the FBI, and Ace Macon's had some down in Austin, but I'd feel better if you were there."

"I wouldn't. I'd feel like hell, and I've had my downer for today. I found out what I needed to know. Anything else you can find will be frosting on the cake."

He walked around the desk, straightening his tan khaki uniform, poking his shirttail back into his pants. "Okay, say we know now where they were killed. I don't see where that helps much, where it leads."

"It's a big step from where we were. I don't know where it will lead. I'll have to give it some thought, let it stew a little. I'm no Sherlock Holmes. I have to sort of feel my way along, from point to point. I can't take a snort of coke and play a fiddle and romp across the rooftops and come up with X equals Y squared. I don't know. Maybe I'll come up with X equals O. You never know what's at the fair until you get there, and at least this is a new and better direction."

He smiled and opened the drawer in a filing cabinet. He took out a thick, square briefcase, "Our technical kit," he said dryly. "I only used it once before to take some finger-prints at a robbery. Didn't turn out worth a shit." He slid the

127

case onto his desk and worked the clasps, then turned with an annoyed look as the office door burst open.

Theron Alldyce stood in the opening, one pudgy hand still on the doorknob. He smiled at me and bobbed his head.

"Good day, Mr. Roman. Please don't get up. I saw you come in and I just wanted to say hello and ask if there was anything new to report." Before I could answer he looked at Ward standing by his desk. "Chief Bannion, would you please tell Mr. Roman that I am indeed the mayor of our fair city. I don't think he quite believed me when I told him that."

Ward glanced at me and shrugged. "Yeah, he's our mayor all right. Been the mayor ever since I been back. I don't know what the town would do without Mayor Alldyce. He's our biggest booster, our best civic organizer, always got something cooking to promote the town, right, Mr. Mayor?"

Mayor Alldyce wiggled his fingers at me. "I'll just be running along now. I do hope I get to meet your lovely wife while she's here, Mr. Roman. We watch her all the time. Please give her our best."

"I will," I said, but I was talking to a closing door. We watched silently through the glass as he bounced off down the corridor, head bowed, shoulders rounded under the mighty load of civic responsibility.

I stood up. "I really didn't not believe him," I said. "He just seems so . . . so innocent for public office."

"He's a joke," Ward said. "And a pain in the ass most of the time. But nobody else wants the blamed job, and you'll have to give him credit for trying."

I opened the door.

"Sure you won't change your mind and come with me? I ain't too hot about taking Ace Macon out there. He sees a snake or a horned toad or something, he's likely to shoot up the whole countryside."

"Your cross, buddy. I've got to pick up some groceries and get out to the motor home in time to burn a couple of steaks before dark. I intend to spend a quiet peaceful evening with my wife, a little intelligent talk about the state of the economy, world peace, and what we can do to further women's lib.''

He gave me a slant-eyed look and a lopsided grin. ''Get out of here. I'm drowning in bullshit.''

''See you tomorrow,'' I said, and left.

23

We ate sitting side by side in the tiny vinyl booth between the coffin shower and the cooking area. Occasionally our shoulders touched as one or the other leaned too far to the left or right. Once in a while our shoulders met on purpose, for emphasis, just for fun. The meal, as promised, was simple all-American fare, seared rib eye and baked potato and salad, natural grain rolls as a concession to good nutrition. No green onions although I had bought a couple of bunches. A good sign.

We talked about the state of the economy, world affairs, and how best to further the cause of women in a man's world. Susie had some interesting views. I kept most of mine to myself.

We were silent more than we talked, though, engrossed in the meal. Halfway through, I had an inspirational flash and congratulated her on an excellent dinner although her only contribution had been the salad. She blushed prettily and said thank you, dark eyes promising more substantial rewards later. You can't reach forty without learning something.

It was cozy in the little motor home, a sense of intimate immediacy, but maybe that was due in part to the proximity of the bed, the falling darkness. The garage was closed and silent, the cows gathered under a nearby stand of trees. Bob-whites whistled, and whippoorwills called, and somewhere nearby an uneasy dog defied the rising moon. I let out a notch in my belt and had a smoke while Susie cleaned up the mess. She wouldn't have it any other way. Woman's work, she said, but with that little lopsided smile that said it wasn't really so. I kept my own counsel.

I watched her flitting around, supple and lithe, humming, moving to her own graceful beat. I thought of potentates and sheiks, slave girls and concubines, erotic visions that paled and faded before my memories of early afternoon. I needed no fantasies with Susie, no aphrodisiac to stir my blood. That was her magic—silent, silken bonds I no longer wanted to break. Once, awash with emotions somewhere between ancient love and honest lust, I stood up and caught her to me, held her tightly and kissed her, the dark eyes firing with immediate response, soft lips curving in a gentle knowing smile.

"You forgot my magazines," she said later, back, seated next to me again. "And that reminds me." She slipped out of the booth once again, went into the living area—a matter of a couple of feet—and picked up the black Bible from the second shelf of an end table.

She sat down, an odd look on her face. "And you're probably going to yell at me, accuse me of prying, but just remember it was your idea for me to read the Bible."

"Never happen," I said. "I never yell. I'm in perfect control at all times."

"Uh-huh." She fanned the pages, stopped, looked, went on.

"No doubt you want an interpretation of some of the more arcane passages," I said. "Well, I did promise, didn't I?"

She nodded without chuckling, without smiling, not even a smothered giggle. She made an exasperated sound and fanned the flimsy pages again, then stopped, backed up, and extracted a yellowed newspaper clipping from between the leaves. She laid it carefully in front of me. "It's old, so be gentle with it."

"Who do you think I am, King Kong?" I used a forefinger

to turn the clipping around, found myself looking at the smiling faces of five young men, or probably boys, judging by the basketball uniforms, light-colored jerseys and dark shorts, the basketball held poised by the taller one in the center. "Aha, allow me to guess. A soccer team? Football? Quoits? Named the Rebels, no less. Possibly from New York?"

"Be serious, Danny. Didn't you say our host was named Nathan?"

"Right, Nathan Barr, and I can tell you right now without half-looking that he has to be the one on the far right. None of the others look like him. He's got the same pale eyes, and a kinda round face—yeah, that could be him."

"I think you're wrong, Danny."

I looked at her. She was deadly serious, a perplexed look on her face.

"What makes you say that?"

"Turn it over—be careful, here let me do it." She gripped the edges between her fingernails and flipped it over on the table. An advertisement for Smith Brothers cough drops took up much of the space, but there was a narrow blank space across the top and someone, a woman, I suspected, had written "Nathan's Father." Written in ink, it had faded to a faint outline, but was still perfectly legible. There was also a date, October 10, 1955.

"Hmmmm," I said, watching her turn the cutting over again. "He kinda looks like I'd think he looked about twelve years ago or so."

She nodded vigorously. "I remembered you said he was around thirty. If that's the case, then that couldn't be him in the picture."

I shrugged. "So it's his old man. Some boys resemble their father." I looked at her. "So, what's all the fuss about?" I leaned closer to read the single line of print below the picture: THE REBELS' STARTING FIVE IN FRIDAY NIGHT'S GAME AGAINST . . . It ended there, the rest obviously lost to the scissors in an effort to make it fit between the pages of the Bible. I turned to Susie. Her face was decidedly pinker than it had been moments before. She went back to flipping through the Bible, head down, absorbed in her efforts.

"There's more," I guessed.

"Danny, I know you're going to think I'm terrible for reading someone else's—but really, it just fell out when I was sorta flipping through—and it's so awful! That poor man!"

"What poor man?" I said automatically, watching her lay two sheets of lined tablet paper before me with the tender solicitude one might reserve for the Dead Sea Scrolls.

"Be real careful, Danny. They're old and fragile and badly faded, but you can still read them okay."

I looked at the salutation: "My Darling son Nathan." I raised my eyes to Susie's rosy face. "You're right. This is terrible. You use a man's motor home, sleep in his bed, and nose around in his personal correspondence."

"Oh, Danny, don't be such a . . . a dork. Look at the date on that letter. It's thirty years old almost, well, twenty-eight, at least. And anyway, his mother is dead, his adopted mother, that is, and he doesn't even know who his real mother was— not really." She paused for a deep breath. "And the really tragic part of it is, he can't even be sure which one of those boys is his real father."

"Susie, what the hell are you talking about?"

She folded her arms and clamped her lips and gave me a taunting, defiant look. "I'm not saying another word. If you want to know, you'll have to read the letter."

"What's a dork?"

Her mouth tightened and she shook her head, slowly and deliberately.

"Tell me what a dork is and maybe I'll read the letter."

"Afterwards," she said, the edges of her mouth creeping upward. "After you read it."

"Okay," I said. "But I take no blame for this. I'm being blackmailed and blackmail is a crime in this state. Punishable by . . . well, I'll think of something."

"I'll bet you will," she said sweetly, and tapped the faded papers with a slender forefinger. "Read."

I read.

24

My Darling son Nathan:

I hope you will never see this letter. I hope that you will go through your lifetime believing that Sally and Moser are your real parents. They are fine decent people and I'm certain you will have a good life. If I did not believe that with all my heart I would not allow them to take you as their own.

It breaks my heart that I can no longer care for you. I am growing weaker day by day. I can no longer trust myself alone to take care of your needs. That is why the Barrs have taken us in. Without them we would both be wards of the county or the state. I have an incurable disease of the blood and there is nothing more that can be done.

The fact that you are reading this means that the Barrs are prematurely dead, before your twenty-first birthday. After that they were to destroy this letter and the picture of your father, leave you to live out your life believing they were your parents. They are good honest people. I'm sure they will respect my wishes in this as irrational as they may seem.

I wish I could tell you that one of the boys in the photograph was my sweetheart, that we had been madly in love and could not wait and conceived you out of love.

Sadly that is not the case. As you may have already guessed, you were conceived out of wedlock, but your conception was the result of rape, not an act of love. One of them raped me and I have no idea which one.

I have paused here for two whole days to consider my motives in writing this letter. By the time I finish it will have been a week since I started.

I suppose, in the beginning, I had visions of you finding your father someday, confronting him with the proof of his deed, and ruining his life as he has surely ruined mine. But as I look at you in your little bed, I can see no resemblance to any one of the five boys and I realize what an impossible task it would be for you, what it would do to you.

I know that I must soon die, but I know also that this will be left, as everything is, in the hands of God.

I cannot tell you how much I love you. I cannot tell you how much I hate to die.

Your loving mother
Carlotta Valdez

I leaned back and dug in my shirt pocket for cigarettes. "Something must have misfired."

Susie paused in the act of replacing the letter in the Bible. "What do you mean, misfired?"

"According to the letter, he was supposed to get it only if both the Barrs died prematurely, namely before he was twenty-one. His father is having a heart attack right now. That's why he went back to Missouri."

"Maybe he found the Bible after his stepmother died."

"That could be, I suppose. Well, at any rate, are you through nosing around in his private papers?"

"Doesn't that letter make you sad?" She got up and put the Bible on its shelf. When she came back her eyes were moist. "And to top it off he's got diabetes."

"How do you know?"

135

"There's two bottles of insulin in the fridge, one about half-full, and there's a big package of needles in one of the cabinet drawers."

"Very good. We'll have him arrested right away. Diabetes is not lawful in this state."

"And in the medicine cabinet in the bathroom there's one of those tapes you use to measure your sugar content."

"I'll bet you'd run off the scale on that one."

"Anyway, smarty, I feel sorry for him, and thinking about his life and his poor mother makes me want to cry. Don't you feel sorry for him?"

"No, not particularly. A thirty year old tragedy. Enough tragedies going on right here and now to cry about."

"Hah! I can see you crying. You wouldn't be caught dead crying. Big tough macho brute." She picked up one of my hands, worked my fingers into a fist, then tried her best to bite one of my knuckles. It hurt like hell. I smiled at her.

She let go, made a contrite face, and kissed her teeth marks. "I'm sorry, Danny." She brought my hand to her face, rubbed it against her cheek, then turned it over and nuzzled my palm. "You have magical hands."

"You're angling for a back rub, right?"

"Noooo," she said, beginning to blush again. "Not exactly . . ." She let it drift away.

"What are you angling for . . . exactly?"

She smiled and tossed her glossy mane of hair, the color creeping lower into her neck. She mauled my hand and didn't answer. It embarrassed her to blush, and that usually made her blush harder.

"My grandpa used to say that if you wanted to pick the dance you had to name the music."

"Your grandpa had something to say about everything, to hear you tell it."

"Yeah. He wasn't chary with his words or with his advice. He would've sure loved you. He had an eye for fine horseflesh and luscious women. Said the only way you could tell them apart sometimes is by the way they held their tail."

She laughed despite a visible effort not to. I lit a cigarette and suddenly all my bites were itching, as if they had been lurking just below the level of my awareness.

I stood up and pulled up my right pants leg. Four of the bites were on my right leg, three of them confined to a space no larger than a silver dollar.

Susie took one look at the small red bumps. "Chigger bites. Oh, lord, don't tell me we've got chiggers in the grass around here. They eat on me like ice cream."

"Not chiggers. Fire ants. Look in the medicine cabinet. I think I saw some bottles of antiseptic creams in there."

She went into the bathroom. Moments later I heard an exclamation: "Aha!" She came back unscrewing the cap from a small white tube of ointment.

"Caldocel," she said. "This is what you need. Remember last year when I worked the South Texas flood? The water ran the ants out of their nests. They were on everything you touched. A druggist gave us some of this. Worked like magic. Two minutes, and the pain and burning were gone. It seemed to help heal the bites too."

I watched while she smeared the greasy ointment on the bites. The itching and stinging diminished immediately. "That's great, Suse, thanks."

"Men are such babies," she mused. "Lower pain thresholds than women."

"That right?" I felt a prickle of inexplicable irritation. "I suppose that's nature's way of compensating women for the pain of childbirth. Not to mention all that pain and drudgery around the house."

She gave me a quick sharp look, half amused, half quizzical, then apparently decided to let it pass. She put the cap on the ointment tube and changed the subject.

"Did you know that snakes have the same poison as bees and wasps?"

"No! I didn't know that!" There must have been more sarcasm in my voice than I intended; a moment later I heard the screen door slam, and when I looked out the door she was sitting in one of the aluminum chairs, arms crossed, looking out across the moonlit slope.

"Hey," I said, "if we're gonna sit out there I'll bring you a jacket. It gets chilly pretty quick after the moon comes up."

"No thanks, I'm fine." Her voice was rigid and controlled, stiffly formal.

I grinned and took down her blue windbreaker from the hook behind the door. I stared at it for a second, then shrugged and put it back. I put on my coat and went outside.

"Nice out here," I said. I lit a cigarette and dropped into the other chair. I hopped the chair around so I could join her in watching the pasture. Out of the corner of my eye, I saw her rubbing her bare arms below the short puffed sleeves of her blouse.

"Peaceful," I said.

A large dark shape swooped out of the line of trees down by the creek, whooshed low over the pasture, and landed in the top of a tree adjacent to the motor home. It made a hooting sound.

"Owl," I said.

Seconds later a coyote moaned somewhere not far away, ended his wail with short yelping barks.

"Coyote," I said.

Behind us, from some back yard in the row of houses across from Nash's Garage, a dog answered the coyote's howl, a dispirited, mechanical bark.

"Dog," I said. I saw her turn her head slightly to the right, away from me, and knew I was getting to her. I smoked contentedly and waited. It wasn't long. Over by the stand of trees where the cattle had gathered for the night a calf bawled plaintively.

"Calf," I said. Her head dipped, hair cascading forward to hide her face. Almost immediately the foliage directly above us rustled, a bird twittered angrily.

"Don't," she said, her voice thick and husky. "If you say bird, I'll . . . I swear I'll . . ." She broke off, shaking, unable to complete her threat, rocking with helpless laughter.

I got up and reached inside the motor home and took down

her jacket. I helped her into it, hugged her a couple of times. It wasn't much of an apology but she accepted it as such.

"You take advantage of me," she said when we were back seated again. "You don't fight fair. You know I can't stay mad when you make me laugh—"

"Gee whiz, I didn't know you were mad."

She shook her head and sighed. We went back to watching the pasture, lit up like some ghostly arena in the amphitheater of trees. The moon was full and bright, and I've heard it said that a new moon brings out the wanting in those of us still young enough, or young at heart enough, to care—or maybe I heard it in a song.

Whatever the source, it appeared to be true. Before long we were looking at each other more than the moonlit pasture. Electric, meaningful glances that probably would have looked damn silly to anyone watching. But then again maybe not, people being pretty much the same about some things.

At any rate, we were soon on our feet, climbing the steps into the motor home. I might even have carried her if the entrance had been a little wider.

Later, a short time later, looking into dark depthless eyes, I asked her: "Are you sure? I don't want to take advantage of—" She closed my mouth with warm lips, a not unexpected response under the circumstances, a totally acceptable way to be shushed.

Somewhere on the hill our coyote moaned again, a choppy, mournful lament. From out of its nearby tree the owl hooted a reply, then swept away in a crashing flurry of wings. Our friend the dog had another go at it, irate and hoarse, giving it a little more heart.

I felt her belly tremble with laughter way down deep, and heard a muffled joyous sound. I made my kind of noises and did some trembling of my own, but for entirely different reasons.

25

DONNA GILCREST WORKED FOR DESMOND'S REALTY. Located on the south side of the square in an old red brick
building with a flat roof and a high false front, the realty
office itself was bright and cheery with pastel-pink walls,
drapes, indirect lighting, and fiercely contemporary furnish-
ings. Without knowing why, I immediately got the idea that
Desmond's Realty was a relatively new enterprise. It may
have been the obviously new furniture, the refurbishment of
the interior, or possibly the attitude and reaction of the three
female occupants who snapped to rigid attention as I sauntered through the door.

The one nearest the door appeared to be the youngest. She
had been hunkered over her desk reading a magazine when
I glanced through the glass before entering. Her two com-
panions across the room were chatting over large mugs of
something I took to be coffee.

But when I turned back from closing the door the magazine was gone, the mugs out of sight, all three women intent
and absorbed, paperwork spread across their desks, pens in
poised hands, momentous decisions only moments away, the
deal of the century awaiting only the slash of a pen.

The young one looked up, the frown of concentration disappearing as if by magic, replaced by a lavish smile. She was pretty in a cheerful, non-intimidating way, white teeth, squared off in front, a little crooked at the sides, not objectionably so. She wore a pale green sweater, sleeves pushed to the center of her forearms, à la Norma Dew. Short brown hair, shorter than most boys', capped her small round head. She had green eyes, friendly eyes, warm, undoubtedly her best feature.

"Good morning, sir. May we help you?" She stood up, revealing a tweed skirt ending exactly at the knee. No tracks on the back of her legs, I thought.

"Good morning. Donna Gilcrest?"

"Yes," she said, a little lilt in her voice, as if pleased that I knew her name. "What can I do for you, Mr.—" She ended on a high suggestive note. Always get their name.

"Dan Roman," I said, and watched her face fall. I had to give her credit, it was only a momentary lapse, and she covered nicely by half-turning toward the two women, still poised over their desks like nervous deer at a scary waterhole.

"Terri Lee, I think I'll take my break now, is that all right?"

"Of course, dear," one of the ladies said, and gave me a friendly nod when I looked at her and smiled. "You go right ahead."

Donna gathered up her purse and took a smartly tailored tweed jacket from the back of her chair. I held the jacket for her and then the door. We went outside.

"Would you like some coffee or something? I noticed a cafe—"

"No, thank you," she said. "I usually walk in the park on nice days."

"That's fine," I said heartily. "I can sure use the exercise."

She didn't reply. We crossed the street, turned into the park, and walked along a well-worn dirt and gravel path around the perimeter. I waited until we passed a knot of old men grouped around two other old men playing checkers. I lit a cigarette.

"I take it you know who I am," I said.

"Yes, Mr. Roman, in certain circles you are becoming famous."

"Or infamous, maybe."

She nodded. "I haven't seen you around before and I was surprised. I expected you to look like . . . oh, I don't know, some heavy in an old movie, I guess. Someone like that ugly little man who played in all the old gangster movies, the one with the raspy voice."

"Edward G. Robinson, I expect you mean. He had a heart of gold, I hear. Loved flowers."

"Does that make you a good guy, loving something?"

"I don't know. I never thought about it much. Nixon loved dogs."

"And Hitler loved music," she said, stepping aside to allow an old woman with a cane right of way. "Good morning, Mrs. Randell." The old lady looked at her with faded, rheumy eyes and finally nodded. "Good morning, dear."

"I guess we all have our good parts and our bad parts," I said, after a time, just to get the conversation going again. "Even the worst of us."

"Even the ones who killed Lisa and Steve?" She cut the green eyes around at me. I had the feeling that in the right light and under the right circumstances they could be devastating.

"Even them," I said. "Or him, or her. It isn't clear yet how many there were."

"Do you know why yet?"

I looked at her, but she was watching a young boy throw a Frisbee for his dog to catch and retrieve. "I have some ideas. I don't know for certain whether they're valid."

She brought her gaze back to the path, walked in silence for a moment. Then she said: "But you think it has something to do with drugs."

"Why would you think that?"

She looked up and smiled wryly. "Word gets around, Mr.

Roman." She stopped abruptly and swung to face me. She pushed the sleeve on her right arm as high as it would go, two inches or so above her elbow. She waited silently while I looked, then repeated the process on the other arm. "I'm sure you've already looked at my legs."

"There are other places."

She shook her head, began walking again. "I never went beyond the pills, the uppers and downers, a few lines of coke. Even the coke scared me. I faked it as often as not. Okay, maybe I was a druggie, but I had my limits. No needles and no crack. The only thing I ever smoked was a little pot."

"Was?"

"Was," she said firmly. "I've been dry for two months."

"Good for you."

She shrugged. "I like to think I never was an addict, not in the sense that Bobby Radcross and Steve and Lisa were. I think mine was more psychological than physical. Maybe I can lick that." She cut her eyes around at me again. "I think Patti and Norma will tell you the same thing."

"You don't have to convince me, Donna. I'm not a cop."

"I know," she said, an unhappy expression on her face. "But I know how you badgered Norma and embarrassed her where she works and I didn't want you to do the same thing to me. That's why I wanted to get out of there."

"Did Norma tell you that?"

"Yes." She took a deep breath. "I know she probably exaggerated some, she usually does, but I didn't want to lose my job. I'm studying for my license—"

"Maybe I did embarrass her," I said. "But not in front of anyone. She was scared when I asked her to show me her arms, and she ran away."

"She would," she said, and brought back the thin little smile. "I saw Bobby Radcross and he told me to watch out for you, that you were out to get us in trouble."

"Do you believe him?"

She looked unhappy again. "I did. But maybe I'm not so sure now. You aren't, are you?"

143

"Not on purpose. Not unless you had something to do with Lisa and Steve's murder."

She stared up at me, eyes wide, startled. "Good heavens, no!"

"Was Steve dealing?"

"I'm not sure what you mean."

"Come on, Donna. Did Steve sell the rest of you drugs?"

"Well, we had to pay for our share, if that's what you mean. Not all the time, though. Sometimes he just gave them to us, him and Bobby."

"You mentioned crack a while ago. That's a fairly new sophisticated drug, or maybe I should say a new way to use coke. Did Steve bring that around, too?"

"He brought some home from Austin once or twice. I saw Bobby freak out after smoking some of that stuff. I think it scared Stevie. He never brought any more after that." We had made a complete turn around the square and were back at the corner near the realty office. She stopped and looked at me. "Can I go back to work now?"

"One more question, Donna, and this is important. Did Steve ever burn anyone that you know about, or even heard about?"

"Burn anyone?"

"Sell them bad drugs, weaker drugs than normal, short change them on weight."

"I don't think so. I don't know why he'd do that, he always seemed to have plenty."

"Who did he get them from?"

"I don't know. He wouldn't talk about that. I heard him tell Bobby some kind of name once, but I don't remember what it was. It wasn't anyone I'd ever heard of."

"Big Bwana?"

She pursed her lips, then rearranged them into a smile. "It could have been. I was high at the time."

"Are you still going around with them?"

The smile tilted, became ironic. "Them? You mean the druggies, Mr. Roman? Yes, sometimes. I don't have many other friends. Kids have their own caste system and druggies

144

are way down on the list, even below the nerds and the wimps and the dorks. Getting high has its price and I don't think you ever stop paying one way or another.''

I took out a cigarette and held it in my hand and waited until she looked up at me. ''We've talked all this time and I haven't asked you. Do you have any idea who killed Lisa and Steve?''

Her small head swung from side to side, the lovely green eyes holding mine. ''No, Mr. Roman, I don't. I wish I did. I'm almost sure I'd tell you.''

''That's fair enough,'' I said. ''Thank you for your time, Ms. Gilcrest.''

She gave me a stingy little smile without showing her teeth, bobbed her head, and crossed the street to her office.

I lit the cigarette I had been holding and walked down the square to where I'd left the Ramcharger. I fired up the engine and wondered where in the unholy name of hell I was going from there.

26

I DIDN'T GO FAR. ONCE AROUND THE SQUARE, AND AN IN-
voluntary stab at the brake as I spotted a sign reading: SUT-
TLER'S HARDWARE. Memory cells tripped, or clicked,
or meshed, or whatever it is they do, and I pulled into the
curb in front of a barber shop with an old-timey twirling
barber pole and a gossip bench along its front wall. I got out
and walked back to the hardware store, a dingy, decrepit
building with a front window display of chain saws and barbecue equipment, walkie-talkies, and a miniature wooden
drilling rig. A handmade poster advertising an upcoming
basketball game between the Jerico Falls Bandits and the
Boonville High School Wildcats was affixed to the inside of
the window with Scotch Tape.

Inside, the store was long and narrow, dimly lighted, a
jumbled collection of old and new side by side, ofteñ over-
lapping and intermingling, as if the proprietor had long ago
given up trying to cope with the vicissitudes of life and the
sloppy habits of paying customers.

At first glance, the room appeared to be empty, penum-
bral, and somber, the unmistakable odor of cat dung rising
above the more palatable smells of oil and leather, the musty

aroma of mildewed clothing, other odors not so readily identifiable, but fully as unpleasant.

I took a couple of steps and tripped over the likely reason for the cat smell, an enormous tiger tom with ragged ears and an almost hairless tail, mute evidence of countless nights on the town.

I caught the edge of a display table and regained my balance. The cat bowed his back and hissed in an almost absent fashion, then sat down in the middle of the aisle again and washed a paw that had at least two toes missing.

"Get out of here, you imp of satan!" The voice came from my left, harsh and strident, yet somehow piping, like a boy imitating a man's command. The cat continued to wash its paw. I turned to my left.

A round hairless head projected above a glass display case, and two berry-bright eyes peered at me around an antique cash register.

"You mean me or the cat," I said, and gave him a friendly smile just in case.

He cackled, one sharp high note I took to be a reassuring laugh. "That damn fool cat. Can't keep him out anymore. He sneaks in with the customers, and I ain't up to chasing him around no more."

I walked toward him, smiling, thinking he must be crippled since he hadn't arisen. Probably arthritis; he looked old enough.

"You want me to throw him out? I worked one summer with a circus wild-animal act. He don't look much bigger'n some of the lions I wrestled."

He cackled again, two notes, same pitch. "That sumbich'll tear your hide off. I seen him whip three bull terriers one day and make eyes at a female cat whilst he was doing it. My old lady's cat. Wished I'd a put him in the coffin with her."

I drew up at the display case, looked down at his shiny pate, blue-veined and slick as plastic wrap above a face as seamed as crinkled shoe leather. He moved back from the counter's edge and I saw why he hadn't stood up: he was already standing.

Not a gnome or a dwarf. A perfectly formed little man about three feet-six, small neat features that had probably been as cute as a Ken doll before the flood of time and erosion. Toothless, a convoluted mouth that tended to slur his words, he still stood as straight as a cottonwood sapling and I would have bet my most valuable postage stamp that he answered to Shorty.

"What can I do you for, mister?"

I took the plastic packet out of my pocket and laid it on the case. "Could you tell me what kind of nail this is?"

He picked it up, turned it over once in his child's fingers, and dropped it back to the counter. "Sure. Horseshoe nail. Got a dozen boxes of them over there on the shelves. This'n of yours ain't no good no more, it's been bent."

"That it has," I said, burrowing into my mind, going back to the blacksmith shop on the ranch where I was born and raised. I could remember watching the cowboys shoe their horses, see them with the nails sticking out of their mouths, the worn rusty horseshoes and nails littering the ground under the shoeing tree. "Are all horseshoe nails the same?"

"Nope. They's different nails for different places. Them boxes over there has got instructions and pictures showing you how to do it. Ain't nothing to it."

I realized abruptly that he thought I was contemplating shoeing a horse. "I, uh, well, maybe I'd better leave it to someone who knows what they're doing."

He scowled and sucked his lips inside his mouth. "Any fool can do it. Man rides, he oughta know how to take care of his mount."

I wanted to ask him what he rode, a St. Bernard dog, but I didn't. He had a right to be a little irascible, being that old and that little couldn't be any fun and here this young whippersnapper was taking up his time and didn't mean to buy anything.

"I, uh, could use some bolts. About half a dozen, I guess."

He gave me a suspicious look. "What kind? Carriage, stove, what?"

"Oh, carriage . . . yeah, carriage."

"What size?"

"About . . . oh, six inches long should do it."

"What size?" he said again, rolling his lips outward in a sneery little smile.

"I just told you . . ." I held my hands about six inches apart.

He sighed. "I got one-quarter, five-sixteenths, three-eighths, five-eighths . . ."

"Oh, you mean the diameter," I said.

"Yeah," he said. "The size. What'll it be?"

"Three-eighths."

"Nuts?"

"Nuts? Oh, yeah, I'll need some nuts . . . and some washers too, if you don't mind."

"I don't mind," he said, and tripped lightly into the area of overloaded tables, disappearing immediately. I lit a cigarette and listened. I thought I could hear him chuckling, but it could have been the cat.

But maybe it was a chuckle I heard after all. He came back with my hardware in a small bag and said blithely: "That'll be twelve dollars."

"Twelve dollars!" The indignation in my voice came not from parsimony, but from shock.

"Things is high," he said piously. "We won't worry about the tax."

"We won't worry about the bolts, either," I said, grinning into the wizened face. I laid a five dollar bill on the counter and picked up my nail. "That's for your time and the information, you old bandit, and the next time you decide to hold someone up you better have a gun handy. He might decide to kick a little ass. No pun intended."

"Oh, yes it was. I always get the little man jokes. You wouldn't say that if we was the same size." He made the five disappear. "I've had to take shit like this all my life."

"Life is often a bitter weed indeed."

He glowered. "Is that some kinda smartass quotation?"

"A simple observation." I turned to go, giving him my friendliest smile. I had enough enemies.

He bounded around the counter, trotted behind me. "I know who you are. I knowed it the minute you come in here kicking my cat. You was pointed out over there in the park talking to that no-good Bannion boy that calls hisself police chief."

I stopped and turned. "Okay, you know me. So what's your point?"

"So what're you doing nosing around over here in my store? You didn't fool me for a minute. You didn't want no horseshoe nails nor no bolts neither. You been talking to somebody says I had something to do with them kids being killed?"

"Did you?"

"Course I didn't! And Ward Bannion knows it. I'll admit I said I'd get even with that Bannion boy and that nutty Radcross kid, but—"

"Get even for what?"

"None of your business, that's what!" He whirled and marched back to the gap in the counter and went inside, eyeing me balefully across the glass counter. "And don't come back in here. Buy your danged bolts somewheres else."

"Well, all right, but I'll miss the ambiance."

The cat came out of nowhere and darted between my legs as I went out the door. He went loping off down the sidewalk in that high-stepping way that felines have, ratty-looking tail at half-mast, looking for sex, food, or adventure, and probably in that order.

I had a visitor waiting when I got back to my truck. The plump lady from the communications console in the police department. She was leaning against a fender smoking a cigarette. When she saw me coming, she threw it down and squashed it with her foot. She looked younger in the natural light, or maybe it was the colorful full skirt and checkered blouse, a new hairdo, dark brown hair down around her face.

She nodded and smiled. "Mr. Roman. Chief Bannion would like to see you if you have a few minutes."

"You bet. I was coming to see him as a matter of fact." I fell in step beside her, as she went up the walk to a set of Spanish double doors I hadn't used. "How did you know I was out here?"

"I saw you through the window a while ago. You went into the realty office and came out with Donna Gilcrest. Then just a few minutes ago I was over at the copying machine by the west window and I saw you park and go into Suttler's." She tilted her head to look at me. "What did you think of Shorty Suttler? Or had you met him before?"

"No, that was the first time, and the last, I hope."

She laughed and beat me to the door handle. "He used to be such a nice little man, back when I was a kid. But then he got old and cranky and his wife died . . ." She let it trail away, lifting a hand to motion to Ward through the glass, then heading for her unmanned console.

"Thank you," I said, but I was sure she didn't hear me.

27

THERE ARE TIMES IN MY LIFE WHEN I MEET A MAN AND know instinctively that I'm not going to like him. It's a gut feeling that I believe results from bits and pieces of random information received and processed instantly by my subconscious, then introduced to my awareness as negative feedback that brings about a tightening of my entire defensive network. Something like strange dogs sniffing, hackles alert.

The man sitting across the desk from Ward had that effect on me. At first glance I wasn't sure why. His expression was amiable enough, a lean pale face with a pencil mustache, a narrow head capped with reddish-blond blow-dried hair. He dressed well, better than me, a two piece tan worsted suit, off-white shirt and a string tie. Narrow, pointed, impossibly shiny boots. He had long fingers studded with rings, his left wrist encircled with a John Wayne copper bracelet, his right wrapped with gold chains. The only incongruous note was the gun rig under his left arm, the handle pointing downward in the latest *Miami Vice* fashion.

"Dan'l," Ward boomed, his voice too hearty, filled with too much good cheer. "I'd like to introduce Deputy Gil Grossman. He's the investigator out of the Sheriff's office who helped us with the preliminary investigation last week. Gil, this is the guy I been telling you about, Dan Roman.''

"Deputy Grossman," I said, wondering what he had done. I had seen no report with his name on it. I took his hand and fought back an urge to ruin a few fingers in the big-stoned rings. Instead, I tugged on it once and let it go, still wondering about my apparently groundless animosity.

"Call me Gil," he said. "I've been hearing a lot about you, Dan. Good work you did there finding the murder spot. Too bad we couldn't have had that seed evidence to go on sooner." He glanced briefly at Ward. "Chief Bannion here needs to tighten up his operation. That old fool Doolittle should have been put out to pasture years ago. We might have had this thing wrapped up already.''

"Can't cut a man out of his pension," Ward said, a tide of pink rising in his face.

"Well," Grossman said graciously, "I don't suppose it matters now that we'll be taking over the case.''

I looked at Ward.

He lifted one big shoulder. "That land out there at my place. It's in the county. I guess that makes it the Sheriff's case.''

"My case," Grossman said smoothly. "That makes a big difference to me. I'm in charge of something, I get it done. I'll have somebody's ass in jail by the end of the week." He turned to me. "I'd like a full report from you, Dan. Everybody you've talked to, what was said, how you happened to stumble on the murder spot . . . well you know the routine. I hear you used to be a city cop years ago. How about, oh, three this afternoon. That give you plenty of time?''

"No," I said.

His eyebrows shot upward. He frowned. "Okay, then. How about tomorrow early? This thing has laid around too long the way it is. Trail's colder'n a polar bear's tit. I think that ought to be enough time, right?''

"No," I said. "No report.''

He stared at me, pale face no longer pale. "I see," he said

softly. "All right." He turned to Ward. "I'll expect his report the minute you get it. Is that understood?"

Ward opened his mouth but I beat him to it.

"He doesn't get one, either," I said, and began to understand. It was arrogance I had sensed, barely suppressed. And ruthlessness. Maybe I had somehow acquired a kind of asshole detector, I thought happily.

"Why the hell not? You're working for him!"

"No, I'm not. I've been working with him. There's a difference. I'm working for the man who's paying me. Now, *he* gets a report."

"Who?"

"Sorry," I said, and grinned into the growing wildness in his eyes. "Client confidentiality."

"Bullshit! I'll haul your ass in for obstruction of—"

"Not in my town, you won't," Ward said quietly. "Not unless you've got a warrant there in your jeans."

"I can damn sure get one!"

I shrugged. "I doubt even that. Not unless you can find a stupid judge or J.P. who isn't too particular about his facts. I have no official capacity here. I'm a private investigator pursuing his client's legitimate interests. That happened to coincide with Ward's legitimate interests, finding a killer, so naturally we worked together." I took a deep breath and looked into his eyes. "I couldn't work with you. I don't think I'd want to if I could."

"Why not?" His voice was harsh and dry, and it was obvious the words cost him a lot.

"My personal reasons are my own," I said. "So let's just say it's because I never said you could call me Dan."

"Shit!" He jumped to his feet. He was taller than I thought, almost eye to eye with my six feet. He ignored me and snapped at Ward. "I'll expect the evidence—that means *all* the evidence—out at the substation by five o'clock. Is that agreeable?"

Ward nodded, then added with a touch of amusement: "I'll see what I can do, Gil."

He looked at me. "You're off this case. As of now. I catch you nosing around and you go to jail. Understand?"

"Real take-charge guy," I said to Ward. "Reckon you oughta tell him he's horsing around with free enterprise here."

Ward shrugged and looked down at his desk, resigning his position as referee.

Grossman shot his cuffs, hiding the gold chains and copper bracelet, rings flashing as he buttoned his coat. Not real silk, I decided, getting a good look at the suit. Seventy percent tops. He picked up his hat from the floor beside his chair and fixed it firmly on his head, a flat-topped, narrow-brimmed Stetson, standard pearl gray.

"I'll see you later, Chief," he said, and went out the door. He closed it quietly.

I lit a cigarette. Ward sighed and lit one of his own. We smoked in silence for a while, listening to an occasional murmur of traffic on the square, the low-pitched unintelligible chatter from the console, the rhythm of the plump lady's voice as she talked into her unit.

Ward leaned back in his chair and laced his hands behind his head. "What made you go and do that?" Smoke trailed up across his nose and into his left eye; he closed it.

"He's a prick."

"I know that but how did you figure it out so fast?"

"Natural talent. My granddaddy said there'd be fools galore and clowns on every corner, but he said watch out for the pricks, they'd hurt you and laugh."

"Your granddaddy was right." He crashed forward in his chair, stubbed out his cigarette. "Gil's mean, all right. And he's sneaky. Watch out for him."

"He head of the Sheriff's homicide team?"

Ward laughed. "The Sheriff don't have a homicide team. People don't get murdered in Saragache County. They get robbed, burgled, killed on the highways, and some overdose on drugs. Once in a while somebody will take an axe or a shotgun to their spouse, but they generally call in themselves,

155

want to tell why they did it. Real homicides like Lisa and Steve? First in years.''

"Sounds like a good place to live.''

"If you're over sixty and a good Baptist.'' He drummed his fingers on the desk. "Too bad it had such a sorry ending, Dan.''

"What ending?'' I said. "Nothing's changed that I can see.''

"You're going to defy him?''

"You make it sound like a sacrilege. He didn't hire me, he damned sure can't fire me.''

"But he can make it tough on you. The Sheriff is the highest authority in the county. They can get us cut off from both county and state help with a snap of their finger.''

"What help? From where I sit the only work done on this case before I got here was done by you and Lonnie Caulder. And that was little enough. You talked to some people, but—'' I stopped and crushed out my cigarette, looking him in the eyes. "But what I don't understand, Ward, is why neither of you talked to the kids they hung around with, Patti Dunright, Norma Dew, Radcross, and the others. Was it because you didn't want to hear about the drugs and you knew you would?''

Color moved out of his face, as slowly as a receding tide. A muscle jerked in the dark patch beneath his left eye. His mouth tightened, a thin white line etched in bold relief around his lips. But when he spoke his voice was mild, almost detached: "We talked about this before, Dan. I told you we never had a drug problem around here.''

I stood up. "Yeah, you did. I guess I forgot. You don't have murders around here, either.'' I took the plastic packet out of my pocket and tossed it on his desk. "That goes in with the seed. They took it out of the chunk of boot heel mud you found at the Rodeo Grounds.''

"What is it?'' He was obviously pleased to be away from the subject of drugs.

"A nail. A horseshoe nail.''

"Well, I'll be damned.''

156

"Yeah," I said. I moved to the door.

"Hey, where you going from here? What do you reckon'll be your next step?"

"My next step will be out this door. Then I'm going home to take my wife out to eat. From there I'll have to play it by ear."

"I gotta get over there and meet her before she leaves."

"You better get on with it then. She has to catch the eight o'clock shuttle tonight."

He winced, then brightened. "Maybe I can get out there later this afternoon. I got a two o'clock meeting with Big Bwana and the city treasurer—"

"Who?"

"The Mayor and Stu Sanderson, the city—"

"What did you call him, the Mayor?"

He looked blank, then sheepish. "Oh, Big Bwana. That's what Steve used to call him. I sorta picked it up from him, I guess."

"If you can break loose, come on out. If I'm not there introduce yourself to Susie. She's easy to get to know. She might ask you for some ID, though. I've taught her to be careful. And just remember, buddy, she's taken."

He laughed, broad face back to its normal ruddy hue. "You got nothing to fear from an old lunker like me. Young pretty woman scare the pants off me."

"Yeah," I said, and went out the door. We were back on an even keel again, but walking to my truck I felt a faint stirring of uneasiness, a combination of low-grade anxiety and dread I couldn't find a reason for. After a while, I wasn't sure I wanted to try.

28

WE ATE LUNCH AT A RESTAURANT A FEW MILES OUT ON THE highway. I had a pork loin sandwich and fries with a beer. Susie had a salad and unsweetened iced tea. She swiped a couple of my fries but shook her head vigorously when I offered her half.

"I have to watch it," she said, patting herself on the hip.

"Let me do the watching," I said. "You eat all you want."

"Don't kid me," she said. "You like me trim and tidy."

"Trim and tidy is fine, but fat and sloppy has its place."

"Uh-huh. We'll save that for when we get pregnant."

I stopped masticating and swallowed. "Are we getting pregnant?"

She smiled demurely and ruthlessly pierced a tiny red tomato with her fork. "We might if we don't stop . . ." She lowered her voice. ". . . stop doing you-know-what so much."

I took my last bite of sandwich and chewed, gazing at her thoughtfully, watching the red gathering beneath the curve of her jaw, massing for an assault on her face. Finally, I shook my head and swallowed. She took a sip of tea. Timing was everything.

"I don't get the connection."

She whooped and broke up, stabbing at her mouth with her napkin, spilling her tea with a spastic hand. Our waitress, ever alert, dashed toward us, eyes wide with concern, a tea towel appearing magically in her hand. She drew up beside Susie, staring at the round head bobbing low over the salad. At first glance she appeared to be eating out of her bowl.

"Is she all right?"

"Doc says she's better, says next week we'll let her use a fork."

Susie gave up; she threw back her head and yodeled, caroled, trumpeted laughter, holding her sides, a look akin to pain crossing her crimson face, dark eyes seeping tears, darting glances at me filled with promises of retaliation, mutilation, and dismemberment. Around us heads turned, some staring openly, others discreetly from the corners of their eyes. All were smiling.

I scraped back my chair. "I better get her back. First time out . . . you know. Too much excitement. You understand."

"Of course," the waitress said, keeping her distance, accepting the money I shoved at her with a mechanical "Thank you, come again," but never taking her eyes off my shuddering, hiccuping wife with the rounded shoulders and bowed head. Burps and chortles and desperate giggles erupted as I shepherded her tenderly out of the restaurant.

"I'll kill you," she gasped as I closed her door. I climbed behind the wheel feeling great. She had once told me that one of the reasons she loved me was that I could make her laugh, anywhere, anytime, at herself, at me, at the world. I loved making her laugh, maybe more than she loved laughing, and as long as I could reduce her to her present state, nobody—not even Sy Deacon with his high-powered job, handsome face, and sexy baritone—nobody was ever going to steal her away from me.

By the time we got back to town Susie was back to more or less normal. We stopped at the Eckerd's drugstore on the square. I bought a roll of duct tape, a tube of miracle glue, and a baby rattle. Susie bought an armload of magazines and wouldn't look at me until we were safely back in the truck.

On the way out to the motor home, she leafed through one of the magazines. I smoked in silence mostly, listening to crossover country music that was beginning to sound too much like rock and roll.

I parked in our regular spot and she slipped out of her seat and walked ahead of me. I took over watching her hips for a while, right up until she went through the door. I smoked one last cigarette before joining her.

We spent the better part of the afternoon doing this and that, a little you-know-what.

At five o'clock I was waiting under a pecan tree a half-block from the convenience store.

People are creatures of habit. People of low intellect more creatures of habit than most. I was gambling that Bobby Radcross belonged in the latter category. It wasn't much of a gamble. If I lost I'd just have to find another way. If he was as much a creature of habit as I imagined, then at any moment he would come barreling down the gravel lane, careen around the corner, lay rubber halfway down the block, and zip into the convenience store parking lot. Inside, he would take up his running battle with the little crab men from outer space.

Which is exactly what he did five minutes later.

I waited until he disappeared inside. I started the Ramcharger's engine and drifted down the block, pulled in beside the little red car, as close as before, maybe a little closer. I got out and closed the Ramcharger's door. I walked around his car and peered inside. He had taken the keys. Even people of low intellect learn. No matter.

I opened his passenger door and pushed down the lock, closed it. I took the vial of miracle, quick-drying glue out of my pocket, cut off the end of the tiny tube with my pocket-knife, and squirted glue into the lock, smeared it liberally over the key cutout itself. I recapped the tube and tested my handiwork a few seconds later with the tip of a paper match.

It was already stiff, changing color as it hardened. I counted ten, lit a cigarette, and tested it again. It was hard. Plan A looked good, but I wasn't kidding myself for a moment that I could handle Bobby Radcross a second time without aid.

I climbed back into the Ramcharger, took the .38 Airweight out of the car pocket and laid it on the seat beside me. I checked the arrangement of the loads again to make sure: two ratshot and three standard unjacketed loads. I didn't want to hurt him unless he forced me to it. With junkies you never knew.

There were fewer cars in the lot than before, and that was good. We were down at the end of the store building again, evidently Bobby's private parking preserve, and there was little chance that anyone would pay any attention to us unless attracted by loud voices or my noisy gun. I hoped to keep both to a bare minimum.

He was in there twenty minutes by my watch, and the war must have gone badly. His face was twisted out of shape, his arms swinging in a pantomime of devastating blows at some unseen enemy.

I was out and crouched beside the truck before he covered five paces, watching his dim outline through the heavily tinted side windows. The setting sun beamed over my shoulder and directly into his eyes, and that probably accounted for the fact that he was almost to his car before he noticed my pickup. He slowed, stopped, shaded his eyes, then moved forward slowly, trying to see into the Ramcharger. I eased back to the corner of the truck and watched him through the rear window.

He stood motionless for a time, watching the truck the way an egg-sucking rat watches the nest of a hawk, assessing possibilities, weighing consequences. Then, suddenly, I saw him smile, saw his hand dip into his pocket, come out with a dangling clip of keys. He ducked low, leaped off the high sidewalk, and crouched beside his car. I could almost hear him chuckle as his hand selected the proper key, jabbed it at the lock . . .

"Goddammit to hell!"

I heard his hand smash the door panel of the car, more profanities, then, rage overwhelming common sense, he charged around the front of both vehicles and stopped at the door of my truck.

This time I could hear the chuckle as he tried the door and found it unlocked, saw the keys dangling in the slot.

He chortled with glee and yanked open the door, ducked to climb inside.

I came up behind him and put the gun against the back of his neck. "Right there! That's fine, old buddy. Don't move, don't twitch, don't even breathe hard. This thing's got a mighty light pull." I shoved him forward across the seat, not giving him time to think, time to gather his scattered wits. I had his right wrist behind his back and cuffed before he made a sound. I had his left almost in position when he came alive in a burst of profanity, kicking backward and upward with one muscular leg, catching his heel on the bottom edge of the door, frustrating him long enough for me to rap him lightly behind the ear, wrench the reluctant arm back into position, and cinch the remaining cuff. He groaned and twisted his thick torso, not even close to being unconscious. But that was fine; it no longer mattered.

I stepped back and watched him wrestle his body around, sit up on the edge of the seat, his face an awesome mass of rage and frustration.

"You sonuvabitch," he said, and drew back a leg to kick me in the groin. I had plenty of time to step aside, but I didn't. I pointed the gun at his foot, let him watch me pull back the hammer.

"Whenever you're ready," I said, surprised at the savagery in my voice, forgetting for the moment that the first two loads were ratshot.

"Bullshit!" He dropped his foot. "You're crazy enough to do it."

"Keep that in mind. Now back up and slide across the seat. It's time for our afternoon drive."

He let out another string of profanities, but he did as he

was told. "What the hell you want now, man? I told you everything I know."

I backed the truck away from his car and turned into the street. "The other time was a rehearsal, Bobby. This one is a take."

He laughed, a harsh rasping little grunt. "Shit, man. You ain't gonna kill me and I can take anything you can hand out. You can't do nothing ain't been done to me before. My old man's been beating on me ever since I can remember, teaching me to be a man. Well, I learned good, man. I'm too much man for you."

"That's okay. I like women better anyway."

He stared at me a moment, then went on, outlining in explicit detail and living color what he was going to do with my gun and my handcuffs when he finally caught me on equal footing at some happy time in the future. I let him ramble. It was better than sullen curses. He had a vivid, if somewhat limited, imagination, and most of the atrocities he planned against my person sounded physically impossible albeit painful.

Shadows were long when I pulled into the Rodeo Grounds. The lights were on in the arena and the sound of pounding hammers drifted faintly across the wide expanse of park. I lit a cigarette, Bobby craned his neck and made a hawking sound of disgust.

"Shit! Here again? You queer for this place, or what?"

"It's close in," I said. "It's secluded. And I noticed the hospital is only a hop, skip, and a jump down the road."

He gave me a thin jeering grin. "You gonna beat me up, huh? I told you, man, I been beat on by experts. I can take the pain, man. Hell, I love pain, wakes you up. So take your best shot, asshole, then start looking over your shoulder." He paused and wet his lips. "Anyhow, I don't know what you want. I told you—"

"I think you do, Bobby. One little item you skipped over and I let slip by. Back in July. A short trip to Houston you and Steve made. You like to tell me about it? The purpose of the trip? What happened?"

"Pleasure trip. A little cooze and a little booze. You know the drill, man."

"That's it, huh? That your last word on the subject?"

"You got it." He wasn't smiling at all, hard glints in his eyes, his face set stubbornly, lips drawn tight, prepared for the assault he expected.

I sighed and tossed the cigarette butt out the window. Time to bring up the reinforcements.

29

I TOOK THE BOX OUT OF THE REAR OF THE RAMCHARGER. An ordinary boot box rubber-banded at each end. Bobby watched me over the back of the seat. He waited silently until I was back behind the wheel, the box placed carefully on the seat between us.

"What've you got, man? Them your kicking shoes or something? How about knives, some knucks, ballcrushers?" His laugh was loud enough, but sounded a little forced.

"You wouldn't believe me if I told you."

"Try me?"

"Hmmmm. How about an old shoe and a baby rattle?"

"Funny. Come on, man, what've you got in there?"

"My sidekick. You watch TV. You know all private eyes have sidekicks. Well, this is mine. He takes over when I come up against somebody as tough as you, somebody who has me buffaloed like you do. I deplore violence, Bobby. I really do. Guns and knives and ballcrushers are not where it's at in the eighties. Finesse, Bobby, is where it's at. Right? What I have in here won't shoot you, cut you, or stomp you—it won't even yell at you. I call it my little truth machine."

He was staring at the box, mesmerized, unblinking. "That's bullshit, man."

I very carefully picked up the box and laid it on his thigh: his leg jerked spasmodically.

"Careful, Bobby. I just wanted to show you how little it weighs. Hardly anything at all." I put it back on the seat and lit a cigarette. I puffed to set the coal, then pressed the glowing ember against one of the rubber bands. After a moment, it snapped. The box vibrated: a faint sound.

Bobby jumped. "Jesus Christ! What is it, man? Jesus—"

"I'll give you one more guess, Bobby. You guess right and you win the game. You guess wrong and you tell me about Houston. Okay? I'll give you a little hint." I picked up the box again, slowly, carefully, held it in my right hand and tapped it gently against the heel of my left palm; something shifted inside.

It made a faint, dry, hollow rattling sound. It sounded like a baby rattle to me, but to Bobby Radcross it was the essence of horror, his worst nightmare come true.

He shrieked, legs stabbing, boot heels tearing my floor mat as he tried to push himself through the door, tried to disappear inside himself, eyes wide, as dark as burned egg yolks. Spittle gathered at the corners of his mouth, sprayed the interior of the cab as he moaned, "Oh Jesus oh Jesus oh Jesus oh Jesus . . ."

"Easy, Bobby," I said, watching his milk-white face in the fading light and feeling a little sick at my stomach. I picked up the box with my left hand and thrust it out the window. "Okay, okay, calm down, dammit! It's outside, okay? Talk to me, Bobby, and I'll put it away. I promise."

It took a while. Hysteria, anxiety attack, or just plain terror, whatever the hell it was, it took a while before he could talk, a while longer before he could talk coherently. I smoked in silence, holding the box out the window, not yet willing to throw away my hole card.

Susie had helped me rig up the box. One of Nathan Barr's old slippers and the baby rattle taped to the box lid at an angle. It didn't sound much like rattlesnakes I had heard, but I was hoping Bobby had never heard one at all. Patti Dun-

166

right had been right on the button: snakes weren't Bobby's favorite thing.

"Talk to me, Bobby. What happened in Houston?"

All the aggressiveness had gone out of him, the arrogance, defiance. For the first time there were traces of the boy in his face, in his muted querulous voice.

"We got burned. They burned me and Steve bad, and on top of that my cousin Petey's men beat us up."

"You got burned. Buying or selling?"

"Selling, man. We had smack, a lot of smack, and Petey set up the deal, then doublecrossed us—"

"Slow down. How much smack?"

He wet his mouth and looked at me as if he didn't expect me to believe him. "We had eleven keys, man, Mexican black tar—"

"Eleven *keys*? Jesus H. Christ! That's . . . That's twenty-four pounds!"

"I know it. Somewhere along in there. It was a heavy suitcase. Man, we were getting a cool million bucks . . . like I said, my cousin Petey set it up. He's a mean bastard, but I never thought he'd burn us like that. Them bastards switched suitcases on us somewhere—but I can't believe that, either, 'cause I never let that money get out of my hand once we made the deal."

"Exactly what happened, Bobby?"

He nodded dully, took a deep breath. "Petey set up the deal. He got one key off the top. We made the trade, ten keys for a million bucks. Some warehouse somewhere. We had Petey and two of his men with us as . . . I don't know, protectors, I guess. They had guns, them little machine guns that look like a tool kit with handles. Everything went okay, though, they had the million and we had the dope. We dumped our dope on the end of this long table and they dumped the money on the other. Steve and Petey checked it out while me and the other two guys watched their other two guys. Steve said okay, loaded the money into our suitcase, and we left. I carried the suitcase in my hand or between my legs all the way to the airport. We put it in a locker Petey had reserved for us and we all went into the bar—''

"Petey had reserved?"

"Yeah, he said there might not be one available otherwise and we had about an hour to wait for our plane and we didn't want to carry around a million dollars. We had it all timed, or Petey did, and—"

"And you two dumb shits handed your million dollars over to Petey."

"No, you're wrong. I had the key to the locker. It was right there in my pocket all the time we was in the bar, about forty five minutes or so. I know. I was nervous and kept checking. Then Petey left and we got our suitcase out of the locker and caught our plane. We didn't know until we got back home that we'd been . . ." His voice trailed off.

"Screwed," I supplied. "You had *a* key to the locker, Bobby, not *the* key. If Petey had it reserved, then he had time to duplicate the key before he turned the original over to you."

He stared straight ahead through the windshield. "That's why—" He broke off.

"That's why what?"

"Well, we hotfooted it right back down there. We had to drive, we didn't have enough money for the plane. But that's why Petey got so mad when I jumped him about getting us mixed up with a bunch of damn crooks. He was drunk and he gets mean when he's drunk and . . . well, one thing led to another and him and his men beat us up and dumped us out in our car, followed us all the way to the city limits." He turned to look at me, a silly expression on his face. "And Petey said we shorted him on his key, that it weighed less than two pounds. He was really pissed off about that."

I shook my head. "They say God protects drunks, fools, and little children. You two were doubly blessed. I don't understand why you didn't end up in a bog somewhere."

"Petey and I was raised together. We was always pretty close."

"Okay, Bobby. Big question. Where did the heroin come from?"

"Man, I can't tell you that. Big Bwana, like I said before. That's all I know. I swear."

"Bullshit, Bobby! No big-time dealer is going to trust two screwups like you and Steve with that much dope. Item number two, a million is too cheap."

"Well, that was our price. Me and Steve decided on that, and—" He paused and wet his lips again. "And, man, I don't think Big Bwana gave the dope to Steve. I think Steve ripped him off."

I stared at him; something lurched in my chest. Motive!

"Do you think Big Bwana knew it? That Steve had ripped him off?" How could he not know it, I wondered, twenty million dollars worth of heroin out on the street.

"I don't think so. Stevie was too calm about it, too cool. He kept saying not to worry, that he'd tapped the main line to Big M. Big M meant Mexico. Stevie had his own code like. If you didn't know it, you couldn't understand him half the time."

Main line to Big M. Steve had obviously found a way to break into someone's pipeline of drugs from Mexico. And someone had been perturbed about that, had finally found out who he was and put a bullet through his head. And Lisa had had the bad luck to be there.

It made sense. More than anything else I'd come across.

"You say that was last July?"

"Yeah, late July, early August, somewhere in there." He looked at the box in my hand, then back at me, and volunteered his first bit of information. "I don't think it was the first time. I think that's where Stevie got the coke last December."

"By ripping off Big Bwana, you mean?"

He shrugged. "Somebody. He sure didn't have that kind of money and he had at least a pound left when I saw it, and he'd had it for a while by then. He was giving it away right and left. That was when we got into the drugs pretty heavy, man. After that."

I got out and put the box in the back of the Ramcharger. I could see him watching me over the seats. "Hey, man, you sure that thing can't get loose?" His voice shuddered, squeaked upscale.

"There's no snake, Bobby. I told you what it was right at first. You're so used to lying, you don't know the truth when you hear it." I picked up the box. "You want to see?"

We stared at each other, the dome light casting his face in shadow. "No," he said.

We each thought our own thoughts on the way back to the convenience store, each kept his own counsel, as they say.

I reached across him and opened the door. He turned without prompting and I unlocked the handcuffs. His shoulders were still slumped, his face devoid of emotion.

"It occurred to me," I said, "that the man who killed Steve may well have tracked him down because of the deal you didn't make in Houston. If that's the case, Bobby, chances are he'll come looking for you one of these days."

"I didn't rip him off." He rubbed his wrists.

"I know that and you know it, but maybe he doesn't. At any rate, you're a dangling thread that must get more irritating every day. I'd be careful if I were you."

He sighed and rubbed his shoulder. "Man, I still don't know who he is."

"I believe you, Bobby. I'm just saying the Virgin Islands are pretty nice this time of year."

He shrugged and turned and strode toward his car, a trifle bowed but not yet broken, a bit more humble but not penitent.

I glanced at my watch. My confab with Bobby had taken longer than I expected. Susie wasn't going to make the eight o'clock shuttle.

Ah, well, there was always the nine o'clock, or the ten o'clock, or . . .

30

Susie caught the eleven o'clock plane to the Dallas/Fort Worth Airport. I waited until the blinking lights were no longer visible in the clear Texas sky, then began the long drive back to Jerico Falls.

Bewitched, bothered, and bewildered are catchy words from an old song, and they accurately described my mood. Still bewitched by the evening hours spent with my lovely wife, bothered and bewildered by what I had learned earlier from Bobby Radcross.

Eleven kilos of heroin was not exactly a small thing. Twenty million dollars more or less when properly diluted and sold on the streets. More than enough motive for a murder, two murders, a dozen murders, depending on who was doing the killing. I had seen people killed for a ten dollar bag, a "dime" bag in the vernacular of the streets, nickel bag back in the days before inflation. I had read somewhere that by the end of the twentieth century drugs would, in all probability, overtake religion as the primary cause of atrocity and murder throughout the history of man.

So now we had a motive. An excellent motive from the viewpoint of the killer. He had lost eleven keys of heroin to a mere stripling, a clever lad by all accounts, but an innocent

171

in the devious ways of the world. The drugs irretrievably lost, he had sought his revenge and at the same time stopped a possible leak in his pipeline.

But why had he waited so long? Steve had obviously obtained the heroin sometime prior to July, exact time and method unknown. The boys had made their ill-fated trip to Houston near the end of July or the first of August. Two and a half months the killer had waited. Why? One reason could be that he didn't know who took his drugs and, as I had suggested to Bobby Radcross, had gotten wind of the deal in Houston and had spent the time tracking it back to the source, back to Jerico Falls and Steve Bannion. That made some sense, not a lot, but a little.

Second question: how? How did Steve manage the rip-off without the owner knowing?

Who left twenty million dollars worth of drugs lying around unattended? Some kind of storage? A cache that Steve had stumbled across? Or could Steve himself have been a part of the pipeline, and if so, why wouldn't Big Bwana have known immediately what happened to the drugs? The answer, of course, was that he would have, and the retaliation would have been swift and deadly. He wouldn't have waited two and a half months.

And then there was Radcross's speculation that it had happened before, that the heroin had been the second rip-off, that the cocaine Steve had been so generous with back in December had also been an inadvertent gift from Big Bwana. Just how stupid could Big Bwana be? One rip-off was possible, two seemed unlikely.

Unless.

Unless what?

Unless there was some connection between Steve and Big Bwana, something that would account for Steve's apparent coolness and aplomb as far as the stolen drugs were concerned. Perhaps some hold Steve had on Big Bwana, some undercurrent that sucked them along the same path, some powerful bond that welded them together and had finally parted when Steve went too far, was trusted too much, got too greedy.

But what kind of bond, I wondered wearily, stopping at Jerico Fall's only traffic light: friendship, blood, love, fear?

I fell into bed physically exhausted but still mentally alert. I lay there for an hour or so watching the curtains on the open windows rise and fall with the moisture-laden air sweeping in from the southwest. Lightning zigzagged and thunder rumbled. I got up and closed the windows. I smoked a cigarette and went back to bed.

The storm came, but sleep got there first and turned down my sensors, closed around me like the comforting arms of a wise and seductive lover.

I had no idea how to contact Nueboldt, the man from DEA. His cryptic command to bring "it" to him had not included routing instructions. That probably meant he wouldn't be hard to find, so maybe the logical route would be the simple one.

After breakfast, a late breakfast, I drove to the city square. Ward's Ford van was in its usual slot. A black GMC pickup occupied the next space, a three-quarter ton with a stake bed. It had large side mirrors and an extra string of lights across the roof, mud-encrusted wheels, and a spotlight. A working truck by the looks of its scratched and dented exterior. I parked three spaces away in a slot marked VISITORS. After all, I was no longer on the case. I had no official capacity. Deputy Gil Grossman had so decreed.

On the way in I figured out that the black pickup probably belonged to one of the Bannion clan. I was right. Cody Bannion sat across the desk from Ward. He was dressed in working clothes, threadbare Wrangler jeans and an old frayed cotton shirt that had seen its heyday in the pointed collar fashions of the fifties. A sleeveless denim jacket topped off the ensemble, gave him a ready to punch a cow or brand a steer look.

We shook hands all around. I took the other visitor's chair and fished out my cigarettes. Ward lit one, also. Cody watched both of us light up with a look of disgust on his round face.

"He's quit," Ward said, by way of explanation. Then added succinctly: "Again."

"Nothing ventured, nothing gained," I said.

"Them things'll ossify your lungs," Cody said. "Thank God I got some will power."

"You've kept it well hidden up until now," Ward said. Then to me: "This is his sixth or tenth time, I've lost count."

"Man has to do what he has to do," I said.

"This time it'll take," Cody said, with all the complacency of the self-righteous. "I was only practicing before." He turned abruptly to me. "Ward here tells me that you're aiming to face down Deputy Grossman."

"Well, I don't exactly plan on a showdown at high noon, but, yeah, I'm going against his orders, so to speak."

"Then you're going ahead with the investigation?"

"Sure, after I talk to Abel Caulder. Could be he might want Grossman to carry the ball."

Cody sat up straight. "What does Abel have to do with anything?"

I looked at Ward. "Explain it to him." I couldn't keep the irritation out of my voice and didn't try very hard. "I thought you already had."

Ward squirmed uneasily. "I thought I told you, Cody. Abel is paying Dan's fee, so it's up to him whether Dan keeps on or not since the case has been taken over by the county."

"Bullshit," Cody snapped. "That was my son killed out there. Ain't no Caulder having a say in whether his killer is caught or not."

"That's not exactly the case," I said, then stopped as Ward lifted a hand.

"Okay, Cody. You wanta take over paying Dan's fee? Then you can have all the say in the matter."

"How much is it?"

"Three hundred a day," Ward said.

"Plus expenses," I added.

"Plus expenses," Ward said.

174

"Jesus Christ! Three—a day? My God, that's twenty-one hundred dollars a week!"

"Plus expenses," I said.

"Well, how about it, Cody?" Ward said quietly. "We put you down for next week, or what?"

Cody Bannion pushed to his feet. He adjusted the vest, his face grim. "I'll have to think on it," he said. He gave me a curt nod, stalked across to the door, and went out. He was back a moment later. "Naw. Leave it to the Sheriff. He gets paid with my taxes. It's his job." He left again.

Ward laughed and slapped his desk. "That's the last we'll see of old Cody for a while. You see that glaze on his eyes? He was in shock. Ain't a man living tighter with a dollar than Cody. I usta feel sorry for Stevie and slip him some spending money along. Cody sure wasn't about to hand out any. Stinginess is what run off his wife Fay back in 1979. She just couldn't handle it anymore."

"How do you think Abel will feel about it?"

Ward shrugged. "I called him last night and told him what happened. He didn't say anything about taking you off the case."

"Okay, I'll call him. In the meantime, do you have any idea where I can connect with a man named Nueboldt? Works for DEA." I went on to describe the man I had met out on the highway.

He nodded. "I know who you mean. I didn't remember his name but he was in here once asking for help on a bust."

"You help him?"

"Sure. You think 'cause we're a dinky little police department that we don't know how to act? Fellow officer asks for help we give it to him—if he asks nice."

"What did you think of Nueboldt?"

"Sorta scroungy looking, as I recall, but I think he'd been doing some undercover work. Seemed competent enough. Wanted to go in like gangbusters, but, thank goodness, cooler heads prevailed, namely mine. He'd ferreted out a speed lab down near the south edge of town. Spangley brothers. Mean dudes, loaded for bear. They had guns in there I hadn't seen the like of since Nam. Enough ordinance to take on Rambo. We took them out without firing a shot.'' He cocked his head, daring me to ask him how.

''Holy cow, how'd you do that?''

His lips quirked, but he went on in solemn tones. ''The Spangley brothers raised redbone hounds. I happened to hear a couple of days before that they had a brand new bitch they'd paid five hundred dollars for. We waited till about dark and I snuck in a neighbor's house and called on the phone and told them I'd just seen their new bitch get hit by a car out in front of their house. All three of them boys came boiling outta there like they'd just invented running. We sorta waltzed on in and lined up between them and their house, about six of us with riot guns, and they saw the light, give up like hardcore sinners at a brush arbor revival.''

''I swear, Ward, that was flat smart. You wanta tell me now where I can find Nueboldt?''

He grinned, unabashed. ''It was, for a fact. Well, okay. Last I heard he was hanging out at the Rockaway Inn on the highway west of town. Sounds sorta fancy, but it's nothing but a honkytonk with a dozen or so rooms upstairs for them hardcore sinners I was talking about before.''

''Is he working undercover again?''

Ward snorted and mashed out his cigarette. ''Maybe he thinks he is, but I doubt if there's a doper in this county who don't know what he is.''

''Have you heard any rumors about a big narcotics burn around here last summer?''

He took a minute lighting another cigarette—finally, somebody who smoked more than I did. ''You mean rip-off?'' he asked quietly.

''That's what I mean, all right.''

He spewed smoke in a long pale stream. ''There was a rumor—not in the summer—back a ways, more like spring, April, May, along in there. Went around for a while, then died out, never heard no more about it. Why? What would that have to do with Lisa and Steve?''

I stood up abruptly. ''I don't know, Ward. Maybe not

a damn thing. Does every damn thing have to have a reason?''

I stomped to the door and went out, catching a glimpse of his face through the glass, filled with perplexity at my sudden irritability.

I couldn't fault him for that. I was wondering about it myself.

31

THE ROCKAWAY INN WAS LOCKED UP TIGHT. NOT PARTIC-
ularly surprising at that time of day. The upper floor had its
own entrance and eleven doors opening off a long dim hall-
way. One door stood ajar, a bathroom, and if there was anyone at home behind the other ten, I couldn't get them to
answer my knock. They were all locked and silent.

I got back into my pickup and smoked a cigarette and
thought about my next move. The man from DEA would
have to wait. I found myself not caring much. My prospects
of getting anything out of him would have been slim at best.
Chances were good that he knew something about the narcotics rip-off, but people like Nueboldt rarely gave anything
away and it was entirely possible that the ''it'' he had mentioned might have been a reference to the twenty-four-odd
pounds of Mexican heroin. Maybe he didn't know about the
Houston transaction and thought the drugs were still floating
around somewhere looking for a home.

I drove back into Jerico Falls. I made one turn around the
square, then nosed into a parking space in front of the Saragache County *Gazette*. Maybe it was time for Tony Caulder's community service piece, after all. With the right slant
it might well stir things up a bit, particularly in the county

law enforcement area. And, too, I hadn't had my picture in the paper recently.

Caulder was in his office alone, standing at a long table moving what appeared to be newspaper clippings around on a wide square board. The door made only a little noise, and he didn't look up until I stopped at a waist-high railing that divided the office approximately in half.

"Mr. Roman," he said, and came toward me with outstretched hand.

"Last time it was Tony and Dan," I said.

He laughed. "Right you are. Come on in and have a seat." He led me to a chipped and dented metal desk pushed against the other wall. He swept a stack of magazines and old newspapers off the seat of a straight-backed chair and pushed it at me. "Don't pay any attention to the clutter. Sara's out today and I'm trying to do her job and mine too and not getting much of anything done." He sank into an old wooden swivel chair with obvious relief. From behind him, beyond a set of double doors, I could hear the clatter and whine of machinery working, feel a faint vibration in the soles of my feet. He appeared to listen for a second, then as if satisfied with what he heard, he looked at me and smiled his engaging smile.

"Well, Dan, have you decided to let me do that James Bond piece on you?"

"James Bond, huh? I was hoping for something a bit more cerebral, like Rambo."

"A little Rambo's no problem."

"Actually, something you said the time we talked before about drugs being flown up out of Mexico and dropped in someone's pasture sorta intrigued me. How can they get away with that? Don't we have radar, intercept planes, that sort of thing?"

"Sure, we have radar and we—the Border Patrol and DEA—have some planes, but not nearly enough, and there are just too many holes in the radar system. A small craft flying low can come in under the radar, zip right up the corridor between Austin and Abilene, and never be detected except by visual sighting. We're right smack in the center of that corridor, by the way.''

''How do they get it down, use some sort of parachute?''

He shrugged. ''Some do, I suppose, but the pros package it in high-impact polystyrene. Come in low and let it go. There's a number of ways you can package it to prevent it breaking open on impact. A parachute keeps it in the air too long, more chance of being seen, plus you lose control in a sense. An unexpected gust of wind could leave your chute high and dry in the top of a tree. Or somewhere in a shinnery thicket. Drug dealers are lazy by nature. They don't like to climb trees, or worse, crawl around in a thicket at night looking for their bundles, and rattlesnakes love shinnery thickets. At any rate, the guys I've talked to prefer the direct method, generally a short time before dark.''

''Guys you've talked to?'' A faint combination of ink and oil wafted in to mix with the musty odor of paper.

He nodded. ''I did a series of articles on drug smuggling for the *Times Herald* not long before I left. I interviewed a bunch of guys in Huntsville.''

''Then someone waiting on the ground takes it the rest of the way?''

''Most of the time. I met one guy in Huntsville who had his own operation going. He'd fly it up in his plane, drop it off on his back forty, take his plane on into town to the airport, drive out, and pick up his dope. Said it worked great till his wife got mad and ratted on him; but usually it's at least a two man operation.''

''Anything like that going on here?''

''I wouldn't be surprised. There's always planes flying around, some of them a hell of a lot lower than they're supposed to be. This is lonely desolate country, a long way between houses once you get back off the highways. Everybody pretty much minds their own business, and we've probably got the most inept sheriff's department in Texas.'' He gave me a small one-sided smile. ''Why? You turn up something interesting?''

"Curious, is all. You hear anything about a big narcotics rip-off around here back in April, May, along in there?"

He shrugged. "There was some talk about the time I took over the *Gazette*. I tried to track it down, back to the source, but it didn't lead anywhere." His eyebrows arched, a look of irony in his eyes. "More curiosity, I suppose."

"A bad habit I have."

"Perhaps not, considering your vocation."

"Rumors can sometimes be traced back to the source if you stay with it long enough. Who told you?"

"Sara," he said promptly. "She heard it from Jenny Westlake, a friend of hers who heard it from Sissy Denker who got it from Norma Dew. That's as far as I got. Norma Dew didn't remember where she heard it."

"Sara's your reporter?"

He smiled crookedly. "And my wife."

"Handy."

"Yeah, until one of the kids get sick, then I have it all to myself, me and old Sam Griswald back there on the presses."

"How often do you go to press?"

"Weekly. Comes out day after tomorrow. Got any good quotes I can use?"

"Sure, couple of favorites of mine: 'Don't shoot till you see the whites of their eyes,' and 'Damn the torpedoes, full speed ahead.' " I stood up.

He laughed and stood up also. "Good old reliable quotes, all right, but I was thinking of something pertaining more or less to the murder case."

"Oh, that. Well, it appears that I have been ordered off the case by the county."

His face sharpened with interest. "County? Sheriff Brindley?"

"No, one of his stalwart minions, a deputy named Grossman."

"That dipshit? Why?"

"I found out where they were killed. It's in county territory, outside the city limits."

"Where?" he reached for pen and paper.

181

I told him and he wrote it down, then twisted to look at me, a ludicrous expression on his face. "You mean *you* found the spot and now the county's forcing you out of the case?"

"Pretty much, although forcing may be a little strong."

"Are you quitting?"

"That's up to your daddy. How far he's willing to back me."

"All the way," he said emphatically. "And so's this paper."

"Good to know," I said, "but I'll need to talk to him."

"Okay." He looked at his watch. "I can reach him at home from twelve to one. If you'll come in . . . oh, around three, I'll have him here. Save you a trip out to the ranch. It's a long dusty drive out there."

"I appreciate it."

"No problem. Dad always comes in one day a week. May as well be today."

We shook hands at the door. "If you write your piece, you might say the investigation is coming right along and that an arrest is expected momentarily."

His eyebrows climbed. "Is that true?"

"No, is truth a prerequisite?"

"Not if I use it in a quote."

"Feel free," I said.

We exchanged smiles. I walked to my truck. I lit a cigarette and wondered if maybe it wasn't time to backtrack a little, cover some ground I had skipped over lightly before. Norma Dew obviously knew more than she had told me, which was practically nothing, and if she had started the rumor about the drug heist, then it was possible she knew some of the details. According to Patti, Norma had been Bobby Radcross's girlfriend, and perhaps Bobby—as unlikely as it seemed—was one of that fraternity of men who indulged in pillow talk, who whispered into shell-pink ears secrets that could not have been plucked from them with red hot pincers or cattle prods to the groin . . . or maybe even snakes in a box.

32

SHE CAME OUT AT TEN MINUTES PAST TWELVE, A SMALL leather purse dangling from her left arm. Dark slacks again, white blouse, some kind of blue leisure jacket that looked like suede. She had an easy, swinging walk that caught the eye, turned heads. Her hair trapped the sunlight like fine strands of burnished gold.

I watched from the truck until she turned into a fast food restaurant down at the end of the block. I got out and stretched, ditched my cigarette, and angled across the street. I could see her through the wide expanse of glass, tall and lissome. One hip propped against the counter, arms folded while she waited for her order. I dawdled near a mailbox on the corner, leaned over to read the mail pickup times on the side. When I straightened she had moved down the counter to the cashier, and a moment later I saw her go out through a side door into a covered area fitted with small metal tables.

I gave her a minute to get settled, watching her sleek blond head above waist-high latticework that separated the eating area from the street. When it appeared that she was fully engrossed, I walked around the corner of the building, through an archway in the latticework, and sat down across the table from her.

She was reading as well as eating, a paperback book curled in one long fingered hand, the other languidly reaching for a french fried potato. She looked up, an annoyed expression on the pretty face, the cool eyes frosty, lips curved to rebuff.

She went from disdain to shock in the batting of an eye; she made an inarticulate sound and let the book slip from her hand, the furled pages uncurling. She threw it into her purse and reached to gather up her hamburger and fries and Coke.

"You can leave," I said, "but it won't matter. I'll come into the store later. If you go home, I'll come there. You're going to talk to me, Norma. If not today, then tomorrow. It's your choice."

"But I don't know anything! I told you that. Lisa and Stevie were my friends, you think I wouldn't help you if I could?"

"You may know more than you think you do. How can you be sure until you hear my questions?"

"You want to get us into trouble over the drugs—"

"No. If Bobby Radcross told you that, he lied. He knows better. You're a beautiful young girl. If you want to spoil your chances of becoming a beautiful young woman by using drugs, then that's your path and you'll have to walk it. All alone, I might add. Dope addicts make damned unreliable friends. I'm interested in the drugs only to the extent they're tied in with Steve and Lisa's deaths."

"You think they are?" She seemed genuinely surprised.

"I don't know. That's what I'm trying to find out. I happen to know Steve and Bobby were involved to a much greater extent than anyone knew." I paused. "Except maybe you and Lisa."

She looked startled again, blue eyes expanding. "Why me? I never had anything to do with . . . all I did was take a few . . ." She let it fade away and lowered her gaze. "I did dope," she said sullenly. "I didn't sell it."

"Eat your hamburger. It's getting cold."

Obediently, she picked up the sandwich and took a small neat bite.

"You are Bobby's girlfriend," I said. "Some men have a habit of telling their women things they won't tell anyone else. For a lot of reasons, none of which have anything to do with this conversation."

"I'm not," she said. "Not anymore. I haven't seen him for over a month."

"But you said he told you I wanted to get you in trouble?"

She nodded and took a small sip of Coke. "He called me and warned me not to talk to you."

"About what?"

She shrugged and nibbled on a french fry. "About anything, I guess."

"About Stevie," I said. "About the way he got the cocaine last December, about the way he got the Mexican black tar in April, or was it May?"

She stared at her fingers holding the french fry; they were trembling. She looked back at me. "I'm afraid of Bobby."

"So am I," I said. "And that's the truth. But I'm also afraid of tornadoes, lightning, cancer . . . we can't let our fears rule our lives, Norma."

"That's easy for you to say," she said, and gave me the smallest ghost of a smile.

"He told you about it, didn't he?"

She put down the sandwich and sighed. "No. Bobby never talked in bed and I suppose that's what you were talking about before. Lisa told me. Stevie did talk in bed. He was smart and he wanted everyone to know it, especially his women." She smiled wryly. "And he had more of them than he thought anyone knew." She flicked a fingernail against her cup of Coke. "He's that much like his daddy, at least."

"Cody? He didn't strike me as the type to be a ladies' man." We were getting away from the subject, but she appeared to be slowly uncoiling from her defensive posture.

She shrugged. "I've always heard rumors about Cody. The latest says he has a woman set up in an apartment in Eastland, a young woman, so the story goes."

"Hard to keep something like that quiet in a small town."

"It would be impossible here, but Eastland is a good deal

larger and pretty far away. On the other hand it may not be true.'' She picked up the sandwich and glanced at her watch. ''I have to go back pretty soon.''

''How did Stevie get the drugs?''

She put the hamburger down. ''You swear you won't tell anyone I told you?''

''I can't promise you that, Norma. I will promise I'll never tell anyone outside the legal system, and I'll most definitely never tell Bobby Radcross.''

She took another sip of Coke, wiped her lips with a paper napkin. She looked around at the empty tables nearby, then let her shoulders fall in a gesture of resignation.

''The first time, back in December of last year, Stevie was out there all by himself—he liked to do that once in a while, get out by himself and study or think. He was kind of a loner sometimes. Anyway, it was beginning to get dark, too dark for him to study anymore and he was getting ready to leave when he heard this airplane.''

''You're talking about his uncle's place, Ward Bannion's place?''

''Yes. Stevie liked it back there by that little lake. Anyway, he saw this airplane coming down that field—that field where they have the milo planted—and at first he thought it was going to crash it was flying so low. He was all set to dive into the lake when the plane pulled up suddenly and he saw something falling. Something small, about big enough to hold a bowling ball, he said. The little box bounced and bounced. Stevie was afraid it was going into the water. But it stopped over near the other bank and he ran over and got it. By then he was almost sure he knew what it was, and he didn't even stop to see. He just jumped in his car and took off, came out the back way—''

''Back way?''

She nodded. ''Nobody uses it much because it's so rough, but there's a dirt road, not hardly even a road at all, just some car tracks that go around the north side of that big hill and run into the county road. You probably wouldn't see it if you didn't know it was there.''

"There was cocaine in the box?"

"Yes. Two pounds and a little more, Lisa said."

"And nobody came nosing around and looking."

"No. Stevie told Lisa he believed the dopers thought their package might have gone into the water. It was well packaged, but it wouldn't have been water-proof, Steve said. If it had gone into the water it would have become waterlogged and sunk. Stevie thought they may have released it a few seconds later than they were supposed to or something."

"The second time?"

She twisted her napkin into a long white cylinder, dropped it into the basket with her uneaten hamburger. "The second time, Stevie was never sure what happened. After he got the coke, he started spending a lot of Saturday evenings back there on that hill behind his uncle's place. All by himself again. He'd show up about an hour or so after dark, looking excited. He'd get high and talk about a big score, about a big killing he was going to make once he got it all figured out. Nobody knew what he was talking about. Bobby would act like he did, but he was as mystified as the rest of us."

"Saturday nights? Did the first one happen on a Saturday night?"

She frowned. "I think so, but I couldn't swear to it. Later he told Lisa they were making drops on Saturday evenings just before dark, always on the nights when his Uncle Ward would be gone out of town. But until that Saturday in April he never had another chance to slip in and pick up the bundle. There was always someone waiting at the side of the field in a pickup truck. As soon as the box hit the ground they'd trot out and pick it up."

"They?"

"Yes. Two of them, Stevie said. Always two of them. And one would carry a gun."

"Steve didn't recognize either of them?"

"If he did, he didn't tell Lisa, or she didn't tell me."

"What happened in April?"

"Well, Stevie kept watching and hoping they'd make some kind of mistake, and getting more and more excited because the bundles were getting bigger and bigger. The planes didn't come every Saturday night. Stevie said they averaged about twice a month, but he never knew when so he was out there for a while every Saturday night.''

"And they finally did?''

"Stevie didn't know what happened. This one night the plane came through right on schedule, dropped the bundle, but the pickup wasn't where it usually was parked. It got dark and still the pickup didn't come. Stevie finally crept out into the field, got down on his hands and knees, and crawled to where he had seen it land. He found the box, a heavy one, so heavy it scared him. He crawled part of the way back but the box was too heavy to slide good, so he just got up and ran the rest of the way.'' She had the napkin again, knotting it around her fingers, her eyes bright and shining. "God, that must have been scary, expecting lights to come on, and somebody to start shooting at you any second.''

"Scary,'' I agreed. "But noble deeds bring out the best in a man.''

"You can poke fun all you want, but Stevie was smart and had a lot of courage. Bobby would never have done that. He'd have been afraid of touching something in the dark that squirmed, not to mention the men with the lights and guns.''

"You're right, bravery should be applauded wherever it's found. Too bad it didn't do him any good, not to mention getting him killed.''

She looked up quickly. "You think that's what it was?''

"It's not a bad motive for murder,'' I said. "Particularly since he and Bobby managed to let the drugs slip through their hands.''

"That was Bobby's fault for trusting that creepy cousin of his. Anyone could look at him and tell he was a crook.''

"Unlike our two young heroes,'' I said. "What I'm wondering is what did Bobby and Stevie and the group do for drugs after Houston?''

She shrugged. "We managed.''

"And Stevie, did he continue his spying on the milo field?''

She shifted uneasily. "I'm not sure. I don't think so. Lisa told me all of this in September, not long before she left for college. She said something about them not using the milo field much anymore, and that she and Stevie went out there sometimes to turn on and . . . like that."

She took a long drink of Coke, rattled the ice in the cup. She picked up the package of french fries and abruptly stood up. "I have to go. I've told you everything I know, Mr. Roman, so I don't expect to see you again."

I stood up and smiled. "Thank you, Ms. Dew. You've not only been very helpful, but you've restored my faith in my own instincts. I don't want to seem ungrateful or to push my luck, but there is one more small thing I'd like to ask."

She dumped the hamburger and empty Coke cup in a nearby trash barrel. She picked up her purse, a thin line creasing her forehead. "Hurry, then, Mr. Roman, I'm going to be late as it is."

"Did Steve tell Lisa who Big Bwana is?"

"Who?" A look of perplexity crowded out the frown.

"Never mind, Ms. Dew. I thank you again for your time."

"You're welcome," she said crisply and swept by me with a curt nod.

I lit a cigarette and followed at a more leisurely pace, feeling a faint, steady, drumbeat of excitement, new speculation smoking in to crowd out the old.

What if, I thought, Big Bwana hadn't tracked Steve through the bungled Houston deal after all? What if he had waited and picked up right where he left off, allowing things to cool down, mellow out? Losing eleven kilos of heroin would have been a devastating blow to anyone other than one of the top dealers in the country, and maybe it had taken a while to recoup, to regroup and continue operations.

What if he had set a trap for his elusive raider, duplicated the events that led up to the shipment in April being left alone in the field long enough to be purloined? It could have been something as simple as a flat tire, faulty ignition, a bad battery—a hundred things.

Perhaps he had been fishing for weeks, an occasional

dummy shipment with no visible reception committee, working under the assumption that if he made it easy enough, sooner or later the raider would strike again.

And, obviously, Steve had taken the bait, seized what he thought was more opportunity at the golden horn of plenty, the natural insouciance of youth and perhaps a drug-addled mind leading him and his unwitting fiancee to their deaths.

On the other hand, maybe by then Lisa knew exactly what she was getting into. She apparently knew everything else with the possible exception of Big Bwana's name. Another thought came sneaking in on sticky feet. What if Steve himself didn't know who Big Bwana was? It wasn't absolutely necessary to know a man's name to steal his horse. No pun intended.

I went back to my truck and drove out to the motor home. Watching Norma not eat had given me an appetite. I opened a beer and stuck a Hungry Man meat and potatoes TV dinner in the midget oven. I went out onto the canvas patio and flopped into one of the aluminum chairs. Hunger always sharpened my mind, brought my senses to a fever pitch.

I lit a cigarette, drank some more beer, gazed at the dark line of trees along the creek, and waited for inspiration.

33

As far as I could tell Abel Caulder was wearing the same worn faded jeans, the same clean but wrinkled work-shirt he had worn the first time I met him. The expression was the same, grim and irascible, as if his features had been seized at some traumatic moment in time and cast in a permanent mold.

But, as before, his voice was friendly, his handshake firm and dry. "Good to see you again, Mr. Roman."

I spoke and nodded at Tony, sitting to one side of the wooden swivel chair, smiling and nodding as if he had just arranged a peace conference between two warring nations. "Three o'clock right on the nose. Like a punctual man."

"An obsession of mine," I said. "The only good one I have." I sat in the only chair left, a straight-backed pedestal swivel that probably belonged to Tony's wife.

"Well, Mr. Roman, Tony tells me you've been busy. He also tells me that Deputy Gil Grossman has been giving you some sass."

"Orders," I said. "He saved his sass for Chief Bannion."

Abel grunted. "Chief Bannion oughta throwed him out on his ass."

"There is a point of law here, Dad," Tony said. "If they were killed on county land then the county has jurisdiction."

"So do I," Abel said. "It was my daughter who was killed. That gives me more jurisdiction than anybody . . . except maybe Cody Bannion."

"I agree with that," I said. "And you have the right to hire anyone you choose to investigate her death." I paused to light a cigarette. "But there are limits to what one man can accomplish. I've learned quite a bit, I think, but so far it hasn't taken me much closer to the killer." I glanced at Tony, then back at the older man. "And a lot of the things I've learned you aren't going to like, Mr. Caulder, maybe some of it you won't even believe."

"Tell me," Abel Caulder said with no discernible change of expression.

I looked at Tony. He shrugged lightly and clasped slender fingers around one knee, his face unreadable.

I took one last drag on my cigarette, mashed it out, and told them. All of it, making my voice dull and toneless, carefully neutral. When I finished we sat in silence: even the muted clamor of the nearby machinery had been mysteriously stilled.

I lit another cigarette and summed it up. "All along it seemed that I was working two different cases, the drugs and the murders. Then gradually they began to come together, to blend into a clearcut case of cause and effect. The drugs caused the murders. Steve went too far. I don't know, maybe the boldness of youth, maybe something else by that time. He was evidently doing a lot of drugs by then and that can make a man foolish and careless."

"Man!" Abel spat suddenly. "He was no man. No man leads a young girl into something like that."

I thought about pointing out that Lisa was already into drugs when she started dating Steve, but decided it wasn't the time. Tony, however, had no such reservations.

"Steve didn't turn her on to drugs, Dad," he said quietly. "She'd been playing around with drugs for years." He looked at me, quickly looked away.

Abel's head swiveled slowly to look at his son. "Why, in the name of God, didn't you tell me?"

"What would you have done, Dad? Whipped her? Chained her to her bedpost? Sent her to bed without supper? What? Lisa was headstrong and willful. Spoiled. We made her that way after Mom died. I say we because we all had a hand in it. The only girl, the youngest child, pretty, cunning, deceitful when she had to be to get her way. We overindulged, we gave her everything because we couldn't stand to see her unhappy. We smoothed out all the hard places and we taught her that whatever she wanted was always right because we saw that she got it. What, Dad? Tell me what the hell you would have done?"

"I was her father," Abel said, his voice thick and strained. "I had a right to know."

Tony sighed and hunched his shoulders, staring at his father's acne-riddled boots. "All you had to do was look."

"I don't know," I said, refocusing the conversation. "I don't know if she was there with Steve that night by accident or design. I don't suppose we'll ever know for sure. It could have been pure bad luck, her being there. Then again, maybe she had thrown in with Steve and they had been staking out the milo field waiting for another opportunity to rip off Big Bwana."

"This Big Bwana," Tony said. "You have no idea who he is?"

"None. That was Steve's name for him, but I understand he used that name for almost anyone in authority."

"Are you sure, Mr. Roman," Abel said. "Are you sure about . . . about Lisa and the drugs?"

"I believe it, Mr. Caulder. That's all I can say. I don't know that it's positively true, no." I returned his listless gaze, puzzled. "I understand that the medical examiner talked to you about drugs found in your daughter's body."

He nodded, one hand coming up to stroke a frozen cheek. "Cody and that doctor cousin of his came to see me, said there were traces of pills . . . said they didn't see any use blackening the kids' names on public documents over some-

193

thing that might have been prescribed by a doctor at the college for the flu or something like that. I agreed.''

"That was it?'' I could feel Tony's gaze on the side of my face.

"They said Ward Bannion had agreed also. I saw no reason not to.'' He turned to look at me, eyes keen and bright again. "She was killed on Bannion land. She was with a Bannion. Don't that tell you something?''

"What, Dad?'' Tony asked, exasperation in his tone. "What should that tell him other than Lisa was in love with a Bannion boy?''

"Love,'' Abel scoffed. "They were too young to know what love is.''

"You were married at their age, Dad,'' Tony said, affection replacing exasperation. "Mom was only eighteen when Ralph was born. You didn't know what you were doing?''

"Probably not. It just happened to turn out all right.'' Abel pushed to his feet and held out his hand. "Keep on with it, Mr. Roman. Until you decide you can't go any farther. If that happens I'll still say thank you for trying.'' He tugged a stained, rounded billfold out of his left rear pocket. "Shouldn't I be paying you something on account?''

"It can wait,'' I said. "I'll send you a bill. I don't like to carry such huge sums of money in case I get mugged.''

Tony laughed. Abel's thin lips quirked, but he didn't change expression. He put the wallet away, nodded his head, and went out the door.

"I guess you're wondering about Dad's face,'' Tony said. "He was in Vietnam. They shot off most of his face and the docs had to rebuild it. Only thing is, the muscles don't work. I think they could've given him a better expression, but there you are, he's lucky to be here at all.''

"Aren't we all,'' I said, easing toward the door. "You count up all the ways there are for a man to die between birth and maturity and it makes you want to run somewhere and hide.''

"Not me,'' Tony said breezily. "I'm a fatalist. It gives me a lot of freedom.''

I stopped at the door and lit a cigarette. "It can give you a lot of pain, too, if you walk in front of a truck and expect him to stop 'cause it isn't your time to go."

He followed me out the door, ready to argue the point. "Yeah, but if it *is* your time to go, then you'll go, and you'll be fulfilling your fate."

"Can't argue with logic like that," I said. We exchanged grins and I sauntered down the street to my Ramcharger, a little wiser than I had been before, but not much.

The park around One Century Plaza was buzzing. A soft beautiful day in early November, crisp clean air, the earth stippled with fallen leaves and balls of sunlight filtering through the multi-colored trees. Texas always has days like that in November, but not often enough that you want to throw one away.

So the populace was out en masse, enjoying the fine weather, doing the things people always do in parks, loitering predominant.

I went into the small savings and loan on the northeast corner of the square, traded the chunky, efficient-looking young lady at the counter a five dollar bill for twenty quarters. I tried to leave one for a tip, but she rejected it with a tiny curl of her lip. Too little, or too much. I wondered.

I found a phone stall outside the bank building. I dropped in a quarter and listened to it tinkle and crash into an empty-sounding reservoir. After a few seconds thought, I dialed my number.

"Captain Sellers' office."

"Hi, Mitsi! This is your old buddy Daniel Boone calling from deep in Indian territory—"

"Please deposit eight quarters for three minutes."

"Jesus Christ! Eight?"

"Yes, sir. Eight. For three minutes."

I fed the quarters into the machine. They took at least thirty seconds to drip through the mechanism.

"Hi, Danny, are you still there?"

195

"Yeah, I am, but two of my hard earned dollars just went south."

"Where in the world have you been? Homer's been trying to get in touch with you for days. Don't you know what time of year it is? He's had glazed eyes for a week now." She finished with her brassy, whinnying laugh; another ten seconds shot to hell.

"Well, you tell him—no wait, I'll tell him myself. Cut me in, will you?"

"He's not here, Danny. They're working the poor man to death—and me too, for that matter."

"How can he work with glazed eyes—no, no, we don't have time to discuss it. I need a few names run through the computer system, Mitsi. Can you just go ahead and do that for me? You'll end up doing it, anyway."

"Golly, Danny, I don't know. We're so busy and you know how mad he gets when I do something for you behind his back."

"Just remind him whose land he's gonna be deer hunting on this year—if he's lucky, that is. You know he'll end up doing it, Mitsi, and I don't have all that much time."

"Please deposit eight quarters for three minutes!"

"Already? Christ sakes, it's only been—"

"It's been three minutes, sir. I'll need another eight quarters."

"Are you a real person or a machine?" I asked, feeding quarters as fast as I could.

"Thank you, sir," she said sweetly. "I'll be back."

"You heard her, Mitsi. She's gonna cut me off sure as hell. Let me give you these names, okay? Homer'll do it, you know he will. Okay?"

She sighed. "Okay, Danny, shoot. And I just hope Homer doesn't when he gets back."

I acknowledged her little funny with a short barking laugh, then read from the list of names I had prepared. I was still three names away from the end when I heard the ominous click and the syrupy voice:

"Eight quarters please for three minutes."

"I don't have eight quarters, but I'll tell you one thing, miss, or my name isn't Robert S. Radcross."

"What was that, Mr. Radcross?"

"Radcross? Why are you calling me Radcross? My name is Anthony T. Caulder. And don't you forget it. C-A-U-L-D-E-R. Now, about your eight quarters. What are they for? More time, I suppose. Well, young lady, I don't need any more time. When James Abel Caulder speaks people listen— you get that last one, Mitsi?"

Mitsi's whinnying laugh answered me.

The line went dead.

I lit a cigarette and stepped away from the phone, grinning at my small victory.

Things like that wouldn't've happened back before they busted up old Ma Bell. That's what happened when the system tinkered with something that wasn't broken.

And that was only a small part of it. What with burgeoning budget deficits, the imbalance of export trade, the ever present threat of atomic annihilation, life for us serious minded folks was getting to be too worrisome to bear. Sometimes I had the feeling that the end was out there crouched and waiting . . . moving . . .

34

As it happened, I didn't have to go looking for Leonard Nueboldt again. He was waiting for me when I got back to the motor home, sprawled in one of the aluminum chairs, as slovenly as before, a noxious mist comprised of cheap whiskey and body odor surrounding him like the lingering aura of a bad dream. He wore the same clothing, the same boots, the same long unkempt hair. He appeared to be asleep. He wasn't. He was watching me through slitted eyes, a bit of melodramatic posing that set my teeth on edge.

I kicked the leg of the chair. "Wake up, Prince Charming, you'll get no kiss from me."

He opened one eye wide and groaned. "Your humor hasn't improved, I see."

"Nor my temper. First of all what are you doing here, and how did you know where to find me?"

He sat up, looking startled. "Chief Bannion. He said you were looking for me." He flipped a sack of tobacco out of his top jacket pocket and fished around for papers.

"I was, but I'm not sure I am anymore. I've already found out what I hoped to learn from you."

"What?"

"That's not the way it works. You tell me what you're looking for and I'll tell you if I've found it."

"If it has to do with drugs, buddy, you tell *me*. That's the way it works."

"Or you'll haul my ass in. I know. You already scared me enough with that one. Why don't you try something really bad? Threaten to hug me or something."

He let the tobacco sack dangle from his teeth while he fashioned the cigarette, brown eyes intent on what he was doing. I couldn't tell if he was smiling or snarling, and I didn't much care which. I was tired and hungry and in no mood for a lot of macho bullshit.

He got the cigarette going before he answered. "I liked that one. I really did. You're a quick man with a quip. I don't smell good, that's a fact, but then I'm in a smelly business. You can't roll around in shit all day and not get some on you. Well, look, I know I rub you the wrong way and that's okay, too. A lot of people have that reaction. But the thing is, one of us is gonna have to trust the other one and say something meaningful or we're just wasting time. I saw you poking around out at the Rockaway Inn and that's why I called Chief Bannion. He confirmed that you were looking for me."

"Why didn't you contact me at the Inn?"

He smiled a faint and enigmatic smile. "I was otherwise occupied at the time. A lady informant. And I couldn't afford to be seen with you."

"Okay," I said. "You go first. Say something meaningful."

He slid his tongue along the seam of his cigarette, the brown eyes dark and unblinking, meeting mine with a riveting force. "Twenty-four and a half pounds of Mexican black tar heroin, give or take an ounce or two. That meaningful enough for you?"

"Ripped off from Big Bwana. Could it be the same twenty-four and a half pounds, I wonder?"

He stared at me, the coated tongue coming out to wet dry lips this time. "Who?" he said hoarsely.

199

"Big Bwana, a sobriquet, a nom de plume. Unless, of course, you can tell me his real name."

He shook his head, looking dazed. "No, we just call him Mr. Big."

I clucked. "No imagination, you government people."

"My God," he said hollowly. "It really exists then?"

"Not in its original form, I wouldn't think. By now it's probably bringing joy to millions of addicts all across the country. What do you mean, it really exists then?"

"We were never sure. The rumors kept coming for six months or more . . . a big shipment of skag. We kept running into it on the streets of Houston, Dallas, Austin . . . Jerico Falls, Texas, a little dump of a country town and there were supposed to be eleven keys of skag floating around, up for grabs."

"Not strictly true. Eleven keys, yes, but they weren't floating around. Local talent ripped them off, then, in turn, got ripped off and bashed around a bit."

"Who?"

"Steve Bannion, the boy who was killed."

He nodded. "Small wonder. But they were too late to get back their dope?"

"By a couple of months or more. The boys took it to Houston and got snookered."

"Boys? Who was the other one? Bobby Radcross?"

"A very good guess."

He shrugged, eyes bright, and tossed away the foul-looking remnant of his cigarette. "Not a guess. They've been into drugs together for a year or more, even did a little pennyante peddling. I bought some high grade blow from Bannion back in the spring. A good price, too. I wondered where he picked that up from."

"Same place, different time. December of last year. Two pounds of coke."

He smiled bleakly and shook his head. "Twice? That's hard to believe."

"Isn't it? But when you say that you're thinking in terms of pros. What if Big Bwana is strictly amateur night at the

Bijou? Maybe he doesn't know that big time dope dealers don't let themselves be ripped off once, let alone twice?''

"It's possible," he said, a touch of humor infiltrating his disbelieving look. "Later on there was another rumor. A half million in cold cash in exchange for the eleven keys, no questions asked, no positions taken. I passed that one up as being a little too far out in orbit." He studied his fingernails, surprisingly well manicured. "That's the kind of thing an amateur might do, a naive amateur."

"Oh, I don't know. I see stuff like that on TV all the time, and insurance companies are always buying back stolen goods. I've handled a few of those transactions. They work. Everyone concerned is happy. The insurance company passes along its loss to the public, the owner gets his goods back, and the thief makes a little something for his trouble."

"I don't suppose you happen to know where this alleged rip-off took place?"

"Yep. A long narrow milo field out behind Chief Ward Bannion's house."

"Jesus Christ! Ward Bannion? You're not telling me he's—"

"All I'm telling you is that it happened in his field. I didn't say he was there. As a matter of fact, he wasn't. He rarely spends a weekend at home and that's when the drops were scheduled."

"Drops? Airplanes? Dammit, I knew they were bringing it in somewhere around here. I tried to tell those assholes in Austin that we needed some spotters spread around on top of some of those hills, but they keep screaming about manpower shortages and budget cuts."

"Same old song and dance. The poor kids don't get breakfast, either; who do you blame?"

He raked a hand down across his face, then made a fist and pounded his thigh. "Jesus Christ, I've been hanging around this dump for almost a year now and you come in here—what's it been, six, seven days?—and you find out all this good—"

"Five, actually," I said thoughtfully. "Or maybe it's only four—"

"—shit about the local dopers. How the hell did you do that? And did you ever think about joining up with the DEA?"

"I'm not much of a joiner. Last time I joined something, I almost got my ass shot off in Vietnam."

"That was a bummer war, man."

"What the hell do you know about it?" I said coldly. "You were still banging knotholes out in the barn—"

"Hey, man, come on, I didn't mean anything—"

"Didn't your Mama ever tell you not to badmouth somebody else's war? It was *our* war, the only one we had, and we fought it damn well. I'd be pleased to hear the name of *your* war. And I'd be pleased to shake your hand and say well done brother for defending your country like we did." I wasn't nearly as heated as I sounded, but I was tired and hungry and he appeared to be in no hurry to go.

"Shit!" He bounced to his feet, his expression somewhere between sullen and angry. "I wasn't *badmouthing* your damned war! I *loved* your damned war! I saw Rambo *three* times! I *admired* you guys although most of you didn't have sense enough to pour piss out of a boot!" At some point during his tirade, he had puffed up, eyes sparking fire, color bleeding into his face—Cagney facing down Bogart, Mickey Rooney on the prod.

We stared at each other. I could feel myself relenting, but before I could form a forgiving smile, he stormed off the canvas patio, out of the sphere of light, maybe if I was lucky, out of my life.

After a moment, I shrugged and lit a cigarette, went inside the motor home looking for something to eat.

Oh well, he'd never be a close friend anyway.

It was my night for visitors. An hour or so later Ward Bannion and Nathan Barr showed up on my metal doorstep, clamoring for admittance, demanding wine, women, and song and, failing that, the next best thing, a beer. I judged by the shine in their eyes and their boisterous manner that they had already had a few, or many.

"Well, my friend, how goes the battle?" Nathan Barr asked, popping the tab on a can of beer, eyeing me with the solemn dignity of the near drunk. "Old Ward here tells me you've been making some giant strides in your investigation."

"Baby steps might be a more apt description."

"Don't be modest," Ward rumbled. "It don't become you. You're good at what you do, so come on and admit it. It ain't a brag if you can do it."

"How's your dad, Nate?"

He held out a hand and waggled it. "No better and not much worse, I guess. It was sorta a false alarm. My sister tends to get hysterical every time Dad snorts in his sleep."

"Won't take me but a minute to get my stuff together," I said. "I sure appreciate your hospitality—"

"Hey, wait a minute, man! I didn't come over here to put you out. I'm spending the night with Ward, and as many nights as it takes. Okay? I came by to pick up a bottle of insulin and some needles. Drugstore's already closed and I ain't had my shot for the day. All right? Now let's don't hear any more about it."

"I appreciate the offer, Nate, but I can't just walk in and take over your home this—"

"Thought I said I didn't want to hear any more about it. Now, let's just break out another beer and you guys tell me what's happened while I was gone."

I let Ward do most of the telling, partly because I could see he enjoyed it, partly because I was tired of talking. Tired of telling the same thing over and over and resolving nothing in the process. When Ward finished, Nate leaned back in the little booth, cerulean eyes brighter in a face that had gone several shades paler.

"Jesus, Dan, that was great detective work, man, figuring out where it happened like that. That's like magic, man. How the hell do you do it? I'm serious, how the hell do you do it?"

Ward laughed and I shrugged. "No magic. The best I can say for myself is that I'm a good listener. I listen when people talk and they tell me things, sometimes things they don't intend to tell, or don't know they're telling."

Ward snorted. "Modest. Didn't I tell you? Same way in Nam. I find him fighting the whole damn VC army and he just says 'hi,' or some damn thing and goes back to chopping VC."

"I was shell-shocked," I said. "And anyway, even a cornered rabbit will sometimes fight back."

"It must have been terrible to be killed like that," Nate said. "It's such a pretty little spot there under the trees."

Ward shook his head. "Too much modesty is as bad as not enough. He wouldn't even take the Silver Star they wanted to give him, so how in hell could I take mine?" The scowl he threw my way was too real to be faked.

"Had nothing to do with me," I said. "Mine was a conscience call. I didn't deserve it. I was fighting for my life, nothing more, nothing less."

"Gloomy as hell at night, though," Nate said, looking at me then back at Ward, trying to bring the conversation back on track. "You figured out why they moved the bodies?"

Ward gave him a disgusted look, the scowl lingering. "If they were using my milo field for a Saturday night dope drop, then they wouldn't be wanting to call attention to it, now would they?"

Nate's lips pursed. "Yeah, hey, I guess that's right."

"Give the kid from Missouri a gold star," Ward said, affable again, rising and stretching his big body until it creaked. He winked at me and I wondered if I had imagined the fleeting glimpse of animosity I had seen in his face.

"Come on, kid, get your insulin and let's get out of here and let the man get his sleep."

"It's early," I protested, but without much conviction, and Ward laughed.

"It's plain to see you've been missing a lot of beauty sleep lately. You want to keep that purty wife of yours, you'd better be catching up."

"I keep trying and trying," I said. "But I don't see any results in the mirror."

Nate slammed the refrigerator door, scooped up a handful of packaged needles out of a drawer. He held up the bottle of insulin. "Gotta take a chaser for all this beer."

"You ought to see it," Ward said. "He sticks that damn needle right in his belly." He shuddered and rubbed his stomach. "God, I couldn't do that. In the ass, maybe."

Nate shrugged. "You could if you had to. You can do anything if you have to."

Ward herded him through the door. "Well, right now we have to go. So go. See you later, Dan."

"Take it easy," I said. "And thanks again, Nate."

"Stay cool, man," Nate said, then jumped away from Ward's prodding thumb. "Dammit, Ward, if you wasn't such a big bastard—"

I closed the door on the rest of it. I dumped the empty cans and the ashtray and wiped the table. I cleaned up my mess from dinner and decided against another beer. I took a cold shower, had one last cigarette, and went to bed.

I couldn't sleep. Something nagged. Nibbled at the outer reaches of my mind like a school of minnows around a crippled mayfly. Something heard or something seen. I had no idea when or where or what. I knew from experience that struggling only made it worse, sent it burrowing deeper into the labyrinth. So I cleared my mind of Jerico Falls and environs, of murders and felons pushing dope.

Instead I thought of warm places and soothing sounds, of loving glances from liquid eyes, of cloudless skies. But that didn't work either, so I went directly to my ruse of last resort: counting highway buzzards around an armadillo kill.

It's an old Texas remedy for insomnia that's not for everyone, but, as always, it worked for me.

35

I SLEPT POORLY, BUCOLIC DREAMS ETCHED WITH AMOR-
phous menace and nameless dread. Sometime during the
early morning hours it grew colder and I awoke chilled and
stiff as old sun dried leather. Nothing resolved. No miracu-
lous enlightenment during my troubled sleep. The puzzle
remained, unsolved, and I realized with a cold sodden lump
in my chest that I didn't know where to go next, who to see,
what to say.

A cigarette helped some, as did bacon and eggs, and for
one of the few times in my life I wished I could stand the
taste of coffee. I had cold milk instead, three fingers of orange juice as a chaser. I cleaned up my mess and went outside, thinking the brisk air might clear the cobwebs out of
my mind.

The air was more than brisk, it was downright chilly. I
went back inside and put on a coat.

I was coming through the door a second time when I caught
the flash of movement in the pasture, down by the line of
trees that bordered the creek. Flashes of movement weren't
at all uncommon out in the field; cows moved all the time,
as did birds, an occasional dog, or wild animal, a human
being now and again.

But this flash seemed somehow different, a splash of vivid yellow against the dark trees, too large to be a bird, too high off the ground to be a dog, too fast moving to be a cow. That left human, an odd erratic human to be sure, zigzagging up the gentle slope in short staggering bursts, only to fall to all fours, head hanging low as if sniffing out the spoor of some unknown prey, rising again to resume the awkward run, veering sometimes to the left or to the right, but always heading in my general direction. I watched his painful progress up the hill and realized that I had known almost from the first that it was Bobby Radcross and that he was heading straight for me.

I went inside the motor home again, picked up the Smith & Wesson Airweight, and went back outside.

Bobby Radcross was standing twenty feet from the fence, weaving back and forth like a drunken highwire act. I could hear his rasping breath, a sobbing sound as he tried to swallow and talk at the same time and could do neither. The lower half of his face was smeared with blood, his yellow shirt ripped and flapping; the right knee was gone out of his jeans, his hair plastered to his forehead with what looked like a thin coating of slime, his lower pants legs mud-smeared.

We looked at each other while he gathered breath; I let him see me put the gun in my waistband. I lit a cigarette and waited.

"They not—" He stopped, swallowed, and tried again. "They're not here yet?"

There was desperation in his voice, a touch of humility I couldn't quite believe. "Who's not here?" I asked kindly, wondering if he could be coming down from some strange new trip.

"Paw—Paw and my two brothers." He staggered forward as far as the fence and stared at me, a pleading look in his wild eyes. "Maybe Lucy had . . . had some trouble finding them. I called—God, it seems like hours ago."

"You called . . . from out there?"

"From Stafford's Crossing where this creek goes under the highway."

"You used a phone, though?" I felt it was a point that needed clarification.

"Hell yes! Of course I used—" He broke off, teetering, catching a fence post with one beefy hand, staring at the five strands of barbwire as if they presented an insurmountable obstacle. "Jesus Christ, Mr. Roman. They—you was right all along. Them sonsabitches tried to kill me!"

"Which sonsabitches were those, Bobby?"

"Right out there in broad daylight! I was on my way to work, out on the county road. Right down from our lane. Paw and Lace and Drew was already gone, and I was in a hurry and this damn big black pickup had the road blocked and when I slowed down to see if I could help, them bastards stepped around that truck and cut down on me with automatics. Man, I mean machine guns! MAC-10's or Uzi's, or like that. They got the front end with the first burst, the windshield and the front tires, and that little car zipped straight into the ditch. Only thing that kept them from killing me. I fell out the door on the far side and crawled into that overflow drain they got across there to help out when Crooked Creek is in flood. Man, I was hauling ass. I knew sooner or later they'd hit the gas tank and that car would go up like a rocket. I was coming out the other side when she went off and I just dove headfirst into them high weeds along there figuring they'd be watching the car. Guess they was. They got out of there pretty fast after that." He pressed down on the top strand of wire, gauging his chances of straddling the fence. It didn't give. He cursed and kicked the post.

"What were you doing out there? I think I remember seeing a sign at Stafford's Crossing. That's a long way from here."

"You telling me, man? Must be three miles at least. And I don't know how many more following this damn crooked creek—no wonder they call it that—and I run near about every step of the way."

"Why?"

"Because I know where you were staying, man. I knowed

208

that creek would bring me out over here behind Nash's Garage.''

"Why, Bobby? So you could tell me I was right?''

"Oh, hell no, man. Just because—'' He broke off and made an ironic grimace. "Man, I know it's crazy as hell. You come in here hassling me, beating on me, kidnaping my ass, putting on handcuffs and threatening me with guns and snakes and . . . and, Christ knows it's crazy, but you're the only bastard in this town right now I trust.'' He gave me a silly grin. "Ain't that the shits?'' He wiped a rivulet of blood trickling into his left eye. "That don't include my family, of course.''

"What's wrong with the Sheriff, with Ward Bannion? You'd have saved yourself a lot of exercise and they would have picked you up—''

"Hell, man. Gil Grossman is our deputy and I wouldn't trust that crooked bastard as far as I could throw him. He shook me and Stevie down lots of times, took our money and our dope and kicked our asses, but he kept the money and the dope for himself.'' He kicked the fence post again, yanked on the top wire. "Man, I've got to get over there and sit down or I'm gonna wipe out.''

I walked over and held the wires open for him, keeping my right hand free. He crawled through slowly, like an old dog with arthritis. I watched him hobble to the patio and drop limply into one of the chairs. He groaned, his head dropping forward into his hands.

"You need a drink?''

"Yeah. Make it a beer. I had plenty of water on the way.''

I got him a can of beer and moved the other chair a few feet away, facing him. The gun gouged my stomach. I laid it on the canvas deck beside me. Radcross drank half the beer in one gulp, wiped his mouth carefully and grinned crookedly. "You won't need that gun. I swear.''

"Where'd you get the cuts on your face? Glass?''

He touched his cheek tenderly. "I guess so. I started ducking soon as I saw what they was up to, but that windshield just kinda seemed to explode. And too, there's thickets all along the creek. I followed the cow trails, but they ain't tall as a man and there was a lot of brush."

"You could have called Ward Bannion. Even if it was outside the city limits, he'd have picked you up. You trust Ward, don't you?"

He emptied the beer can into his mouth, then absently crushed it between long thick fingers. "I always thought so. I used to see him a lot when me and Stevie—but I don't know anymore, man. Blood is thicker'n water."

"What the hell has that got to do with it?"

His shoulders hunched, short neck disappearing into his shirt collar. His bloodshot eyes came up to meet mine and I felt a faint chill creep across the back of my head, into the pockets behind my ears.

"Big Bwana, man. That was Big Bwana out there trying to waste me today. It had to be, man, who else would it be?"

I stared at him silently. It was his ball, he'd have to run with it.

"Blood kin, man. The closest there is and I'm betting he killed Stevie too, shot him down like somebody's stray dog and all over a pot full of skag that Stevie never got a dime out of."

"You recognized him then," I said mechanically. "The man who shot at you?"

"I've knowed him all my life, and it was broad daylight."

"Who?" I knew the answer, but I had to hear him say it.

"Cody Bannion. How was I gonna tell Ward his brother Cody was the one shot at me? Maybe he wouldn't've even believed me. Maybe he would and . . ." He let it trail away and shrugged. "Blood's thicker'n water."

"The other man?"

"I've seen him around a lot lately. I've never heard his name. If I have I've forgot it." He went on to describe Leonard Nueboldt right down to his biker clothes and ungodly smell. "Everybody thought he was a narc, man, ain't that rich?"

"Rich," I echoed hollowly, suddenly realizing that I had told Nueboldt about Bobby Radcross, that evidently Steve had told them nothing the night he was killed, that they had not known about the Houston fiasco or that Steve had a partner in crime. They had known nothing beyond the fact that they had lost eleven kilos of heroin, not until I had obligingly filled Nueboldt in. The thought left a bitter taste in my mouth.

I took out a cigarette. A car door slammed out on the parking lot next to the garage.

Radcross got up and limped to the front of the motor home. "There's Paw and them. They got our guns. Good. I hope them sonsabitches try it again." He lifted a thick arm and waved, then turned back to me. "I ain't going to no Virgins Islands or nothing, but I am going to kin in Dallas for a while, until this all gets straightened out." He hesitated, moved around in a small half-circle. "I guess I should have guessed it was Steve's daddy all along. Mainly 'cause Stevie was too cool. Like he wasn't worried about being found out or nothing, like he thought his daddy wouldn't really do anything to him, not anything bad." He chuckled harshly. "I guess he was wrong, huh?"

I didn't answer. After a moment, he went out of sight around the corner of the motor home.

I finished the cigarette.

36

"I DON'T BELIEVE IT!" WARD THUNDERED, SLAPPING THE top of his desk with a plate-sized hand. "That Radcross kid is lying through his goddamned teeth!" He leaped to his feet and stomped to the window, stood looking out over his view of the square, broad powerful body stiffly upright, hands on hips balled into fists. He whirled on me. "Do you believe him?"

"He didn't lie about the car. We both saw that. I counted more than thirty bullet holes not counting the ones that went through the windows—"

"I know that! I saw that too, dammit! So somebody tried to fry his ass. That don't mean it was Cody."

"Why would he say it was if it wasn't, Ward? Does he have anything against Cody? Cody's son was his best friend. He told me Cody always treated him well. So, why would he lie?"

"I don't know, dammit, but he did. And why the hell did he run off like he did?"

"He's scared. Without having to give it much thought, I'd say he has a right to be. A government man and a man he's known all his life try to gun him down on an open road?

212

Wouldn't you be a little afraid in his shoes? He's got a man's body, Ward, but he's still a kid.''

He walked slowly back to his chair and sat down, raked both hands through his tangled mass of silver hair. He shook his head. ''No way Cody could have shot Stevie. Even . . . even if he is involved in the drug thing, there's just no way he could have—could have shot his own son.''

''It's hard to believe,'' I said.

''I don't believe it,'' he said emphatically. ''There's not one shred of evidence that says he did.''

''You've got that right,'' I said. ''There's not one shred of evidence that anyone killed them, but somebody did. We know that because we have the bodies.''

A puzzled frown rippled across his brow. ''What the hell does that mean?''

''Nothing. And that's my point. We have two dead bodies with no physical evidence linking anyone to their death. That means the human factors become that much more important, the two primary factors being motive and opportunity. We know Cody had a motive, assuming that he is Big Bwana, but has anyone ever asked him where he was between eight and ten o'clock on the night of the murders? Have you?''

''Hell, no, that would have been—'' He broke off, obviously groping for the right word.

''Indelicate? Impertinent? Or just gross? Hold on, don't get all hot and sweaty. I haven't asked him either and we both are at fault. Parents kill their offspring for a multitude of reasons. Cody had a good one ready-made and waiting. He hates the Caulders. How much does he hate the Caulders? Only he knows that. Only he knows whether he'd rather see his son dead than married to one.''

''My God, I can't believe that,'' Ward said, his voice scratchy, just above a whisper.

''I'm having some problems with it myself, but don't you think we should at least ask him?''

''I guess we'll have to,'' he said, the words trickling off his tongue like lumps of toxic waste.

''And if we don't hurry a bit,'' I said, ''the county will

beat us to him. You don't think Bobby Radcross's dad is going to let this pass, do you?''

"No, he won't,'' he said soberly. "He might even try to settle it himself, him and them other two sons of his. He's not one to go running to the law much.'' He stood up abruptly and crossed to a metal locker pushed into one corner of the room. He opened the door and took down a gunbelt and holstered gun, a thick heavy belt and a long bone-handled gun. He strapped it around his waist, settled it snugly on his hips. He took out the gun and checked the cylinder, snapped it back into the scabbard, tested it for ease of pull. He looked up and found me watching.

"Cody's gun. Usta be, anyway. Belonged to Dad. Cody gave it to me when I took this job. Too damn big and uncomfortable to wear it all the time. I use a clip-on .38 mostly, Police Chief Special. I hate carrying a gun, but it's part of the job. So far I haven't had to shoot anybody.''

"Why are you wearing that one this time?''

He lifted the gun and let it slip back into the holster. "I'm not sure. Making a statement, maybe. Letting Cody know we're serious about this. Most of the time he don't take me very seriously. I guess that comes from being the older brother, I don't know.'' He looked me over. "You got a gun?''

"It's in the truck.''

"Well, get it,'' he said. He took a hat off the top of the cabinet, a low-crowned Stetson I'd never seen him wear. It went well with his uniform. For the first time he looked like a cop.

"Beats the hell out of that silly little black beret,'' I said as we left the office.

"Maybe,'' he said, "but things were a hell of a lot simpler back then.''

Cody Bannion's ranchhouse was less than a five minute drive from Ward's old yellow frame. A well-tended, one-story brick veneer, it had obviously been built during a time when energy was cheap. A huge picture window fronted the wrap-around white rock driveway, aimed fearlessly into the western sun. The roof had the rugged, dull-gray patina of hand-worked cedar shingles, another daring innovation in this hot dry land where fire stations were few and far between, where water to fight a fire came from wells and tanker trucks rather than a corner hydrant.

Cody Bannion's stake bed pickup was parked near the top of the looping driveway. A dark brown Dodge sat next to it, vaguely familiar, mud-splashed and road-grimed, windows so darkly tinted and dirty it was next to impossible to see inside. Ward parked beside it.

We sat looking at the house, forty feet or so away. I lit a cigarette and shoved the Airweight into my waistband. Ward lit a cigarette and sneered, a feeble attempt at humor I knew he didn't feel.

"Better watch it, little buddy, you'll shoot off your reason for living."

"First smart thing you've said today."

He sighed and flipped the cigarette out the window. "Might as well get this over, he won't come to us."

But he was wrong. We were out and walking when the front door opened. Cody came stumbling through, his hands behind his back, hatless and coatless. He stopped in the middle of the porch as if on command; a short, bulky figure appeared behind him. From his free-flowing unkempt hair to his drooping untidy boots, Leonard Nueboldt looked exactly the same. He turned and closed the door and looked at us and added a smile.

"Sorry, gents, if you've come to arrest him. I reckon I've beat you to it." He lifted a suitcase he held in his left hand. "Enough skag in here to keep the whole damn country happy for a week." He laughed and appeared to notice the large black automatic in his right hand for the first time. He shoved it into his waistband. "Sorry about this, Chief, but I guess by now you know about your brother here. Killed some kid out on the county road east of here this morning, but you've probably already heard about that. If I hadn't of happened along, he'da got away with it, too." He took Cody's arm and moved him forward to the steps. They stepped down, slowly, carefully.

"This is bullshit, Ward," I said, feeling the muscles contract in my stomach, a quick sharp jolt of adrenaline. "They're running a number on us."

"Yeah," Ward growled, then raised his voice. "What about it, Cody, what's going on here?"

Cody raised his head, his face pale and emotionless. He lifted his shoulders in a shrug—and kept on lifting, right arm swinging wide to clear the stubby little machine gun he had been holding behind his back.

"Watch it!" Ward roared, right hand driving for his gun.

I was already watching it, the blur of Nueboldt's hand slapping for the gun, ripping it free, coming up to eye level.

He was faster than me. I realized that from the beginning, duplicating his movements but lagging one click behind—right up to the precious split second he wasted to aim.

I was turning as I drew, firing the second my gun was clear, firing instinctively, the way I had been taught to do.

And I flat out beat him to it. He never got off his shot. Nerveless fingers can't pull triggers, and my bullet shattered the life in his arm. The gun fell. He staggered backwards, hit the edge of the porch, and sat down hard.

Cody lay sprawled in the yard, his gun lying in the dirt, the selector set on automatic. Ward stood swaying, the long gun hanging from his hand, his face deathly pale. Try as I might, I couldn't remember hearing another shot.

I leaned over Cody, but Ward stopped me with an inarticulate sound. He put away the gun. "Leave him, Dan. He's dead."

I nodded and continued on to where Nueboldt sat moaning and rocking on the edge of the porch. The injured hand lay limply in his lap, curled slightly, palm covered with blood. I helped him off with his leather coat.

"You sonuvabitch," he said weakly. "You've ruined my arm."

"Bit of a mess, all right." I took out my handkerchief, gripped two corners, and whipped it into a roll. The bullet had entered his arm through the center of the bicep and I suspected a shattered bone. Anytime now the shock would be wearing off and he would need something stronger than aspirin.

"You're lucky I didn't go for an eye," I said. "No way to apply a tourniquet." I found a short stick and twisted the rolled handkerchief snug around his arm. "Here, you take over. If it's still bleeding too much to suit you, just twist it a little more." I scooped up his gun and went over to Ward, standing beside his van, smoking, head down.

"We'd better get somebody out here with some painkiller. Any minute now Howdy Doody over there is going to start climbing the porch posts. You want to get on the horn?"

"Jesus Christ, Dan, I killed him!" His voice was thick, breaking.

"Jesus Christ, Ward," I said, imitating him without meaning to. "What the hell do you think he was gonna do with that stutter gun? Prune his trees? He had it on rock and roll, man! That was a goddamn gook trick they almost pulled on us. A gook trick on his own brother. Don't waste your grief on him." I stared at his stricken face, breathing deeply, the anger draining as swiftly as it had come. I pushed Nueboldt's gun into his hand. "Do your job, Ward. He could bleed to death on us."

He nodded jerkily and stepped into the van. He reached behind the seat and placed Nueboldt's gun beside the MAC-10 he had taken from Cody. He picked up the mike, then put it down again, and looked at me.

"When I left Nam, man, I swore I'd never kill another man. Then they sent me into the field in the Feebies and I had to do that, I had to kill a man. I quit. Eventually, that cost me my wife and kids. I came back here figuring this would be safe. But I guess no place is safe. It hurt like hell the other times I killed, even the gooks." He stopped and wet his lips. "But not like this, never like this." He shook his head. "I'll have to quit again. Move on."

"It's a long road, man, when you're running." I turned on my heel and walked away from him, understanding how he felt, unable to do more than silently commiserate with him. It was something he would have to work through by himself, balance self-preservation against fraternal love. He wouldn't believe it at the moment, but self-preservation would win hands down. Years, months, perhaps even weeks from now he would think of this day and feel a twinge of sorrow at what had happened, a rush of gratitude that it had ended as well as it had.

I sat down beside Nueboldt and checked the bleeding. It was barely oozing. His face was as white as the gravel in the driveway, eyes squinted with pain. Sweat glistened across his forehead, above his upper lip.

"Jesus, man, are they on the way?"

"Well," I said, and paused to light a cigarette. "Old Ward there is waiting for my signal. Once they get here you'll be out of our hands and there's some things I need to know first."

"You sonuvabitch!"

"That's twice, Nueboldt, and you haven't smiled either time. One more time and I'll take back my hanky." I shoved the cigarette between his lips and lit another. He puffed hungrily, tilting his eyes away from the smoke.

"I want to know about Steve and Lisa. Who killed them, you or Cody?"

He took one last drag and spat out the cigarette. "You're crazy, man, we didn't kill them two kids. I don't know what the hell you're talking about."

"Wrong answer, Leonard. Look, I know you set a trap for Steve, a dummy shipment and nobody there to pick it up. You'd done it before without results. But this time, this Saturday night, it worked. Steve went out for the box and you and Cody were waiting. You tied them up and put on blindfolds, and I guess now I know why you did that. Cody couldn't stand to have them looking at him when you killed them."

"No way, man," he said earnestly, leaning forward, weaving. "Okay, we were there. What you said about the trap was true. I caught them. I tied them up, then I went and

218

got Cody. He made me put blindfolds on them before he would even come close. He thought Steve didn't know about him, but I knew he did. But you couldn't tell Cody anything. It had to be his way or not at all. He just watched while I tried to scare Steve into telling what happened to the eleven keys. I'll have to give the little bastard credit. He was cool. He stood there grinning, telling me I'd better check with the boss before I touched a hair on his head. I wanted to kill the little shit, but Cody just shook his head. He drug me off out of earshot of the kids and told me to let them go. Then he walked back down to where we parked the car and waited while I—'' He broke off, shivering. "Man, I'm hurting."

"While you what?" I spoke loudly to drown out the first faint sounds of wailing sirens. "While you went back and shot them?"

"Hell, no, man! I told you. I didn't cut them loose like Cody wanted, though. I just left them where they were, blindfolds and all. I told Steve I'd be watching his ass and then I took off with Cody." His head lifted as the siren sounds became unmistakable. He looked at me. "You lied to me, man."

"Yeah, I guess I did. Well, fair's fair, Leonard. You've been lying like hell for the past few minutes yourself. You're asking me to believe someone came along after you and Cody left, found the kids all trussed up like Christmas turkeys, and decided to blow out their brains. You hang on to that story, Leonard, it oughta slide you right into the little blue room with the gurney and disposable needles."

"It's the truth, man," he said, his voice muted, almost indifferent, as if he had lost interest in the subject. He made a gagging sound and began to tilt forward, eyes rolling back in his head.

I caught him and eased him back on the porch. I checked the wound. He had relaxed his hold on the tourniquet and blood was flowing again. I twisted it tight and wedged the stick beneath his arm.

I stood up and lit a cigarette, wiped blood from my fingertips on Nueboldt's trouser leg. The sirens were close. I could see flashes of movement through the line of trees out on the highway. Ward was still in the van, head resting on his arms folded around the steering wheel. Cody lay where we had left him, blood trickling out from beneath his body. Big blue flies buzzed around his head, dive-bombed the leaking blood.

My stomach rolled. I looked back at the highway and guessed I had about a minute left.

I walked over and leaned against an oak tree and vomited.

37

IT TOOK A WHILE TO GET IT ALL STRAIGHTENED OUT. IT involved telling our stories to a tall corpulent deputy with big ears and nervous hands and, later, telling them again to Sheriff James Brindley in Ward's office in Jerico Falls. Sheriff Brindley was also corpulent, red-faced, and bald. He had an irregular tic under his left eye, a mole on his cheek with three long curling hairs. His manner was affable, however, his smile large and toothy and always wet at the edges. He oozed camaraderie, fellowship, and seemed to genuinely want to understand.

"Where do you reckon them fellers were going with all that money?" He looked first at Ward, then at me. I looked at Ward.

Ward shrugged. "My guess is they were getting ready to run. After the Radcross boy got away this morning they must have known everything was going to come undone. Cody didn't like it here, anyway. Never has. He always wanted to go back east somewhere, somewhere there ain't no rocks or cactus or mesquite. He wasn't any good at ranching and he knew it. But he just kept on trying, selling off a piece of land every year or two to keep his head above water. I don't know, maybe that's what got him started in all this dope business."

"A million dollars," Brindley marveled. "I've never seen that much money before all in one place." He opened the suitcase and stared at the neat rows of bills as if to make sure they were still there. "I'll have to keep this as evidence. If it turns out it is drug money, then it'll have to go to the state." He looked at Ward.

Ward shrugged again. "It's not mine, that's for sure."

"And there's our other case," Brindley said. "Your nephew and the Caulder girl. You think we can make a case against Nueboldt?"

Ward hooked a thumb in my direction. "Dan here can tell you more about that than I can."

Brindley turned bright inquisitive eyes on me. "What do you think, Mr. Roman?"

"I don't know. Unless he confesses, and I doubt that very seriously, all you have is my word that he told me he was there. My word against his, and he is, after all, a government man. Offhand, I'd say no."

"But you think he did it?"

"It makes sense that way. I have no proof one way or the other."

"We can charge him with assault with a deadly weapon." He glanced at Ward, then back at me. "You can both attest to that."

"Yeah, we can do that," Ward said. "But he's the one who got shot."

"Your best bet," I said, "is to charge him with attempted murder."

Brindley frowned. "You mean the Radcross boy?"

I nodded.

"But you said the boy left town for Dallas or somewhere."

"That's what he said, but he may change his mind now that he has nothing to fear."

"Well," he said, and passed a large hairy hand across his florid face. "I'll do that then. I'll charge Nueboldt with assault with a deadly weapon and attempted murder. He's a bad cop, whatever we can get him for won't be enough to suit me." He struggled out of Ward's swivel chair and held out his hand. "We'll need you to come back down here for the hearing and trial, Mr. Roman. I appreciate your cooperation."

"Glad to help."

He picked up the suitcase and crossed to the door. He opened it and gave the heavy bag to one of his two waiting deputies. "Guard that with your lives, men," he said, and looked back at us and winked. He laughed, lifted a long beefy arm in a friendly wave, and left.

Ward pushed away from the cabinet he was leaning on and sat down in his chair. He took out a cigarette, lit it, then leaned back, washing his face with both hands.

I lit a Carlton and smoked silently, waiting for him. I had nothing much to say and if I found he felt the same way, then I could go. On the other hand I'd stay and talk as long as he wanted to talk. I owed him much more than that.

After what seemed like a long time he mashed out the cigarette and came forward in the chair, spatulate fingers coming together in the center of the desk. He stared down at them.

"I guess it's finished."

"I guess so," I said.

"You think he—you think Cody killed them, don't you?"

"I can't say that, Ward. The only one who can is Nueboldt and he says no."

"You can't believe him. He's smart enough to know he'd draw an accessory if he told the truth."

"Maybe," I said. "And maybe he's the one who pulled the trigger."

"That's possible," he said, and sighed deeply. "Carol Anne is coming in tonight." His face reshaped itself along pleasant lines.

"Good. That's good. I was gonna suggest we tie one on, but Carol Anne is definitely better."

"Yeah, well maybe. She can be a firesnorter when she gets mad and she left here mad."

"Not really. She was smiling. Anyway, you've talked to her since then."

"Yeah, until you cut us off."

"Sorry."

He smiled faintly. "I've always wondered how women could be so soft on the outside and so tough inside. You ever wonder about that?"

"No, as a matter of fact, I never did. You think about deep stuff like that a lot?"

"Some of the things Cody's been doing make more sense now," he said, abruptly changing the subject. "Back in June he mortgaged the ranch. All of it. He didn't know I knew, but you can't keep secrets in a small town. I figure now it was to pay somebody back for the drugs Steve stole off him."

"Makes sense. He was part of a pipeline and he would have been responsible for the drugs until they were passed on to the next phase of the operation."

"Nueboldt?"

"No, I think Nueboldt and Cody were partners. Norma Dew said there were always two men waiting for the drop. Lisa told Norma. She got her information from Steve."

"Makes you wonder who Cody passed the drugs to."

"No it doesn't. I'm not even curious. That's somebody else's chestnut."

He pushed back from his desk and stood up. He laid the Stetson on the cabinet and took off the gunbelt. He hung it carefully in the metal locker, then moved to the window and stood looking out, one hand braced on the frame.

"I'd like to be alone for a while, Dan, if you don't mind."

I stood up. "You bet, Ward. I'll stop by before I leave . . . I guess that'll be in the morning."

He nodded without turning.

I left.

I called Abel Caulder from one of the public phones along the east wall of the Civic Center. He had already heard from Tony and knew much of what had happened; I filled him in on the rest.

Ultimately, we agreed that the case for me was finished, that with Cody dead and Leonard Nueboldt out of reach there was little more I could do, that the story Nueboldt had told me didn't make a lot of sense but it would now be up to the ponderous machinery of the law to accept or reject, to establish a germ of truth and bring about a measure of justice.

Neither of us had much faith in that.

"I'll be in town tomorrow," he said. "I'll be at the *Gazette* with Tony from about ten to twelve. If you'd like we can take a walk over to the bank and I can give you your fee in cash."

"That won't be necessary. Tony has my address. Just send me a check."

"That'll be fine, Mr. Roman. I want to add my thanks."

"I wish the answer could be more clearcut. I wish I could say to you that Cody killed your girl, or that Nueboldt did. I can't do that, and I'm sorry."

"Don't be," he said shortly. "I'm satisfied that one of them did. Which one doesn't seem to matter as much as it did. If it was Cody, he's dead, and I intend to see that Nueboldt goes to prison."

We talked for a few minutes more, then said our goodbyes and I hung up the receiver feeling resigned but vaguely dissatisfied. I had correctly expressed my feelings to Abel Caulder. I liked precise, well-defined answers, and not knowing exactly what had happened that night in the milo field left me with an empty gnawing feeling of incompleteness, of failure. If Nueboldt was telling the truth then I had accomplished nothing beyond a temporary disruption of a drug pipeline from Mexico. There were other fields, plenty of other greedy people waiting to replace Nueboldt and Cody. If, on the other hand, Nueboldt was lying—and that seemed likely—and one of them, or both, had committed the two murders, then a measure of justice had already been achieved with Cody's death, more to be realized when and if Nueboldt was convicted and sent to Huntsville. As an ex-cop he would live an extremely precarious life in a prison system that boasted more murders each year than a lot of medium-sized cities.

In the end justice would more than likely prevail, but it

was the not knowing, the little black bug of uncertainty, that I found discomfiting.

I ate a hamburger at a fast food restaurant out on the highway and drove to the motor home in a sort of gray-blue funk. Even the weather had changed to match my mood, dark thunderheads off in the west, a dreary gray ceiling hanging low and ominous just above the treetops. The air was steeped with damp slippery moisture and my ant bites began to itch again. I scratched lightly, carefully, while I drove, but that served only to aggravate, and by the time I reached the motor home they were burning and stinging as much as they ever had.

I went inside and found the tube of Caldocel and came back outside again. I propped my foot on one of the aluminum chairs and slipped up my pants leg. To my layman's eye the bites looked much better, smaller and not as red, a kind of sickly pink instead. I wondered why they were burning and itching, then decided it must either be the humidity or my prickly frame of mind.

I was applying the ointment straight out of the tube when I heard the crunch of dried grass behind me, the scuff of feet on the canvas patio, a muffled mirthful noise that sounded more like a giggle than a laugh. I turned my head.

Nathan Barr stood watching me, weaving, a loosely co-ordinated grin on his face, eyelids at half-mast over blue eyes shot with blood. He wore a cowboy hat, a lightweight denim jacket, and faded jeans. The tail of a crisp white dress shirt dangled outside his pants.

"Howdy, pardner," he said, waving a half-pint bottle of something I strongly suspected was whiskey under my nose. "What'cha doing?" He peered at my leg and made the smothered laughing sound again. "Gotcha some ant bites, huh? Little buggers itch like hell, don't they? Mine's about all cleared up, though." He waved the bottle again. "How about a little drinkee? Good old Tennessee stuff. Guaranteed to blow your . . . hat off." Off balance, he took an involuntary step sideways and stopped himself with a hand against the motor home. "How about it?"

"I was about ready to have a beer, Nate. When I get started with the hard stuff I usually don't know when to stop, so I'd better stick with the beer."

"Hell, ain't nobody around here gonna tell you to stop. You can drink as much as you damn well want."

"Yeah, but that little old half-pint you got there wouldn't go far with a couple of hard-knockers like me and you."

"I've got more," he said earnestly, leaning forward, taking a leg-jerking step to keep from falling. "I got some more in the car and there's them two bottles you didn't even touch in there in the cabinet."

I shook my head and laughed. "I'd better not, Nate. I'll be pulling out in the morning and if there's anything I hate to do it's drive with a hangover."

"Pulling out—" He straightened, his face suddenly solemn. "I heard about . . . about Cody and that other feller. I guess old Ward's plenty low. I wish I knew what to say to him, but I don't guess it matters what you say, it don't help much at a time like this."

"Not much," I agreed. I doctored the bumps on my other leg and let the pants drop around my boot. I inspected the tube of ointment and shook my head ruefully. "I've about used up your Caldocel. I'll replace it before I leave—"

"No way, man. I don't need it anymore; anyhow, I bought another tube while I was gone to . . . to Missouri." He hiccuped and removed the top from the whiskey bottle. He held it out. "You sure you don't want a little nip?"

"No, thanks, Nate. I'll take a raincheck."

"Okay, man," he said, and tilted the bottle. I watched his Adams's apple bob up and down.

"Look, Nate, why don't you bunk here tonight? I can—"

"Hey, no, man." He lurched away from the motor home, an almost frightened look on his face. "I gotta lot of celebrating to do yet tonight. I promised old Ward I'd be back out to his place, too. I can't let him down, man. He might need me."

Like he needs a case of poison ivy, I thought. "You're in no condition to drive. At least let me—"

He made a shushing motion and dropped his voice to a stage whisper. "I gotta driver, man. A redheaded driver named Virginia. She's a real looker, too. I think I got lucky tonight!" He quit trying to put the cap back on the whiskey bottle and stuck a finger into the neck. He brought back the loose smile, his eyes trying to focus on my face. "I'll be seeing you, man. Ginny'll be gettin' anxious. I can't keep her waiting no more. She's a helluva driver, and I can't afford to lose her." He staggered to the front of the motor home, then stopped and looked back. "Thanks a lot, man, for everything." He nodded for emphasis, gave me a thumbs up sign, then weaved on out of sight.

"You're welcome, Nate," I said, wondering what I had done, wondering also if I had ever been that sloppily drunk, that puerile and helpless before the world.

I told myself that I hadn't, then paid no attention to my lies because I knew damned well that I had, and, what was worse, could very well be so again.

38

I GOT A LATE START THE NEXT DAY. A LONG FITFUL NIGHT and a cold overcast morning combined to keep me abed longer than usual. I ate a leisurely breakfast of bacon and eggs and spent an hour making sure the motor home was sparkling clean as I had found it.

I left Nate a note thanking him for his more-than-generous hospitality, and wishing him well. I invited him to visit me in Midway City and declared that I would look him up when I came down for the hearing.

As promised, I drove downtown to One Century Plaza to say goodbye to Ward. He wasn't in. A little relieved, I asked the plump lady at the communications console to tell him I'd come by, but couldn't hang around and wait, pleading pressing business engagements in oil, timber, and high tech, and a burning desire to see the Fort Worth skyline again.

Back in my truck, I lit a cigarette and sighed. All my commitments met, promises kept. I was free to go, nothing to keep me in Jerico Falls. Home only four hours and a pit stop away. Color TV with remote control. VCR. Stereo with high fidelity tape deck. Space. My own bed. Books, records, tapes. Friends. Susie . . . soon.

So what the hell was I doing sitting there?

I flipped the cigarette out the window, started the engine, and drove off the square.

Jerico Falls wasn't much of a town, I reminded myself, and what happened here mattered little in the grand scheme of things, mattered not at all to the people in the world I was going back to. A glitch, an aberration that might rate three minutes on a slow news night in Dallas, a single headline in a Forth Worth paper: DEAD RANCHER DRUG KINGPIN. Justice is served.

So why did I have a sinking feeling of defeat? Why did I feel that I was a quitter?

The sign was old, half the size of a standard billboard. The right side sagged drunkenly, the support pole obviously rotted off at ground level. Bare-limbed oak saplings grew up around it, almost hiding it from view, and I probably wouldn't have noticed it at all if I hadn't been following the flight of a chicken hawk streaking across the road with something wriggling in its claws.

The bird landed on top of the sign, its spiky beak immediately slicing into its morning meal, rising, driving downward again, rising . . .

The hawk flew, prey still clutched firmly in its spiny grip. But I hardly noticed. I was reading the sign:

You are now leaving the city of Jerico Falls, Texas, Home of the Jerico Falls High School REBELS, 1956 Winners of the Saragache County Basketball Championship.

                                Please come again.

Rebels?

I lit a cigarette and read the sign again, trying to make sense out of what was clearly nonsense, a bad joke perhaps, an inside joke that only the citizens of Jerico Falls could understand.

Rebels?

Not so! The Jerico Falls High basketball team was called

the Bandits. I clearly recalled seeing the poster in Suttler's window. The Jerico Bandits vs the Boonville Wildcats.

The Rebels were Nathan Barr's team . . . or to be more precise, Nathan Barr's *daddy's* team . . .

Without understanding why, I was suddenly sitting stiffly upright, hands locked on the wheel, staring at the sign as if it held all the secrets of the ages, as if it could reveal the dubious future of mankind.

A tiny rill of shock tickled somewhere in my brain, tightened the muscles across my back. I had a tingling sense of impending epiphany, a breathless expectation of revelation on the tip of my mind.

I closed my eyes and shrank into myself to aid the rejuvenation going on inside my head, the assimilation of jumbled bits and pieces and facts, the meaningless trivia that I had blithely passed over on my way to better places and bigger things, on my way to ignominious defeat. I sat enthralled, juggling facts like the individual notes of a brilliant jazz improvisation, fragile crystals of conjecture exploding, forming a new and nebulous mosaic.

There were what-if's and but's and maybe's to mar the cutting edge of my new vision, but there was also a clear cold logic no longer blinkered by intangibles like friendship and gratitude. I was processing information like a computer running wild, stepping back and looking on, sifting scenes and conversations, coldly tabulating the tiny kernels of truth.

When I finished I lit another cigarette and sat for a while, getting my jangled nerves back under control.

Then I turned the Ramcharger around and drove back into Jerico Falls.

I stopped the first adult I saw, an elderly man making his way along the sidewalk with the aid of a crooked wooden cane.

I eased up to the curb beside him, rolled down my window, and gave him a friendly smile. He smiled back, but the faded blue eyes beneath the Ford gimme cap were bright and suspicious.

"Excuse me, sir, are you familiar with the Jerico Falls High School basketball team?"

He shuffled around to face me without lifting his feet. He stabbed the sidewalk with his cane. "Course I am. What kinda question is that?"

"I was just curious. They're named the Bandits, I understand."

"That's right. Best danged team in the county."

"How long—"

"How long have I lived here? All my life up to this minute. I was born here, young fellow."

"Actually, sir, what I meant was how long has the team been named the Bandits?"

"Oh. Well . . . let's see . . . how long has that actor fellow been in the White House, six years? About that long. We was doing fine with the name we had, the Rebels, and then some black kids playing on the team wouldn't play no more until we changed the name. You ever hear of such tomfoolery as that?" He scowled and sucked his lower lip inside his mouth. "Ain't won the county tourney since we changed either, I can tell you that. Bad luck changing a team's name thataway."

"Never can tell, maybe this is the year. Thanks a lot for your time and I hope you have a good walk."

"Ain't walkin," he said, his voice rising as I let the truck drift away from the curb. "Creepin is what you'd have to call it."

I laughed and waved and drove off, pleased with the encounter, leaving one of my what-if's lying dead on the damp black asphalt.

I had left the keys inside when I locked the motor home, so I had to break one of the small square panes in the glass door panel, wincing as I did so, muttering an apology to Nathan Barr. I reached through and unlocked the door and went inside.

I was out in less than two minutes. I locked it up again, ignoring the broken window, wondering for perhaps the ten thousandth time where one might go to learn to pick locks the way they do in all the P.I. TV shows. I rarely failed to get through a door if I wanted to badly enough, but I usually had to kick it down first.

I drove directly to the square. I found a parking space three or four doors down from the Saragache County *Gazette*. I eased the truck into the narrow space, averting my eyes from a sign that read: PARKING FOR MILDRED'S BEAUTY SALON ONLY.

I crossed in front of the pickup and sauntered up the sidewalk past Mildred's Beauty Salon expecting a hail at the very least, a confrontation at the very worst, an angry Amazon armed with hot curling irons and blow-dry guns. But nothing happened. Small town folks, courteous to a fault, giving the dumbass north Texas yankee a little slack.

Tony Caulder and his wife Sara were huddled shoulder to shoulder over the long table. Abel Caulder sat at Tony's desk, in Tony's chair, booted feet propped against an open drawer. From behind him came the dull monotonous hum of the laboring presses.

Tony looked up. I made a negative gesture and pointed toward his father. He smiled and nodded and turned back to whatever it was he and his wife were doing. I pushed through the swinging gate in the dividing railing and approached Abel.

He looked up, lips quirking in his angry face. "Changed your mind." It was a statement more than a question. "Don't blame you a bit. This day and time a man needs to get his money quick while the getting's good, 'fore chapter eleven sets in." He made his smothered laughing sound, got to his feet, and held out his hand, his eyes on the Bible in mine.

I shook his hand, then sat down in the straight chair at the corner of the desk. I put down the Bible and took out a cigarette.

"It's not the money, Mr. Caulder. I need to ask you a question and I know your first reaction is going to be that it's none of my business, and maybe it isn't, but please believe me when I say it is important."

233

"Sounds serious," he said lightly, reclaiming his seat, removing his sweat-darkened gray hat and dropping it on the floor beside him, his dark eyes never leaving my face. "Go ahead, Mr. Roman, ask your question. If I think it's none of your business, I won't answer it."

"Fair enough." I lit the cigarette, using the time to marshal my thoughts, deciding on my line of approach. I coughed and cleared my throat.

"Approximately thirty-one years ago something happened here in Jerico Falls or maybe somewhere around here, I'm not exactly sure where. It involved five young men and a young girl named Carlotta." I stopped and studied his face; his expression remained unchanged, as always, not even a flicker in his eye. "The girl was raped by one of the boys. As strange as it may seem, she didn't know which boy was the rapist, didn't know which one of the boys fathered her child."

He made a sound then, a low sibilant sigh, eyes shuttered for one brief moment, as if in pain. "My God . . . a child. We didn't know . . . there were rumors, but . . ." His thin scratchy voice faded, returned, stronger. "I—we thought it was only . . . was only a rumor after the . . . after Carlotta disappeared. Some said her father kicked her out, some said he sent her to relatives in Arizona, New Mexico, somewhere like that."

"It's true, then?"

"It's true, yes, the rape is true. I didn't know about the child. We—none of us did."

"Five of you involved. How could it happen that she didn't know which one?"

He brushed a hand through his bushy hair, lingered to finger the frozen muscles of his cheek, then scrubbed lightly a two day growth of stubble on his chin. "I won't go into the details, Mr. Roman, but it involved one of those early summer storms we sometimes get in Texas, the kind we called gully-washers in the old days. It involved five boys, teammates on the Rebels basketball team, gathering to celebrate graduation from high school, a night of poker playing and boozing it up out at my Uncle Charlie's place. He was off on a week's fishing trip to Mexico and I was watching the place for him, feeding his stock, putting out chicken scratch and things like that. A perfect place for our little celebration. Back off the county road a half-mile or so, no neighbors for a couple of miles—a perfect place, like I said.'' He stopped and lifted his head and I realized the muted rumble of the presses had ceased. I saw Tony Caulder stride briskly through the double doors.

"We never counted on no women . . . girls. Strictly male, drinking beer and telling dirty jokes. Like that. She came on her own, looking like a little drowned pullet, hair plastered to her face, shivering with cold, crying, I guess, along with it, it was hard to tell. She'd gone off the county road into the ditch and almost got caught in the rising water. She'd come to our lights, straight across the field, mud and burrs and stickers all over her jeans. But she was a purty little thing. You could see that easy enough. Built, you know. I scrounged around and found some stuff Ella Mae, one of my cousins, had left there and sent her upstairs to the bathroom.'' He stopped, lips puckered thoughtfully.

"You were right,'' I said, smiling. "I don't need all the details.''

"Oh, yeah, I see what you mean. Well, to shorten it some, she got all dried out and came down looking a little different. Tom Scurry fixed her a . . . I think it was a screwdriver out of some of my uncle's liquor, and she went after it like she knew exactly what it was for. She livened up some after that. We all took turns dancing with her after a while. But that only lasted a little while before the electricity went off. We had to scrounge around and find some lanterns and lamps, and maybe that's what caused it to happen. She'd had another screwdriver or two and she was doing a lot of giggling, bumping into us in the dark and bouncing away before we could grab her good. I guess you coulda called her a tease, but that ain't no excuse for what happened.''

"What happened?''

"Well, after a while we decided chasing her around wasn't

much fun anymore, and we took one of the lamps to the dining room table and started playing poker. She watched for a time, then I noticed her yawning, and the first thing I knew she was gone. I sorta forgot about her and I guess the other guys did too, except maybe the one who raped her. Anyway, Jesse Culliwell came down from the bathroom a while later and said she was asleep on one of the beds upstairs. I went up there myself later on and she was where he had said she was, curled up under a comforter on my uncle's bed. Sound asleep, as far as I could tell. We went on playing poker.'' He stopped as the hum of the machinery started again, his head bobbing minutely in satisfaction. ''Need some new presses back there.''

I nodded, trying not to let my impatience show in my face.

''Well, we broke up about two, I suppose it was. The storm was still going strong, lots of lightning and thunder, raining bucketfuls. It didn't matter much to us, though, since we'd planned to stay all night in the first place. To make it short, we all found us a place to sleep, and I don't know if it was by some sorta unspoken agreement or what, but we all stayed down on the first floor. My uncle had two bedrooms down and two up, but the ones downstairs had been his boys' rooms and they were all twin beds. So that gave us four beds. I slept on the couch in the living room.''

''So sometime during the morning hours someone went upstairs and raped her?''

He looked at me. I was sure he was scowling, but couldn't show it on his face. ''That's about the size of it,'' he said crisply. ''Somebody did exactly that. He blew out that little lamp she had and climbed in there and raped her. More than once, she said.''

''Why didn't she cry out?''

''He had the butcher knife from the kitchen. He left it up there with her. I thought for a while she was gonna stick me when I went up to wake her up about seven. She was all huddled in my uncle's big chair with the comforter around her. When I got close, she showed me the knife and said she'd stick me if I came any closer.'' He stopped and sighed.

"It took a while to get it out of her, to get the knife away from her."

"Nobody had any idea who it was?"

"No. It could have been any one of us. We all died away when we hit the sack. We wasn't used to being up that late, or drinking like that. All, that is, except the raper. He musta been laying there waiting, counting the snores."

I laid the Bible on the desk in front of him, opened it to the newspaper photo.

He stared at it for a moment, then looked up at me, his eyes bright. "God almighty, where'd you get that?"

"Is that the first five on the Rebels team? The ones we've been discussing?"

"Sure is . . . yeah, I remember when they took this . . . back in the fall of '55 sometime—"

I jabbed my finger at the tall boy in the center, the one with the ball. "That's you?"

"Right. These two on my right are Tom Scurry and Jesse Culliwell, and these two here are—"

"Let me guess," I said, and pointed to the one in the lower left of the picture. "Cody Bannion?"

"Yeah, old Cody hisself. That other one is Theron Alldyce."

"Alldyce? Mayor Alldyce?" I must have sounded as shocked as I felt.

His head lifted, lips quirking. "Wouldn't think it to look at him now, huh? He was purty little, but, boy, was he fast on the floor."

I closed the Bible and stood up, my head swirling. It had taken a while to get there, but we had just welded another link in my fragile chain, a big one, maybe the linchpin that held it all together. We had also demolished another one of my what-if's, but's and maybe's, and I could tell by the thrumming in my body, my adrenaline high, that a part of me was already convinced, already homing in for the kill.

"Thanks for your candor, Mr. Caulder. I know it must have been hard to tell after keeping it a secret all these years."

His eyebrows lifted, a dark wryness in his eyes. He

237

shrugged. "What secret? Probably five hundred oldtimers in this town coulda told you about it. Six people know a secret, it don't stay a secret very long."

I nodded and shook his hand and thanked him again. I waved at Tony Caulder and smiled at his young wife and went out the door, a bit of youthful bounce back in my step.

It seemed I wasn't quite finished in Jerico Falls after all.

I stopped at the truck, thought it over for a moment, then crossed the street and went into One Century Plaza. Ward still wasn't there, but his telephone was, and I sat down and put in a call to the Midway City Police Department. It had occurred to me that if I ever wanted Captain Homer Sellers to help me again, it behooved me to at least show a little interest in the eleven-odd names I had given his secretary Mitsi.

Homer was at his desk for once and, after enduring a bit of more-or-less goodnatured complaining, I nudged him into telling me what he had found out. Seven of the eleven people had no record, three had only minor skirmishes with the law. He left the best for last and I listened to his rumbling baritone recital with a kind of morbid fascination. It was almost anticlimactic, like plugging in the last piece of a giant jigsaw puzzle, a great deal of satisfaction but no real surprise.

"Thanks, Homer," I said when he finished. "I appreciate it."

"Yeah. Well, when the hell you coming home? We got work to do down there on your place, stands to fix, firewood to cut—"

"Dig out your coonskin cap, Homer, and listen to your tape of buck farts, I'll be home tonight, I hope."

"I'm gonna take a couple days vacation. We'll run down there and check out the sign, maybe build a new stand over on that second hill, a ground stand, you know how I hate climbing trees. Man, I'm getting the fever. I can't wait to blast one of them little critters right between the eyes!"

"Uh-huh. The way you did last year, huh? And the year before that? How long's it been since you killed a deer, Homer?"

"About the last time you did. I ain't no meat hunter. Nothing less than a Boone and Crockett head for me. You know—"

"I know if bullshit was music you'd be a rock and roll band. I'll see you later, Homer." I hung up gently.

39

He had already hitched the trailer on the back of the motor home, the little foreign car firmly tied down. The awning was neatly rolled and lashed, and he was packing the aluminum chairs and the canvas groundcover in the storage bin when he looked up and saw me standing there.

He jumped, then grinned. "Shit! Man, you scared me." He slammed the cover on the bin and turned the handle.

"Sorry," I said.

"It's okay, man. I was just thinking about something else, is all." He came toward me, wiping his hands on a red-checkered handkerchief. "I thought you'd already taken off. I saw all your stuff was gone." He studiously avoided looking at my left hand, the one holding the Bible. I lifted it.

"Had to bring this back. I borrowed it this morning. Sorry I had to break the pane of glass, but I locked the keys inside the first time." I stepped forward and handed him the Bible.

"Hey, that's okay, man. Don't worry about it." He jerked his head toward the motor home. "Come on in. I got some coffee made. I was getting ready to have a cup, anyway." He bounded up the steps without waiting for an answer, leaving the door swinging wide. I followed him.

"Sit down, Dan. I'll get us a cup."

I slid into the booth. "No, thanks. Coffee's one bad habit I don't have."

"How about a beer, then? Come on, man, you gotta have something. Keep me company." He poured coffee into a cup; the cup rattled against the glass percolator.

"Maybe a beer," I said. I took out a Carlton, held it in my hand. "You don't want to know what I was doing with your Bible, Nate?"

"Naw, man, it don't matter. You don't have to explain anything to me. I read the Bible all the time." He handed me the beer, unopened, and set his coffee cup on the arm of the small couch across the aisle from the booth. "It ain't nothing to be ashamed of." His face was starkly pale, the bloodshot blue eyes trying for humor that wasn't there.

I opened the beer and lit the cigarette. He opened a drawer and slid a small ashtray toward me across the table. He took a deep breath and tasted his coffee; his hand was still shaking. He abruptly sat down on the couch. "Crap, this stuff is still hot." He tried for a wry smile; it simply looked foolish, vacant, reflecting a kind of sick despair that matched his eyes. "Guess I'm still hungover."

I took a drink of beer, feeling a little sick despair of my own. "Why in God's name did you kill them, Nate?"

We stared at each other.

His hand closed around the cup; coffee sloshed onto the arm of the couch, onto the vinyl floor, onto his hand; he didn't seem to notice. His tongue came out and tried to wet his lips without success. He cleared his throat and brushed hair out of his eyes.

"What . . . kill who? I don't understand—" He appeared to run out of saliva, or maybe his throat closed on the words. Whatever the cause, he made a dry, sick gagging sound and collapsed in on himself, his round face working above the beard, stricken.

I waited, feeling no need to repeat my question. The answer was there, had been there all along if I had only taken the time to look, to question, to use my brain for something besides a storage box for cold irrelevant facts. The tree had always been there, but I hadn't seen it because of the forest, as they say. I had been up to my eyeballs in drugs and drug lore, drug users and drug pushers, drug money. And when it came right down to it, drugs had nothing to do with it at all. At least not much.

I finished the cigarette and took another sip of beer. Nate hadn't moved, hardly blinked, blank eyes fixed on some unreachable goal, crouched into the corner of the couch like a disabled fly caught in some sticky spider web.

"I don't think you meant to do it, Nate, I mean, I don't think you set out to kill them. I think it just happened. They were there, all tied up, and you were watching and you had the gun and you suddenly realized that you could kill them and that Cody would be blamed. That's what you wanted, wasn't it? You wanted your daddy to suffer for what he had done to your mother, your real mother. You could kill his son and hurt him that way, then make him hurt more when they punished him for killing his own son. Was that the way it was, Nate?"

A shudder rippled through him; his right hand jerked and the coffee cup fell to the floor. He didn't appear to notice. "No—yes—no, not . . . not exactly . . . that way. I wanted to . . . to hurt him. Yes. But not for . . . not only for her. For me too. I called him . . . told him I was his son . . . told him I wanted . . . all I wanted was to come and . . . and talk to him. Just *talk* to him goddammit! He said I was . . . was crazy, that Steve was his only son, and . . . and that if I came around he'd . . . he'd set the dogs on me!"

"You didn't tell him who you were, that you were Nathan Barr?"

He shook his head. "No, I didn't tell him my name. I just told him I was his son, the son he . . . he got by raping my mother Carlotta Valdez over thirty years ago. He just laughed . . . just laughed and cursed me and hung up."

"When was that?"

His trembling fingers plucked at his curly beard, touched his hidden lips, moved back to clasp his other hand in a white-knuckled grip.

242

"I don't know . . . a month ago, maybe a little more. My God, it took me five years to get . . . get up the courage to do that much."

"How could you be so sure it was Cody and not one—"

"Jesus Christ! Look at me! I—I'm built exactly like him and under this beard I'm wearing his goddamned face!"

I looked at him, really looked for perhaps the first time— and he was right. I couldn't tell much about the face, but the contours were the same, the slender compact body the same, the pale blue eyes, even the short straight nose that flared slightly at the nostrils.

"Man, I knew the first time I saw him. Jesus. It took so long. Five years. Drifting around Texas looking for a small town with a basketball team named the Rebels. That's all I knew, man. Texas and the Rebels. And, by God, I found him, and I almost had a heart attack. I couldn't breathe . . . I saw his face and I knew he was the one . . . even before I knew his name, I knew. That was six years ago. I was in Fort Worth working the Fat Stock Show when I heard on TV about the small town where they were having trouble with black players over the name of the team. The Rebels. They wanted to change it to something else. Two days after I got here I saw him on the street. I already had a mustache and long sideburns or I think he would have known. We met face to face in front of the Eat-A-Bite restaurant. I turned right around and left town. I didn't come back until my beard was thick enough to hide my face."

"You've been here ever since?"

"No, not exactly. I come and go. I spent most of my time here, though, particularly after I met Ward. He's my uncle, you know. We got to be good friends. I did some horseshoeing work for him was the way it started. I—I guess I was just looking for . . . for a family."

"You had a family," I said gently, wondering if I should tell him what I knew, what Homer had found out about him through the magic of computers. "The Barrs, the people who adopted you."

His teeth glinted briefly, a bitter grimace. "She was . . .

243

fine, a good woman and I—I loved her. But she died when I was eleven. They had two children of their own by then, a boy and a girl. After she died I became their caretaker. Moser Barr made no bones about it. My job was to raise the other kids. When I was thirteen I rebelled. That was when he gave me the Bible with the letter, told me that I was not of his blood and that if I wanted a place to live I'd do what he told me to do. We were at war all the time after that. When I was sixteen, he gave me five hundred dollars and kicked me out." He paused, studying his interlaced fingers, as if trying to decide whether to tell me the rest.

I lit a cigarette and, when he made no attempt to resume, I said: "I know about the fire, Nate, about Moser's death."

"If you know that," he said without looking up, his voice barely above a whisper, "then you know that I was exonerated."

"Yes, I know that. I also know that you were remanded for psychiatric examination and that the last record of Nathan Barr in Missouri was when you walked off the grounds of the state mental hospital when you were twenty."

He shrugged. "They thought I was a firebug. I'll admit I set some fires when I was a teenager, but it was Moser Barr's property I was burning, nobody else's." He appeared to notice the fallen cup for the first time. He picked it up. "I need another cup. You want another beer?"

"No, thanks, Nate."

He stood up and poured coffee into his cup. His hand was steady. "How did you find out about me?"

"Computers," I said. "Big Brother looking over your shoulder. You'd be surprised at what they know about you, about all of us, for that matter."

"I didn't mean that," he said, sitting on the couch again. "I meant what made you think it was me who . . ." He let it trail away, sipping coffee, watching me over the rim of the cup.

"I'm not sure, Nate, not exactly. A lot of little things, unrelated things. You were like a bad penny standing on edge in a crack—hard to see clearly. I thought of you when I found out about the horseshoe nail, but that was reaching, I reasoned. Anyone could pick up a discarded nail with a muddy boot, even though the percentages would have been in your favor. I thought of you again when I got bit by the fire ants and Susie found the ointment in your medicine cabinet. But there again I thought I was reaching. I knew your bites weren't flea bites the way you said they were, but I thought you may have gotten into some chiggers somewhere. Anyway, your bites looked too new that night out at Ward's and that was more than two weeks after the murders. And even when I learned that you were a diabetic, and remembered that it sometimes takes two to three times as long for diabetics to heal, even then I didn't make a direct connection between your bites and mine." I paused and mashed out the cigarette, feeling his burning gaze on my face. "And even last night when you were drunk and called them your ant bites it didn't really mean much. There were other fire ant mounds around."

"That's pretty flimsy stuff," he said softly.

"You're right, it is. But there was more. At one point you said you didn't know about the lake behind Ward's mountain, and then later you said it was a pretty little place, but gloomy under the trees, or words to that effect. All little things, Nate. Almost meaningless out of proper context, or without continuity."

"You're right, meaningless."

I nodded and took another sip of beer. "A bad penny in a crack, Nate. But I was looking higher, looking for a pot of dope at the end of my rainbow, looking for a big dope dealer called Big Bwana. I was obsessed by that and nothing else made much of an impression. It took a dead man and a crooked cop to blow a hole in my little bubble. Nueboldt told me the truth and somewhere deep inside I think I believed him. But everything fit so goddamned perfectly. I had my drug kingpin, ergo I had my killer. Nueboldt admitted he had tied up the kids, but said that he left them that way. That was hard to accept. It meant there was someone else in the picture, some shadowy image that marred my beautiful portrait.'' I smiled at him across the narrow aisle. ''A cool little spider in a hidden corner of the web. That was you, Nate. And I simply overlooked you. The times I did think of you, I couldn't find a motive.''

He sipped coffee and watched me, unblinking.

''Until,'' I said, ''I saw the sign out at the city limits about a basketball team called the Rebels. The name clicked. I remembered your father's picture, the Rebel team. My mind came out of hibernation. I realized suddenly that this was your town, Nate, your mother's town before she was banished, that your father was here in all likelihood, and that you were probably here because of that. I remember your resemblance to one of the faces in the picture, the face that I thought belonged to you until we read the date on the back and read the letter written by your mother. That uneasy void I felt inside began to fill, began to fill with you, Nate. You were no longer the penny in the crack, the little hidden spider, you were the star of your own little drama. Everything all at once looked different. I remembered your mother's plea for vengeance. You began to make sense. There were some gaps in my line of thinking, some holes in my picture, but for the most part I've been able to plug them up, to my own satisfaction, at least.''

He sipped coffee silently, then abruptly made a face and looked down at the cup. ''Sugar. I need some sugar.'' He pushed to his feet, took the two steps necessary to reach the cabinet to the left of the stove.

I heard the squeaky slide of a cabinet drawer, but I didn't bother to look around. Seconds later he came back into view, the gun held out before him in both hands. The hands trembled only a little.

He had to wet his lips again before he could speak, had to hawk something out of his throat. ''Take—take out your gun, Dan. Lay it on the table.'' His features were hard and bunched, set in granite, blue eyes cold and empty, bottomless. His voice was dull, didactic, almost detached. It was a startling transformation and despite my feeling of confidence, I felt a tiny ripple of fear.

246

I placed both hands on the table palms down, fingers spread. "I don't have a gun, Nate. I didn't think I'd need one."

"I don't believe you! Open your coat."

I opened my jacket, turning so he could see both sides.

"Jesus Christ! You came after me without a gun! You're either the coolest son-of-a-bitch I've ever seen, or you think I'm . . . I'm a . . . a sorry—" He choked, voice cracking like a teenager, icy composure breaking, fading.

"What I think is that you're not a killer, Nate. I think you did something terrible in a moment of passion, acting out of hate, or, hell, maybe love, I don't pretend to know. Unless I'm badly mistaken, you regret it, regretted it almost at once. Why else would you take the bodies, at great risk I might add, to a place where they would be found quickly? Why else would you cover them with the blanket?"

"I—I couldn't . . . I couldn't just leave them lying there . . . Jesus, not with the insects, the ants and the animals out there in the dark field . . ."

"That's what I mean, Nate. It was a rash act, maybe even a deranged one, but you treated the bodies with care. That was an act of humanity, not the hallmark of a cold blooded killer."

"I could hear them . . . hear them talking. The . . . the other man and . . . and Daddy. The other man was mad, he wanted to kill them. Daddy said no, that he had gathered together the money to pay for the drugs, that Steve was his blood, his son, that he would handle it in his own way." He stopped, staring at me, through me, the blue eyes wide with something like wonder. "He—he told the other man he had a million . . . a million dollars to pay for some drugs that Steve had taken. God! He was willing to pay a million dollars for Steve's life and . . . and he was going . . . was going to set the goddamned dogs on me!" His voice was thick and hoarse, his face stricken again behind the beard. "A million dollars," he breathed.

I held out my hand. "Give me the gun, Nate. This is foolishness. You can't run. Where would you go? Wherever you go, they'll find you. At any rate, Ward should be here any second now. I left a message on his desk.''

"You told him . . . you told Ward?''

"I had no choice. It doesn't matter—''

"Oh, Jesus, what's he gonna think of me!'' His hands drooped as if the gun had suddenly assumed an intolerable gravitational weight.

"I think Ward will understand, Nate, if anyone can. He knows how it is to kill someone because you're compelled to do it. It's not the reason why so much as it is the having to do it.'' It was a convoluted rationale at best, but it appeared to be reaching him. "Give me the gun.''

I held out my hand again. His head bobbed jerkily and he laid the heavy automatic in my palm.

I slipped it into my pocket, deciding it wasn't the right time to tell him I had unloaded it when I stopped to pick up the Bible.

"What were you doing back there, Nate?''

"Taking . . . taking a walk. I had my fishing gear and some worms. I—I love to fish. Ward said there were a lot of catfish . . . I wanted to surprise him with . . . I saw the kids go by from where I sat on the bank. They couldn't see me for the bushes and I decided to wait until dark then leave 'cause I figured they were back there to . . . to make out. But just before dark the plane came in low over the field. I saw a bundle drop. I waited a while. I saw Steve run out there and pick it up. And . . . and then I heard the truck coming up the road without lights. I saw two men. Daddy and another man. They stopped close to where I was hidden. The other man got out and walked around the lake to where Steve and the girl were parked. I heard voices, loud, angry. After a while he came back and . . . and Daddy went back with him. That's when I heard them arguing.'' He ended his weary recital and dropped limply on the couch, body flaccid, his eyes dull, trembling fingers plucking at his beard.

I waited a while, then prodded gently. "And?''

He sucked in a deep breath, let it out slowly. "After Daddy and the man left I—I waited . . . and after a while I slipped

up the road to where the kids were. I guess I expected to find
. . . I don't know, maybe find them dead or something. But
they were trying to untie each other . . . God, I don't know
why I . . . why I did it! I just couldn't seem to help myself . . . I know it's crazy. I had the gun out of my tackle
box—I always take it for snakes—and . . . and it was just
like watching someone else . . . I was just standing there
watching someone else do that terrible thing! Just watching
this other person . . . this cold heartless other person . . .
do it!'' His smudged blue eyes peered hopelessly out of deep
sockets, haunted by unclean memories. He built a small
twisted smile out of the raw pain in his face. ''All the time I
spent—wasted, waiting, hoping something would happen to
make me a part . . . a part of this family . . . and . . . and
Steve was nothing but a thief, a thief and a junkie . . . Daddy,
he was . . . well, you know what he was.''

''Why did you go to Missouri? Or did you? With Moser
Barr dead—''

He shook his head. ''That was a . . . a lie. I went to New
Orleans. I was afraid . . . I was afraid Ward would look at
me and know. I'm no good at hiding things, and Ward he
. . . he can see right through you sometimes. He's the only
one in the family worth a damn.''

There was nothing I could say to that, no words of comfort
that wouldn't have stuck in my throat, and condemnation
seemed fruitless. So I lit another cigarette and slid out of the
booth.

I helped him clean up the coffee on the floor, waited while
he changed into his Sunday best, then drove him to One
Century Plaza. It was a silent ride. I kept thinking about him
and Ward being related, about him growing up in a stunted
part of the forest.

Like Susie had said, everything about his life was a little
sad.

Unlike Susie, I didn't feel much like crying.

ABOUT THE AUTHOR

Edward Mathis is the author of FROM A HIGH PLACE,
DARK STREAKS AND EMPTY PLACES and NATURAL
PREY, all published by Ballantine.